The last thing Tommy Lovell expects is death in a family business. It's 1986, and Tommy's dream restaurant has failed, taking his shaky marriage along with it. Now he's licking his wounds back in his childhood bedroom, while he takes stock of his life at the end of his 20s. Reluctantly, Tommy agrees to tag along when his father offers to help his friend Otto Jonker save Otto's struggling appliance/TV store in a dying Berkshires town. Tommy is ready for a change of scenery, maybe a bit of romance, and—if he's lucky—a chance to fly his father's Cessna. But the trip takes a disastrous turn after Otto skids off the road during a midnight motorcycle ride and is critically injured, forcing Tommy and his father into unexpected danger as they make disturbing discoveries about Otto's personal and professional troubles.

Also by Wally Wood

Getting Oriented: A Novel About Japan

The Girl in the Photo

With Jerry Acuff

The Relationship Edge

Stop Acting Like a Seller and Start Thinking Like a Buyer

Death in a Family Business

A Tommy Lovell mystery by

Wally Wood

This is a work of fiction. Names, characters, places, and incidents are either the product of the author's imagination or are used fictitiously. Any resemblance to actual persons living or dead, events or locales is entirely coincidental.

Copyright © 2015 by Wallis E. Wood

All rights reserved. This book, or parts thereof, may not be reproduced in any form without permission.

A reading group guide is available at:
www.MysteriesOfWriting.blogspot.com

Published in the United States by Wally Wood

ISBN-13: 978-1511993173
ISBN-10: 1511993170

Printed in the United States of America

This book is for

Gregory, Victoria, and Jefferson, with love

1 / Thursday evening

As I stood in Otto Jonker's basement, watching him awkwardly fumble for the right words, I was struck by how big he was—like 6-foot-2, 250-pound big. A red-faced guy with a booming laugh that seemed forced. He'd rolled up the sleeves of his white shirt and cracked a couple windows so the October night would cool the room, but he was sweating anyway, wiping his forehead periodically with a blue-and-white hanky from a back pocket. Watching him pace, I thought he was working on a heart attack.

Otto wouldn't even talk about the business and why he needed Dad and the others to come save his ass until he'd blasted the quadraphonic sound system and demonstrated the Super Betamax video player, which Sony had begun to ship.

He'd insisted on holding the orientation meeting at his house rather than at the store. Watching him prance from the wet bar to the giant projection TV, I thought that showing off his house was Otto's way to let Dad and the others know he wasn't a total loser. No, he was a good provider, giving his family a gigantic modern house and filling it with toys.

I could see Dad trying to be polite while growing impatient, his expression of friendly interest becoming tight as he waited for Otto to get down to business.

Of course, I didn't care how much time Otto wasted. I was

pretty much along for the ride. Dad said he thought I could be helpful, but I think he mostly wanted me for company, a father-son bonding opportunity. After all, we hadn't spent a whole lot of time together during the last ten years or so.

Dad's impatience finally overrode his restraint, and he said something in a low tone to Otto, who instantly turned off the sound from the four speakers—cutting off the realistic roar of a freight train as it seemed to chug around all four corners of the knotty-pine paneled rec room. The room was suddenly quiet enough I could hear Otto say, "I suppose we should get started. Everyone got something to drink?" He shot a glance at Christine, his wife, as if she might be slacking off as hostess, and began again, this time with an embarrassed giggle. "I suppose you're all wondering why I've called you here for this meeting."

No one was wondering. I'd overheard Dad's end of the conversation last week when Otto phoned to say his business—Jonker Appliance & TV in Pittsfield—was in a bad way and could he come out and look at the situation? Why Dad? The two of them had been roommates a couple times at some management seminars, and Dad ran a thriving two-store appliance-TV business north of Boston, Lovell & Son Appliance/TV. Dad thought Otto had to be desperate to reach out to him.

"He sounded like a drowning man going down for the third time," Dad told Mom when he hung up.

"Sounds serious."

"And he thinks I know something he doesn't."

"You probably do," Mom said with a smile.

Perched on a high bar stool next to him was Joanne McQuilkin, one of Dad's dealer friends who was almost as tall as Otto. She was dressed in a conservative pants suit that, I couldn't help noticing, showed nothing of her figure. As soon as I realized my mind wandering in this direction, I had to wonder: Why am I looking for the figure of a woman old enough to be my mother? I thought I caught Dad checking out Joanne's ass. The way they'd stood together earlier, drinks in hand, suggested a closer relationship than retailing colleagues, but what did I know?

Joanne had her long graying blond hair tied back in a careless bun and she seemed to be wearing no makeup except pale lipstick. When she and I had walked downstairs to Otto's rec room an hour before, she remarked that she was sorry to hear about my restaurant. "I still remember the meal you served us two years ago when my son and I were visiting Northeastern and Tufts." She gave me a smile and added, "It was a rigatoni, followed by a wonderful tiramisu for dessert." It gave me a warm feeling that she could recall it; the tiramisu *was* one of Si Accomodi's specialties. "Your Dad says you're living at home?"

"For the time being." I nodded, but kept my head down so she couldn't see me struggle to keep my face neutral.

"Do you have any plans?" She inspected me like a teacher with a new student.

"I've renewed my student pilot's license and Dad's going to help me get a full license." Of course, that wasn't what she was asking. She wanted to know what I was going to do with the rest of my life. As if I knew.

"Do you want to work as a pilot? Fly big jets?" She sounded interested.

"Pilot jobs are tough to get. I'm considering my options."

With a dismissive wave, Joanne rejected that as the bullshit answer it was. "Tommy, do you want to start another restaurant? Or do something else?"

She was generous to show any interest when I was sure she didn't give a shit. I put my hand out, palm up, and told her, "If you have any suggestions, I'm wide open."

"I'll think about it." She sounded as if she would seriously consider it, too, which surprised me.

Now Joanne was sitting on the bar stool, following Otto's

constant pacing with her eyes as the other two dealers, Dan Wald and Nick Carvainis, settled into the fake leather couch across the room. Dad pulled the other bar stool over next to Joanne as Otto continued his agitated pacing in front of the TV screen. Once he had everybody's attention, Otto told Christine to hand out the folders as he began to explain the background information he'd prepared: First-half financial statements ("I'm waiting for third-quarter figures"); employee records, which were names, titles, and years of employment ("I couldn't get the payroll stuff together fast enough"); newspaper ads from the store and its competitors ("Just to show you what I'm up against").

When Otto's briefing ran down, Dad let the others ask their questions first. Dan, who'd come out of the service side of the business before buying the busy appliance store he now owned, asked a few questions about the service operation. Otto assured us that he had a cracker-jack service manager and boasted that Jonker Appliance & TV service was the best in town.

I watched Nick run his fingers down a row of numbers as he asked about third-quarter results. Otto said he'd talked to his accountant just that afternoon and the accountant had promised to deliver a profit/loss statement and balance sheet tomorrow afternoon. In other words, he didn't answer.

Joanne wanted to know about customer relations. Nobody's eyebrows went up when Otto said they were terrific, but by that time, even I could feel the skepticism in the room. "They buy all their appliances and consumer electronics from us. I have three generations in a family buying from us," Otto said with a straight face.

When Dad's turn came around he asked what Otto thought his three biggest problems were. Otto gave a helpless shrug and pulled out his hanky to wipe his face. Several seconds ticked by in silence, then he muttered, "Well, Tom, obviously there's more money going out than coming in." Dad started to say something, but Otto held up his hand and said in a louder voice, "I know, I know. That's too goddamn simple. It's just that I don't know what to do about it. I don't even know where to start." He made me think of a man in a minefield, afraid to move forward, afraid to move back, and bewildered by how he got there. His head swung back and forth as if looking for answers in our faces.

Dad said, "Well, that's why we're here."

But what did I know? I sure didn't know that by the end of the weekend there'd be a death in the family business.

2 / Friday morning

The next morning I woke to the steam of Dad's shower billowing into our hotel room. I blinked blearily while he moved around the room in his usual full-speed-ahead morning mode. I was still adjusting to the concept of morning after years of late nights in the restaurant, but Dad had always been a caffeine-optional early riser. That's us, I thought, Tommy and Tom, just like night and day. Literally.

When I came out of the bathroom to dress, Dad was on the phone. "I heard there's a storm moving in. Could you check—" Giving the airport ground service its marching orders. Dad was always double- and triple-checking the Cessna. He'd told me yesterday's flight in had been smooth and easy, but there always seemed to be something to check.

I picked up my pace so Dad and I could get downstairs to breakfast and I could jump-start my system with a couple cups of black coffee.

After a pedestrian breakfast together in the Hilton dining room, Dad, Nick, Joanne, Dan, and I walked the two blocks to Jonker's store, right on the dot for our eight o'clock appointment. We were starting our day two hours before the store opened; Dad said we needed the time to start digging into the business before customers arrived to, quote, distract the staff, unquote. He set a brisk pace along North Street to stay warm in the October air.

As we walked, I looked up and couldn't help but think it was another good day to fly, even if the Weather Channel said it would be clouding up with rain after midnight. I noticed, as I'd noticed on the drive yesterday, the reds and golds of the oaks, maples, and birches on the hills around town. It was peak leaf-peeping season, and somebody had to twist a couple arms for us to secure rooms at the Hilton and even then Nick and Dan shared a room as did Dad and I—which sure as hell wasn't my choice.

The store's front door was locked, the inside dark. I'd expected to see big old Otto bouncing up and down like a kid doing the pee dance, eager to welcome us into his domain. He was excited enough last night.

Based on Otto's rec room performance, I thought he was scared shitless. I'd recognized that fear in my bathroom mirror. A tightness around the eyes—eyes shifting from side to side, looking for aid from somewhere, anywhere; tongue licking lips that insisted on cracking, dry throat making it hard to speak easily. Or think clearly.

My analysis, which I didn't bother to share with Dad: Otto was in over his head and was afraid to do anything. He relaxed toward evening's end, as if absorbing Dad's confidence. As the meeting broke up, Otto announced in his booming voice, "If anybody knows what to do about things, it's you guys! You guys are the best!"

Standing outside Otto's store, the window displays looked jumbled and junky to my eyes. Stepping closer and cupping my hands to shut out the sun, I could see the so-called white goods on one side of the entrance: almond and white refrigerators, washers, dryers, dishwashers, microwave ovens, and ranges. Jammed together on the other side were the electronics, the brown goods: television sets in wood-grain vinyl, console stereos in particleboard printed to look like walnut, hi-fi equipment, videocassette recorders. It looked as if Otto wanted to showcase every single goddamn item the store sold right up front.

Very different from our stores. Dad put one high-end refrigerator in one window and the store's biggest color TV console in the other. Put a spotlight on them. Have a tiny tent card to identify the brand, model, a couple key features. But no price. "You want the price of this beautiful piece of merchandise, you come into the store," Dad told me once. "You want to tell people subliminally there's no hard sell. Shop here and you'll be treated with the same respect as we treat the products."

I thought the explanation was one of those justifications Dad made up on the spot to impress me, then a high-school senior. Fast-forward to my time with Gina at the restaurant, however, and I realized that presentation actually meant a lot, if not everything. Gina liked to say, "People eat with their eyes first." Too bad more of them didn't open their wallets and come back with friends after seeing her artistically arranged entrées. One of these days I'll remember to tell Dad he was right. Display worked for Lovell's appliances, even if it couldn't keep Si Accomodi in business.

Thinking Otto was hiding somewhere in the back, Dad pounded on the front door hard enough to make the little "Open at 10:00" sign on the other side of the glass shake on its string.

Nothing happened. No light clicked on at the back. No movement inside. Nothing. If something didn't happen soon, a cop would come along to shoo us away, no matter how respectable we looked in our dress shirts, suit jackets, and polished shoes. Store's closed! Come back during store hours.

"What is this?" Nick said, narrowing his eyes and raising a fist. "I drive all the way from Scranton for this, and Otto oversleeps?"

Joanne swiveled her head to check out the area and told us, "There's a pay phone across the street. We can call his house and find out what's happening."

Dad agreed, "Good idea," and started across.

Although North Street appeared to be the town's main shopping drag, it was so early and so empty we could jaywalk without dodging a single car. The tobacco shop/newsstand with the phone was a hole-in-the-wall, not big enough for all of us, so I hung back. The pay phone was on the wall by the door and the others crowded around Dad, leaving no room for even a skinny customer to squeeze past. Finally wide awake after my coffee kicked in, I thought they should have more consideration for the poor old guy behind the counter who saw all this prospective business evaporate into one phone call.

They dialed and I read the October 3rd headlines on the local paper: "President Ronald Reagan Signs the Goldwater-Nichols Act into Law," "Apparent Attempt Made to Kill Rajiv Gandhi," "Faculty at BCC Votes No Confidence in Daube."

I didn't give a damn about the Goldwater-Nichols Act, Indian politics, or Berkshire Community College, so I walked to the curb to look up and down North Street. At one time, it must have been a thriving commercial street in a prosperous New England mill town. Now it looked sad and, well, tacky. There were a couple of once-grand movie theaters with empty marquees. The Woolworth's display windows were covered with sheets of plywood. A men's clothing store looked as if it was hanging on, but it also looked as if half the retail spaces along the street were out of business. A bank two blocks down did appear to be a going concern. A non-profit state housing office took up a large store across the street. I could see a Goodwill Industries sign up the street. Jonker's, the clothing shop, the bank, and Goodwill were the few enterprises that showed any life.

No wonder Otto had been so antsy last night. His town was dying around him.

3 / Friday morning

Nick, Dan, and Joanne hustled out of the tobacco shop behind Dad, who was shaking his head. "What?" they wanted to know. "What'd she say?" Dad seemed stunned, the others distressed. Dad stopped in the middle of the sidewalk and we circled him like players around the coach. He took a deep breath to compose himself and told us the story.

Wendy, Otto's daughter, had answered the phone. We hadn't met her last night because she was a student at Clark University in Worcester and had arrived at the house only after the meeting broke up.

Not long after we left, Otto rumbled away on his Harley to blow off steam—she said he did that when he felt stressed—and he'd gotten into some kind of accident. The police rang the bell around four in the morning and woke her and her mom with the news. They'd both gone to the hospital. Wendy didn't know how badly Otto was injured, but it was serious.

Her mother was so distraught, she didn't think to call any of us. But around dawn she remembered Dad and the rest of us were supposed to be at the store, so she sent Wendy back home to wait for Dad's call. (At this point, I wondered: Why not send Wendy to wait for us at the store? But I guess if my father was clinging to life in a hospital bed, my mind would be fuzzy too.)

When Dad stopped, Nick asked, "What should we do now?"

"The store's still in trouble." Dad had become abnormally calm. He was shifting into Focus Mode, in which nothing could—should—distract him. I'd seen it before. One time, our Cessna's engine began running ragged and I thought we might wind up ditching in some farmer's field—if we were lucky. But Dad, at the controls, shifted into Focus Mode and concentrated on exactly what should be done, and did it (add carburetor heat, drop to a lower altitude, look for a spot to land). To my relief, the engine caught and we were able to fly on. It was as if Dad instantly ordered a mental to-do list, and began working on one item after another. "We have to save the store," he pronounced. "If we don't turn this store around, and fast, Otto and Christine will be out on the street."

That seemed extreme. The store must be in worse shape than anybody imagined. I hadn't studied Otto's financials, but Dad had; he was still working at our room's desk when I fell asleep last night and he sure could sniff out trouble.

"What, leave Christine all alone at the hospital? We should be with her, see what's happening with Otto," said Joanne.

Dad thought for a second. "Good point. You and Tommy go. Make sure she's all right. Let her know we're going ahead with the analysis."

"See if she's got a key to the store," said Nick.

Dad shook that off. "Service manager's due any minute. Wendy told me. He'll let us in."

As Joanne and I walked back to the hotel parking garage, I offered to drive. She said, with a raised eyebrow, "I thought you flew up here with Tom."

I told her he'd flown up alone after flying to a meeting on Long Island earlier in the day. I'd have gladly gone along to put in another couple hours at the controls, but I had a whole different kind of meeting in Boston yesterday morning. A showdown in Bean Town: me and my lawyer versus Gina and her lawyer. That's how come I was driving Dad's Buick back and forth across Massachusetts.

"I . . . I heard about your restaurant, but I didn't realize you were in the middle of a divorce. That sounds absolutely miserable." Joanne made ordinary words resonate with kindness and concern.

I didn't know what to say. Bitch about the unfairness of it all? Tell her I'd learned a good lesson, that hard work isn't always rewarded? But I didn't want to whine, sound like a loser. Dad wasn't a loser, and he didn't raise his only child to be a loser.

"Well." To deflect any more of Joanne's sympathy, I put on a cheerful face and shrugged to imply I was putting it all behind me. "I guess it was a good learning experience." That's what Dad said about almost anything—bad or good. He also liked to say: That which does not kill me makes me stronger.

To which I wanted to say: Just try to keep that in mind when life is beating the crap out of you.

We found Christine sitting at an institutional blond-oak table in the hospital waiting room, staring at the clock. A television set was playing across the room, but Christine was having nothing to do with it. She looked like hell—hair barely combed, eyes red and puffy, her cheeks hollow. None of the brittle brightness she'd shown last night handing around stuffed mushrooms and Vienna sausages. But then who wouldn't look like hell in this hell of a situation?

Joanne and I sat on either side of her at the table. I had no idea what to say. I was there to represent Dad, and he would have been able to murmur something comforting. But Christine Jonker was older than my mother and I had zero experience consoling older women. Fortunately, Joanne knew exactly what to say: "Christine, I am so, so sorry. I want you to know we're all going to support you." She reached out to hold Christine's hand in hers.

Christine made the effort to focus, murmuring, "Thank you," and glanced again at the clock on the waiting room wall. "Almost eight- thirty."

"Have you heard anything?" asked Joanne.

"He's been in the operating room almost four hours."

"Um." Joanne gave me a look I took to mean Go Easy. "We got your message. Tom talked to Wendy," she said in a gentle voice.

"That's good," said Christine tonelessly. I don't know where she was, but I don't think she was with us in the fifth floor waiting room of the Berkshire Medical Center.

"The others went to the store," I said, partly to reassure her and partly so I wouldn't be a total bystander. "They're going to start interviewing the employees."

That was Dad's strategy. Interview the employees, analyze the financials, come up with a plan, show Otto how to execute the plan, and we'd ride out of town as heroes having saved Jonker Appliance & TV from death and dismemberment. Dad would be Analyzer-in-Chief. Nick would be Mr. Operations Management. Dan was Service Department Superman. Joanne was Salesperson of the Century; she could sell sand to Bedouins. And me?

Not so clear. Dad wanted me along to keep him company and to pick up whatever I could pick up. Maybe he thought I'd have special insights because I'd just had my business die a slow and painful death. I'd pointed out that a restaurant was not an appliance-TV store, but Dad insisted he wanted my input. Since I was back living at home in my old bedroom and helping out in the Lovell stores wherever they needed an extra body, I was in no position to argue.

My head snapped back to the here-and-now when a frightened Wendy halted in front of the table. "Here you are!" She might have been twenty-three or twenty-four, short brown-gravy hair, red splotches on her cheeks and neck, a round face, incredibly bloodshot brown eyes. She looked as if she'd been crying non-stop since the cops had come to the house. "How is he?"

Christine stood slowly, as if in pain, to greet Wendy with a hug. "Honey, we don't know yet. He's still in there." She nodded her head toward the No Admittance door. "Have you heard from Brian?" Wendy's younger brother. Otto'd told us Brian worked in the store, but he wasn't at last night's meeting. When Wendy shook her head no, Christine's eyes filled with tears that ran openly down her cheeks.

She held her daughter in wordless communication for several seconds, finally pulling away to ask, "Do you know Joanne McQuilkin? Tommy Lovell?"

Joanne and I had been standing to the side to allow Wendy private time with her mother. Wendy now reached out to shake Joanne's hand and to give me a shy smile. "I'm glad you're here to help my dad," she said to Joanne. "I know Tommy," she said to her mother. "We met at the San Diego convention."

As casually as I could, I checked Wendy out a little more carefully. She was wearing jeans, some kind of green top mostly covered by her gray Clark University sweatshirt. She must have brushed her hair before she left home, and on second look—and with her smile—she seemed almost pert.

"That had to be, what, a decade ago," said Christine.

Eleven years ago last April. I knew because I was eighteen and starting UMass in the fall. Wendy must have been thirteen or so. We'd sat on the Del Coronado's beach to watch the sunset. I was so bored during the convention that I was willing to spend time with a kid.

Now I stared at Wendy, trying to superimpose the image of the young woman in front of me on the image of the skinny little girl on the beach that long-ago evening. I couldn't do it.

Joanne asked Christine and Wendy if they'd had any breakfast. Wendy'd had cereal and juice, Christine half a container of vending machine coffee. Joanne said Christine would make herself sick if she didn't take care of herself. They should go down to the hospital cafeteria. Wendy and I could stay in the waiting room.

Christine didn't want to leave her post, but I could see in her eyes the idea of food appealed, and after a couple pro forma objections, she and Joanne headed out to the elevators.

As Wendy and I sat back at Christine's table, I caught a whiff of a musky odor. It was not offensive and it made Wendy seem vulnerable and womanly. She spoke softly, "I really appreciate what you and your father are doing for us. Mom told me when I got home last night." Wendy's red-rimmed eyes and lack of color didn't help her looks, but when she smiled her half-smile, she was almost cute. "You probably don't remember, but you saved my life once."

"I . . . What?" That had to be one of the world's greatest pickup lines.

She nodded with conviction. "Literally. When I was fourteen." She was serious. "It was at the convention. I went for a swim and didn't realize I was out too far. When I started screaming, you rushed into the water and pulled me to shore."

She gave me sheepish look, a little girl admitting something mischievous. "I'd been watching you, so I knew who you were, and I felt really stupid, like you might think I did it on purpose. I thought you were so brave to come into the water for me." After a pause to push her hair back, she continued. "We sat on the beach together and watched the sunset. I didn't want to go back to the hotel. I just wanted to sit on the beach with you all night. I had a terrible crush on you. I was afraid you'd think I'd done it to make you pay attention to me."

Her story summoned it all back: the warm Pacific, the tiny swells, the small girl waving at me just a little way out and yelling her head off. As I recalled, I hadn't been much of a hero. I swam out to her, but I could stand on the bottom. I held her head above the water and tugged her back to shore. I wrapped her in a giant hotel towel, and we sat on the sand while she calmed down. End of story.

I inspected her with a new attitude. Was anything left of her crush? Of course, being away from the dating scene for so many years, any female who told me she'd had a crush on me would be worth a second look. Or a third.

Wendy's story brought back the memory of my own panic in that ocean.

Dad had headed the organizing committee for that year's convention. I was finishing high school and heading off to college in a couple of months, and Dad and Mom wanted me along for what he called "Our Last Family Vacation Together." Spoken with a heavy sense of passing time and loss, and ignoring the fact that we never took family vacations together. Dad was always too busy with the stores.

Here's what I think was really going on: I was too old for a baby sitter and they thought I was too irresponsible to be left unsupervised for five whole days on my own. I don't know what they thought I'd do. I still had a month of classes. I had my chores at the main store. I thought I was mature and adult, but they clearly thought otherwise, although they didn't come out and say it. They promised me fun at the hotel's Teen Lounge and plenty of beach time. Big whoop.

We flew to California and Dad introduced me to a couple hundred other appliance/TV dealers and their wives and their husbands and their girlfriends and their children and their key employees and whoever else was along for some tax-deductible fun in the sun.

I was bored out of my skull that week. No one else was my age; the few other children were much younger. The guys who were a little older—those I might have hung out with—seemed to be in college or gung ho about the family business. They didn't want to hang out with (or share their pot with) a know-nothing high school kid. Many were actually interested in attending the business sessions. Me? I was stuck at the lame Teen Lounge, decked out with lame ping pong and lame air hockey.

The hotel literature said you could learn to surf, but this was the wrong season or the wrong week or the wrong something because there was no surf. The Pacific's waves were gentle little combers. So while Dad went to the meetings and Mom shopped with other wives, I worked on my tan.

I did try to visit the hotel's kitchens to watch the cooks, being a lot more interested in restaurants than appliances or retailing. Even then I was thinking about what it would be like to own a restaurant. But I was a guest, the hotel's insurance didn't cover an accident, I was in the way, and the cooks politely, firmly shooed me out.

The third evening, with nothing better to do after dinner while the adults swapped store stories, I went down to the beach for a twilight swim. The beach was almost empty, a few old people walking along the shore. No lifeguard. Just a No Swimming sign I ignored. No surf. The gentle breakers barely rose up to my knees. A solid sandy bottom that did not drop off. I had to wade a good way out—a couple hundred feet or more—before the water became neck deep. I lifted my feet and began paddling.

The ocean was a cool bath, the hazy sun was sinking, no other swimmers. I had the entire Pacific to myself. I was strong and free, away from all parental control. I felt strong enough to swim to Mexico . . . or Hawaii. I felt terrific until I needed to rest and dropped my feet to stand.

No bottom.

Looking back at the Del Coronado's lights, I saw that while I'd been playing at swimming, a current was slowly, subtly, inexorably carrying me out to sea.

Sure, I liked playing in the ocean and body-surfing, but I wasn't that good a swimmer. When I looked back at the beach receding, I realized I'd drifted too far out. Terror started to form, a black mist rising somewhere behind my eyes and in my throat to erase every thought but one: You're going to drown.

"Panic and you're dead."

I remember muttering the words aloud.

"Panic and you're dead," I repeated and repeated. The black mist drew back. It didn't vanish, but it stopped overwhelming every other thought.

"Panic and you're dead."

Easy to say, but this blind, mindless, indifferent ocean wanted to exhaust and kill me. It didn't care who I was, what I wanted, what I'd done, or what I hadn't done.

Don't swim against the current. Where had I heard that? A swimming teacher? The Boy Scouts? Something Dad once told me? Don't waste effort fighting the current. Swim with and across the current. I began to swim.

After an interminable period (probably no more than a minute or two), I paused to lift my head. The current was still carrying me down the beach, but I was closer to shore. I was still in water over my head, still in the current, but if I could control my fear and concentrate on my breathing and kicking, I could make it. I instructed myself: Put your head down. Breathe in through your mouth. Blow out through your nose. Kick, kick, kick, kick. Don't panic, swim! Swim!

Then I was standing in water up to my chin, able to push my legs through the water and walk, panting up to the beach several hundred yards away from my towel and sandals. I knelt on the damp sand, shaking with relief, my mind racing: Go for an innocent dip and almost die? How is that fair? I'm safe. Safe as if it never happened. It was an adventure rather than a meaningless, pointless, accidental death.

If I'd never returned to our suite, what would Dad and Mom have thought? That I was in the hotel somewhere having a good time? When would they begin to worry? Where would my body have finally washed ashore? Somewhere in Mexico?

I thought about confessing. But once I was safe, I had nothing to confess. That I ignored the No Swimming sign? Not a good plan. Safe, I was mildly embarrassed by my panic, which seemed no more than a terrifying dream. If I'd told Dad, what would he have said?

He'd have said: Why were you swimming at this time of night with no lifeguard on the beach? What the heck were you thinking? He'd make some stupid rule like: You can't go to the beach alone.

I told no one.

4 / Friday morning

Soon after Joanne and Christine returned from the cafeteria, a doctor in surgical scrubs pushed her way through the No Admittance door into the waiting room. She told Christine that Otto had been moved to the Intensive Care Unit and they'd be monitoring him closely. That was all she could say at the moment. He was badly hurt, and the surgical team was "guardedly optimistic."

It sure didn't sound like a lot of progress to me, but Christine and Wendy seemed less apprehensive, so I kept my mouth shut and my face neutral. Encouraged by Joanne, they agreed to go home, clean up, and come by the store later. Or not. "Don't feel you have to push yourself," Joanne told them, and I nodded like a bobble-head doll even though the advice seemed well-meaning but useless.

The four of us rode an oversized hospital elevator down to the parking garage, then separated to find our cars. Before I turned the Buick's ignition key, I asked Joanne, who seemed distracted, what she thought. She said, "I thought it was curious they haven't heard from Brian."

"Who's Brian?" I asked as I inched the big car out of the garage.

She gave me a where-have-you-been look. "Wendy's

brother. Christine told me over breakfast he has his own apartment but he's not answering his phone and she doesn't know where he is."

"A younger brother?"

"Twenty-one, twenty-two. A couple years younger than Wendy. He works in the store."

If Otto mentioned Brian at last night's meeting, I missed it, although I don't remember Otto mentioning Wendy either. He did say that if we had questions we should ask his office manager, Steffie Gilberti; she knew "where the bodies were buried." I happened to be looking at Christine at the time. It could have been my imagination, but I thought Christine's indulgent mask flickered when Steffie's name came up.

Rather than feed a meter or risk a ticket by parking in front of Otto's, I followed the "Municipal Parking" sign to a lot behind the block of stores and found an empty space. As I locked the car, I took a chance and remarked in a low tone, "I wonder if it was really an accident."

Joanne's eyes widened and she gave me a curious look. "What do you mean?"

"Well, you saw the way he looked last night. I thought he was going to have a heart attack right there in the rec room. Maybe it hit him while he was riding." She didn't look convinced so I tried another idea. "Maybe he was so stressed he lost focus. Or maybe it's his way to escape the store's problems. The way a little kid gets sick before a big test at school."

Okay, that little kid had been me. Throwing up, headache, fever. It wasn't deliberate, and I wasn't doing anything to bring it on, like eating soap or overdosing on children's aspirin. But I had a fifth grade teacher who terrified me (she truly hated me) and every morning of a big test, I started puking so I wouldn't have to go to school.

Joanne shook her head. "Seems like the hard way to avoid

the store's problems."

"I'm not saying it was deliberate. But it makes me wonder. We hear how bad things are at the store, and the next thing we know, Otto's in the ICU."

We'd reached the back of Jonker's store, a cinderblock wall with a concrete loading dock. Five steps climbed from the parking lot's asphalt to the dock and a steel Service Entrance door wide enough for a refrigerator. I stopped for a moment on the dock to look around. A road bordering the parking snaked around behind the North Street stores. A double set of railroad tracks paralleled the road for a few blocks. Beyond the tracks was another street and beyond that street was a steep hill—almost a cliff—crowned with what looked like grand old Victorian homes. And all around, the colors of autumn that I could have been enjoying from the air at the controls of the Cessna, instead of rooting through the wreckage of a fucked-up appliance business. But it sure beat out haggling with lawyers over who would get what from my fucked-up marriage and fucked-up business.

I held the Service Entrance door open for Joanne and followed her into Otto's service shop/warehouse. The inventory, mostly in cardboard shipping cartons, was stacked on either side of a cleared walkway that led to a short hall down the center of the building. Glancing quickly at the stock, it seemed to me, based on our warehouse in Gloucester, that Otto had too much merchandise for the beginning of October. Back home, Dad tried to clear out older products so we had room for the dishwashers, microwave ovens, console stereos, and television sets we would sell for Christmas. This looked as if Otto would have trouble squeezing in another carton.

Otto had created the Service Department in this warehouse space and Dan was sitting at the service bench listening intently to one of the employees. I don't think he noticed us as we passed.

On one side of the hallway was a break/meeting room and a

small office. On the other side was a closed door labeled "Parts/RAs," the employee bathroom, and Otto's office. That door was labeled "Big Boss." Joanne knocked and pushed it open, and there was Dad sitting in Otto's gigantic, black leather executive chair at Otto's gigantic wooden desk.

The office stank of cigar smoke, and Joanne winced as she opened an old-fashioned round humidor on the desk, quickly slamming it shut with a sniff. The sales floor was visible through a picture window cut in the office wall. Virtually every surface—the desk, the credenza behind it, the two leather chairs in front of it, the black leather-covered sofa against one wall, the bookcase, and the low table beside the sofa—was littered with paper. Trade magazines and newspapers, ad proofs, manufacturer spec sheets, three-ring binders from sales training programs, letters, green-and-white computer printouts, warranty forms, bills, order forms.

How could Otto—how could anyone—function in such confusion? Otto could probably lay his hand on any document he needed, but this mountain of litter would drive Dad (and me) nuts in no time. Dad had already shoved aside enough junk to clear a small space in the desktop's center where he could focus on the financial document he was analyzing with the help of an old-fashioned adding machine.

Dad looked up. "How's Otto?"

"He's out of the operating room and in the ICU," said Joanne, clearing a pile of papers from a chair and scooting it up next to Dad at the desk. "I sent Christine and Wendy home to get cleaned up and take a quick nap. No matter what happens, they'll need it."

"Nothing for them to do at the hospital except read old magazines," I said, half to myself.

"Tom," Joanne went on, "Christine did say she'd try to stop in later, to answer questions or help us if we need something."

Dad moved his fingers off the adding machine, giving

Joanne his full attention. "How are they holding up? Really?" The way he leaned in to her showed how much he trusted her opinion.

She shrugged. "Oh, Christine's furious that he went out on his motorcycle after the meeting last night." She did a fair imitation of Christine's voice: "'I'd kill him if he weren't already half dead.' But she's not falling apart. She knows the store is in serious trouble. She knows if it doesn't turn around, everything's going to be worse. Much worse." She paused for a moment, then continued thoughtfully, "I got the impression she's able to compartmentalize. Put Otto and the accident in one compartment. Put the store and what it needs in another. Put Wendy and Brian in another."

"What about Wendy and Brian?" Dad asked.

Joanne looked at me, so I said, "Wendy showed up at the hospital and we had a chat. She's afraid Otto's going to die. I tried to keep her calm, be positive." Dad and Joanne didn't need to hear about my evening on the Del Coronado's beach with Wendy. "We don't know about Brian. They don't know where he is."

"Christine's tried his apartment, but he's not answering his phone and I guess he doesn't have a machine," said Joanne.

I volunteered, "He is supposed to come to work this morning." For no good reason, I was forming an antipathy toward brother Brian.

Dad sat staring thoughtfully at the store beyond the picture window, probably imagining it filled with customers and employees. Joanne shifted a little and asked with much more patience than I could muster, "What do you need us to do?"

That jerked him back into the moment. "When Steffie Gilberti gets in, I'd like you to talk to her, woman-to-woman. See if you can get a sense of the staff's morale. Get a sense of what she's like. Is she really as competent as Otto suggested last night? What's her relationship with Christine? Can they work together?

If Otto's out of the picture for a while, Christine's going to be in charge, and if Steffie is so key, we want to know they can work together."

So Dad had caught Christine's reaction to Steffie's name last night as well. Joanne gave Dad a "You got it." She knew what to do.

"And me?" I asked.

"Tommy, see if you can help Nick with the receivables. If we don't get some cash into the business quickly, nothing else is going to matter. Otto won't have a business when he gets out of the hospital."

That's *if* he gets out of the hospital, I added silently.

5 / Friday morning

Otto had set up an open bullpen for the salespeople at the back of the store, four well-used black metal desks with imitation wood-grain tops. One, I couldn't help noticing, was precisely arranged with a glass jar of hard candies; a calendar; stacked "In," "Out," and "Pending" boxes; and a "Stephanie" name plate. The other desks were jam-packed with order books, product spec sheets, coffee mugs, pencil cups—the litter of any store, anywhere. The cheap desks, worn office chairs, and general disorder made me think of a minor government office.

By the time I pulled up a chair next to Nick he'd unearthed two fat accordion files marked "Receivables," opened one, and was going through it. He pulled out handfuls of sales slips stapled to payment record forms. Instead of neat columns of payment figures, the forms looked like tic-tac-toe boards, lots of empty spaces interspersed with an X here, a sloppy number there.

Nick nodded when I sat down, asked me for the latest about Otto. I shook my head to indicate no news, then leaned over his shoulder to ask, "Can you make sense out of this mess?"

He reached in and fished out one form at random. "Actually, it looks fairly simple. Here." One Henry Costa on Wendell Avenue bought a 19-inch Zenith color television in April, paid $50 down, paid another $50 in May, but had paid nothing since.

The form included a home phone number. "We call this guy and ask him to pretty please catch up with his payments. By now—" Nick looked at the sales receipt, took a moment to calculate. "—by now the whole thing should have been paid off."

Collections from this side of the desk were new to me. Lovell & Son didn't extend credit and neither did Si Accomodi, so I'd never had to try to collect money.

In the last months of Si Accomodi, of course, I'd been on the receiving end of increasingly aggressive collection calls, day after sickening day. Suppliers finally stopped offering terms and demanded cash on delivery. But the calls left me scarred. I knew we owed the money. We didn't have it. All I could do was promise to pay a little bit every week, with every good intention of living up to my promise. All our vendors could do was threaten. And stop deliveries. Goodbye supplies, goodbye customers, goodbye restaurant, goodbye Gina.

It felt strange to be asking for money owed rather than fending off a creditor. It wasn't like asking for money from Gina's parents, which was painful enough. Maybe I could make it a game, a contest: Hi there! We're trying to reach our goal of $1,500 in this hour and we need your pledge of $25 bucks to go toward paying for the color TV you bought in April. Help us save Otto's store.

Nick explained that Otto used a credit company for consumer credit. But when the company turned down a customer's application, Otto made the sale anyway, the store taking on the debt instead. It meant Otto was carrying the least credit-worthy customers himself, the ones most likely to fall behind in their payments or to default. Nick's sigh conveyed his disapproval, and I was sure Dad would feel the same.

I asked how much the store was owed. Nick threw up his hands in a 'who knows?' gesture. "The whole shebang? I'd have to spend a couple hours to add everything up. But there's probably three hundred people on the books."

"Three hundred!"

"Be cool. Be cool. Some are current. Paying ten or fifteen dollars a week as regular as Tuesday. And those are the folks we want because they end up paying eight hundred bucks for a four-hundred-and-fifty-dollar washer. But it looks like a lot of them started making payments, then missed one, didn't make it up, missed another, and no one called to find out what was going on."

"Jonker hasn't been sending out monthly reminders?" Addressing envelopes to announce Lovell's monthly specials had been one of my jobs as a young teenager. Dad wouldn't have let a customer go indefinitely without following up.

"You kidding?" Nick had been triaging the files: those 30 days past due, those 60 days past due, 90 days, and over 120 days. After four months, most businesses would turn the debt over to a collection service, send a truck to pick up the TV, write the debt off as uncollectible, or all three. "If I had to make a ball-park guess of what's outstanding? Seventy-five thousand. Maybe more. Maybe a lot more. Good luck collecting it."

I was stunned. It seemed like too high a mountain to climb. But Nick looked determined and I wanted to be a good boy and do my part. So I picked up a bunch of the older records, crossed to the desk across from Nick, and began pressing numbers on the phone.

First call: ten rings . . . no answer.

Second call: same thing. Don't these people have answering machines?

Third call: a perky recording: "Hi! This is Bobby and Sue. We can't come to the phone right now, but if you leave a message we'll get right back to you."

I tried to be just as perky: "Hi! This is Tommy Lovell down at Jonker Appliance! I wonder if you could get right back to me!" and left the number. Bobby and Sue hadn't paid anything on their washer and dryer since July.

On the seventh ring of the fourth call, someone picked up. "Hello?" Tentative. Elderly. Female.

"Mrs . . . Donaldson? Mrs. Lawrence Donaldson?"

"Yes . . .?" She sounded a hundred years old. Alert, but wary.

"This is Tommy Lovell down at Jonker Appliance & TV. We've been going through our records and we see that you bought a nineteen-inch Zenith color television on April twentieth of this year. You paid twenty-five dollars down and we delivered it on Tuesday, the twenty-second. Is that correct?" I paused to let my words sink in.

"I . . . I guess that's correct. I don't recall the dates precisely." She thought about it for a few seconds. "It was last spring," she said, trying to be helpful. I thought I could hear the TV tuned to *Good Morning America* in the background.

"According to our records, Mr. Donaldson paid twenty-five dollars on May ninth, twenty dollars on June thirteenth, and twenty dollars on July eleventh."

I shut up for a moment to let her dispute that, but she wanted to be obliging. "Yes," she said, "the Social Security comes around the beginning of the month."

"Well, Mrs. Donaldson, since July, we haven't received another payment. You still owe five hundred and eighty-seven dollars and thirty-eight cents. Will Mr. Donaldson come in to make another payment this afternoon or tomorrow?" Give the customer a choice that's no choice.

"Oh." It was more gasp than word. "Larry died on July twenty-third—during that terrible heat we were having."

It took a couple seconds to switch from bill collector to sympathetic stranger. "That's terrible! I'm so sorry to hear about your loss, Mrs. Donaldson." But it doesn't make the $587.38 go away.

"He was working in the garden and he just collapsed onto the tomato plants."

What do you say to an elderly widow? "That's awful . . ."

"Larry was always so proud of his tomatoes. I told him it was too hot to be out there," she added in a querulous voice.

I gave her a moment and then gently steered the conversation back. "What do you think about the payments?"

"Larry always took care of the bills."

"I know that when you lose someone, it takes some time to adjust." I did my best to sound sympathetic and understanding. "If you just sent us something every month . . ."

"Otto said it would be all right when he came to the funeral. I knew his father, you know. Old Herman Jonker. Now *there* was gentleman!" She paused for a moment. "During the war . . . when everything was rationed and you couldn't get anything at the stores anyway . . . some of the farm women would pay him in eggs . . . or butter . . . or meat. And Herman took it. Same as cash."

I wondered if she were suggesting she work off the debt with produce. Whatever happened to Larry's tomatoes? "Those must have been difficult times." I was going to say more about the money, but it hit me: Am I going to squeeze a widow for her last dime? Am I down to that?

I thanked her, said I was sorry I bothered her, and ended the call. I sat staring at the payment sheet. She wasn't my customer. Did I care if the Widow Donaldson paid for her television set? I sure wasn't going to send the delivery guys to pick up a six-month-old TV from an elderly widow. And who'd be that heartless anyway?

What's best? Turn her over to a collection service? See if she's got a son or daughter taking care of her finances? Just forget about it and write it off as a bad debt? I made a note on the payment record, "Try to find a responsible relative," and put it aside to make another call.

Another answering machine. Then I got lucky. On the next call, the woman apologized profusely, said they'd been distracted with two kids going back to college, and said she'd put a check for $278.61 in the mail, the entire balance due on the dishwasher she said she loved.

On the call after that, the man said he'd taken the new television and VCR with him to his apartment when he separated from his wife and he'd start sending $25 a week. I thought he was lying, but I didn't care. It felt like an accomplishment.

I thought I'd struck out on the next call and was about to hang up, when a man picked up. "Yeah? What?" He sounded as if I'd gotten him out of the shower and he wasn't happy about it.

"Mr. Bergquist? Donald Bergquist?"

"Yeah. Who's this?"

"This is Tommy Lovell down at Jonker Appliance & TV. We've been going through our records and we see that you bought a Panasonic video cassette recorder on . . . Saturday, June twenty-first. You paid fifty dollars down and took the VCR with you. Is that correct?"

"Yeah. So what?"

"Our records don't show any further payments. You still owe almost three hundred and fifty dollars."

"I don't owe you shit."

"But the VCR's price—"

Bergquist cut me off. "That piece of crap hasn't worked right since I got it home. The second one, too." The voice seemed to rumble out of an echo chamber. I imagined a large unshaven truck driver or construction worker. That was probably unfair, but his credit application—which the credit company rejected—did list New England Transport as place of employment.

"I'm terribly sorry to hear that," I said as smoothly as I could. "We want all our customers to be happy with their purchases." Bergquist grunted. "Maybe we should send a technician out to look at the machine. See what the trouble—"

"Nobody comes onto my property."

"But Mr. Bergquist—"

"Listen, asshole! You think I don't know what you're thinking? Nobody touches my property. You tell that shithead boss of yours if he keeps harassing me like this I'm coming down to the store and stick the VCR where the sun don't shine."

"Are you making a threat, Mr. Bergquist?"

"You just tell him any more harassing calls, and I won't be responsible for what happens."

"I'll let him know, Mr. Bergquist. You have a nice day now." I cut him off before he could snarl an answer.

I made a note to give the account to a collection agency. They get paid to take abuse. Maybe someone could break Bergquist's kneecaps.

But the conversation made me think. Maybe Otto wasn't as universally loved by his customers as he'd indicated last night.

Joanne, in her usual diplomatic way, had asked about the store's competitive strength in town, and Otto, with obvious satisfaction, had said the store's competitive strength was the relationship he had with his customers. "My customers love me."

"How do you know that?" Nick had asked, not in a challenging way but with genuine curiosity in his voice. Out of the corner of my eye, I saw Dad cock his head ever so slightly. I couldn't mistake that look, having seen it more than once when he didn't believe my homework was all done before we went up together in the Cessna, but he was willing to give me the benefit of the doubt.

Otto said knew it because he said they bought all their appliances and consumer electronics from him—"three generations in a family buying from me."

Maybe. But it didn't sound like Bergquist would be stopping in for a microwave oven any time soon.

6 / Friday morning

Dad stood smiling over my desk and dropped a $20 bill in front of me. I hung up the phone without leaving another callback message to look up at him. "We need coffee," he said. "There's got to be a place to get good coffee around here." Emphasis on "good."

"And donuts," said Nick, stretching as he stood up. "I'll go with you. Hey, any word on Otto yet?"

Dad shook his head. Nick plucked his jacket off the back of the chair. We got to the door just as Dad called out, "See what Joanne and Dan want."

I might have been more pissed at being Dad's delivery boy if I weren't already sick of making collection calls.

Nick and I walked back up the side street to North Street. As we stood on the corner, unsure which way to turn, a man in a Red Sox cap carrying a Dunkin' Donuts coffee container crossed toward us. Nick stopped him, pointed at the cup, and asked, "Where can we buy one of those?" The man said the shop was one block down and two over. Nick thanked him with a sincere "Go Sox!"

Problem solved, we moved on and Nick said without preamble or introduction, as if picking up a conversation we'd dropped last night at Otto's, "Tell me more about your restaurant."

"Nothing to tell. It's gone."

"Yeah, I heard that. So what happened?" He sounded genuinely interested.

I hesitated before answering. "A lot of things." Because my answer seemed inadequate, I added, "Everything."

We were walking past an imposing white-and-gray marble First Agricultural Bank building. Nearby I could see the city hall, town offices, and a police station. Like Dad, I enjoyed knowing where things were, the relationships between streets and buildings and rivers and mountains, creating a mental map. Whenever we flew, he was always scanning the ground for a possible place to land in an emergency.

Nick wasn't going to let it go. "Anything special?"

I sorted through the differences Gina and I fought about. The personal stuff was none of Nick's business. He prompted, gently but firmly, "Start with the location."

We'd leased space in a shopping strip instead of a mall or upscale commercial building. The strip was cheap and the landlord gave us a deal on the first year's rent. "The space had been a restaurant, so we didn't have to spend a lot on equipment—not that we had a lot to spend." In fact, we burned through most of our savings before we opened the doors.

Nick asked the obvious, "What happened to the former tenant?"

"He'd gone bust. Which should have told us something. But Gina and I thought we'd do better because we'd have a better menu, better service. We'd have a better atmosphere. When we saw the place, it was a dump." When we'd first pushed open the door, we were surprised the former tenant had stayed in business more than a week. The room was dark, dirty, and depressing; the black walls and ceiling made even the empty space feel claustrophobic.

"So what happened?"

We walked another half block in silence. Most people, when they ask a question, expect an immediate answer. If they don't get one, they ask the question again, as if you didn't hear it the first time. Or they ask another question, as if you didn't understand the first one. Nick acted as if he could wait the rest of the morning for an answer. It gave me a funny feeling to have my fucked-up business under Nick's sympathetic but relentless microscope.

I shrugged and blurted out my tale of woe. "No one thing. A lot of things. We were under-capitalized. Not enough money meant we were cutting corners. Trying to do everything ourselves. Not enough loyal, regular customers. By the time we woke up and tried to get a bank loan, no one would touch us so we borrowed from her parents. Gina was trying to do everything in the kitchen and it was too much and we couldn't afford any decent help, so we had a revolving door, which meant the expense of finding, dressing, and training someone new every few weeks. Gina's an incredible cook, but running a kitchen for a thirty-seat restaurant is very different from making a great Sunday dinner. She burned out. We both did. We reached the point where we didn't have enough cash, so we couldn't buy supplies. One day we ran out of butter. Can you believe it? A restaurant running out of butter? I was going to use tips and send the waiter to the supermarket for a couple pounds of butter when I woke up: 'This is it,' I told myself. 'We're over the edge. It's too late.' That day, we closed early and told the staff—the three of them—we were finished. Don't come in tomorrow. We just gave up."

Recalling that horrible evening, I could feel my throat tighten once again, my eyes sting with tears. Killing Si Accomodi felt like turning off the life support of a dying loved one. Click— and it was all over and all you had was grief.

Nick shook his head. "That's got to hurt. You work so hard,

and it's not enough."

"It hurts like hell," I agreed and added silently, You can't imagine what it feels like. "So anyway, the restaurant was big a waste of time. Four years down the toilet."

"Could be." Nick seemed to consider the idea. "But you never know going in, do you? What's going to be a waste of time."

What could I say? Was the restaurant really a waste of time? The days—months!—Gina and I spent planning, redecorating, creating the menu, working seventy hours a week to make it successful, had all that been a waste? Considering the way Si Accomodi had eaten my life, maybe it was.

Had my marriage been a waste? Even though I was still raw from the restaurant's collapse, Gina's fury, and yesterday's meeting with the lawyers, I wouldn't call the time entirely wasted. We'd had some good times. When we were working together to get the doors open, we'd go back to our condo, shower, and make love, excited by what we were creating and by the other's excitement. Saying with our bodies what we hadn't said while we worked. Or at least that's the way I wanted to remember it.

Another of Dad's "can-do" sayings popped into my mind—he liked to say that every new experience, good or bad, was a learning experience. Maybe I learned things I didn't want to know—like love doesn't always conquer all.

Rather than keep on dissecting my troubles, I changed the subject. "If Otto's going to be in the hospital for a while, and the store's teetering on the edge, can our help really make much of a difference?"

Nick said nothing for a couple steps. "Otto's been a friend to Tom and to me. He needs help. It's like the neighbor kid who falls out of a tree and breaks his arm. You drive him to the hospital. You show up and you do what you can do." As if Nick had planned the commotion to make his point, an ambulance came tearing up the street, siren screaming.

Nick's analogy was flawed somehow, but I didn't debate him. His heart was in the right place. I knew what it was like to need help, and how hard it was to accept it. This time, I was in a position to offer some. Still, I wasn't convinced that Dad and his friends, parachuting in for a weekend, could really save Otto and his store. "But what if Otto is Wile E. Coyote? He's run off the cliff and is just standing in mid-air, waiting to fall."

"We don't know that yet, do we?" Nick gave me a hard look. "We don't know jack shit about Otto's business yet, do we?" I muttered agreement. "Maybe he's not off the cliff. Maybe he is and we can throw him a line. But Tom's got the right idea. Here's a business that's been providing a living to—what?—a couple dozen people—more—for years. You don't want to see it fold unless there's no other choice."

The Dunkin' Donuts was like every Dunkin' Donuts, all pink and cream. The three girls behind the counter looked as if they should be in high school. Brandi, a cute blond with thin lips and a button nose, filled out her uniform nicely. I could see a white ribbed undershirt where the uniform gapped. She asked if she could help us, and Nick, all smiles and charm, asked if the coffee was fresh and the donuts hot.

Brandi apparently couldn't tell if this gray-haired guy in the fedora and black leather jacket was serious, so she played it safe, returned his smile, and said, "Hot donuts melt the icing—but we just brewed a fresh pot of coffee."

I thought the "fresh pot" line was something the clerks were trained to say, day and night, fresh pot or no. And the "hot donut" excuse was bullshit because the donuts came from a central facility. Yet Brandi managed to come off as friendly and helpful, not a robotic corporate tool. The shop was lucky to have her.

Nick said, "Fresh coffee—just what we're looking for," and turned to me for the orders. As Brandi jammed containers into a cardboard carrier, I noticed she was a nail biter; her nails were ragged and down to the quick. Nick played Mr. Decision-maker, picking out a dozen donuts.

Brandi rang up the sale, I gave her Dad's twenty, she entered the amount, and she began pulling singles out of the cash drawer. "You don't have to count back?" I said. She looked confused.

Mom taught me to make change when I was old enough to reach the cash register. If the order came to, say, $15.57, and the customer handed over a twenty, I would count back three pennies to make $15.60, a nickel and a dime to make $15.75, a quarter to make $16.00, and four singles to make $20.00. Quick and simple and I didn't have to subtract mentally to calculate the $4.43. Now the machine was taking over.

I explained and Brandi said, "No need. It"—the cash register—"tells me how much change to give." She flashed a sweet grin as she handed over the bills, coins, and a machine-printed receipt. I felt old. A skill I'd been proud to hone was obsolete.

Nick ostentatiously stuffed another twenty into the tip cup. He picked up the donuts. I carried the coffee.

Nick must have seen me react at the tip—Brandi's brown eyes, a little heavy on the mascara, certainly widened when she saw what he was doing—because back on the street, Nick bent close to speak softly into my ear. "You know what gets good service?"

"A big tip?" It always encouraged good service at Si Accomodi.

Nick seemed disappointed that I'd guessed correctly, but he stood upright and said with authority, "You bet your ass. They'll talk about us for the rest of the shift."

7 / Friday morning

Dad held a closed-door strategy meeting in the break room over the coffee and donuts. I stood to the side, nibbling the last glazed donut, while the experts poked through the figures to diagnose what sounded like one very sick business.

Otto's store had lost almost $25,000 on sales of $682,751 in the first six months of 1986. Even worse, Dad thought Otto bled more red ink in the third quarter.

Nick wondered out loud about the store's problems. Something out of whack with Otto's prices? Not charging enough to make a profit? Competition so harsh he couldn't charge more? Or were expenses totally out of line: advertising, salaries and wages, rent, travel?

Dad agreed with Nick's speculation but said we needed more information to pinpoint the real reasons for the loss.

Joanne asked if Otto might be taking too much money out of the business for himself.

Again, Dad said he couldn't tell without more information, but if so, Otto should fire his accountant; the taxes on their personal income would be killing him and Christine. Dad did think something might have happened to Otto's financials two or three years ago—it would take a few years for a business to slip into the disorder he saw here.

I felt vaguely embarrassed I wasn't able to contribute to the discussion. (Of course, as Mom always told me, "If you have nothing to say, say nothing.") At the same time I was impressed by Dad's knowledge and attitude. He was determined that if Otto's store could be saved, he and his friends were going to save it. And he was including me in his inner circle, which both pleased me and put me on the spot to be productive in some way.

Dan was just talking about interviewing the rest of the employees, in search of some ideas, when we were startled by a hard rap on the door. It flew open and the worried face of a middle-aged woman appeared. "I just heard about Otto! That's terrible! Terrible! How is he? It he all right?"

Dad half-stood. "You are . . . ?"

"On his motorcycle? Oh, that damned motorcycle! But he couldn't!" She came into the break room on a flood of words and fluttering hands.

"I'm Tom Lovell. You are . . .?"

She stopped in front of him, wringing her hands, trying to regain control of her feelings. "Stephanie. Stephanie Gilberti. The office manager. Vernon just told me." So this was the Steffie person Otto had mentioned last night. She'd come in through the back entrance and passed the service manager who was probably feeling self-important as the bearer of bad news about the boss.

Dad spoke calmly. "Otto's still in intensive care. We don't know exactly how he's doing, but we should be getting an update very soon." Then he summed up the reason for our visit—Otto called for help—and introduced Joanne, Nick, Dan, and me. We nodded at Steffie, she nodded back, clearly not taking everything in.

I would have put Steffie in her late forties, a little younger than Christine. She had blue eyes and was wearing heavy mascara and eye shadow. A hefty woman, she wore a green sweater that seemed too small. Her thick auburn curls were a hair salon's triumph. She might be pushing fifty, but she was pushing back.

"That motorcycle! That damned motorcycle! I'm not surprised—the way he used to go off on it." She sounded put out, a parent pissed off by her child's wayward behavior.

Joanne moved closer to Steffie and followed up: "You're the office manager?"

"And executive secretary *and* personnel manager *and* bookkeeper *and* chief cook and bottle washer."

Steffie's tone suggested that, despite her chores, she was proud of everything she was doing. She was an important—in her eyes, the most important—member of the staff, the indispensible one. I wondered about Steffie's relationship with Otto's wife. If Steffie was the indispensible one, what was Christine? Otto's words stuck in my mind: "If you need anything I can't answer, ask Steffie—Stephanie Gilberti. She knows where all the bodies are buried."

Dad asked her, "Do you know where Otto kept the key to his desk?"

She looked blank, as if she didn't understand the question. "Another key? I mean—he had one with his usual set of keys."

"Do you know what he keeps in it?"

She had to think a moment. "Personnel files . . . financial records." She looked vaguely around the room. "Things he doesn't want lying around." Her attitude said, And what's wrong with that?

Dad dropped his voice and leaned toward her. "Mrs. Gilberti, Otto asked us to help him with the store. We've just been going through the numbers. What's your take on how the business is doing?"

Steffie's right hand smoothed the front of her sweater. She hesitated. "I . . . I know Otto's been worried." We waited for her to say more. She licked her upper lip, and scanned the room without looking anyone in the eye. "I know we've done better in the past."

"You're the bookkeeper. Do you talk to the accountant?"

Now she sounded a little defensive. "Just to send him papers . . . figures. He doesn't talk to me about what he does. Just if he needs more information. His reports go directly to Otto, of course."

"So you don't know if the business is making money or how much."

"I . . . I know it's not making much. This year has been very difficult."

I noticed Dad hesitated before his next question, as if trying to decide how much to reveal. "Would it surprise you to know the store lost money in the first half?"

We all watched her. She didn't seem surprised, but she did look uncomfortable. "I think I knew that." She sounded as if she were confessing personal failure.

"It wasn't a lot of money, but—" Dad broke off. I could almost see the gears turning. He was never one to rub anyone's nose in bad news. But if Jonker's continued to lose money, it would be out of business. What kind of losses could the store sustain . . . and for how long? A sensitive subject, for sure. No wonder the office manager seemed uneasy.

I caught Dad's eye and he made an almost imperceptible "go ahead" gesture. Adopting a conversational tone, I combined a touch of flattery with a real question. "Otto told us how much he depends on you, how much you know about the store. If you were running the business, what changes would you make?"

Some of the tension left Steffie's face, tension I hadn't recognized until it disappeared. "We have too many people," she said promptly. "I work really hard, but some of the employees spend all day just drinking coffee and sitting around, having a cigarette and gossiping. Otto's just too big-hearted. He doesn't want to let anyone go. Whether they're working hard or not." She stopped and looked at Dad, maybe concerned she'd said too much.

He nodded thoughtfully, letting her know we were taking her seriously. I thought it was a good time for me to fade into the background and let the others continue the interview. "Anything else?" Joanne prodded gently.

Steffie didn't hesitate. "Run more ads. Sears is in the paper almost every day, but sometimes we don't run an ad for a week or even two. I think people want to see you're in the paper all the time."

Dad made a note on his pad and encouraged her to keep going. "Anything else?"

A hint of tension reappeared around Steffie's eyes and mouth. "I don't want to tell tales out of school."

Dad adopted the professional and trustworthy voice I'd heard so many times: "If it will help the business, we should know about it."

"Well . . . it has to do with Mrs. Jonker. Christine." Why was I not surprised? "She doesn't understand him." Steffie pulled at a button on her sweater. "He's been under a lot of pressure lately." She licked her lips. "He doesn't need her second-guessing his decisions."

Joanne put her two cents in: "Christine is questioning his decisions?" Steffie nodded vigorously. "How do you know?"

"My desk is right on the other side of his office wall." The neat desk under the picture window; Otto could just tap on the window and Steffie would come running. "She comes right through the front door, bold as brass, walks right into his office, pulls down the Venetian blind, and goes at it. I can't hear what they're saying exactly, but they really go at it, if you know what I mean."

No way was I going to touch this. I mean, what married (or

recently separated) man would go down that road? Luckily, Joanne asked, in a quiet, woman-to-woman voice, "Often?"

Steffie had to think. Finally she admitted, "I wouldn't say *often*. Maybe every couple months or so. And at top volume."

Joanne pressed her a little further. "You must have some idea what they argued about."

Steffie only shook her head and pursed her lips, again giving me the impression she feared she'd said too much already. "No. They're just loud voices." She jerked her head around at a noise and motioned. "There's someone at the front door." I thought she looked relieved to be off the hot seat.

Dan, who was closest to the break room door, glanced down the hall and through the showroom. "Looks like a salesman." Curious, I stuck my head out the break room door to see. Customers don't usually show up an hour before opening and not wearing tie and jacket. Dan amended his opinion as the man pulled out his wallet and held it up. "It's a cop," said Dan.

Steffie went to the back to turn off the alarm and fished in her purse for the front door key. When she unlocked the door, the man again flashed his badge, introduced himself as Detective Wilkins from the Pittsfield police department, and eased his way inside. "Just tying up some loose ends. You work here?" he asked Dad, ignoring Steffie.

"No, just visiting. Mrs. Gilberti works here." After she explained who she was and what she did in the store, she deferred to Dad as they walked down the hall to the break room and sat down. Dad extracted a business card from his shirt pocket and handed it to the detective as he introduced Nick, Dan, Joanne, and me. They all offered their business cards. All except me. I'd thrown away all my Si Accomodi/Thomas W. Lovell, Prop. cards in a general purging.

The detective carefully arranged the cards in front of him and looked slowly around the group to connect the names to the faces. I wondered why a simple motorcycle accident needed a detective. Once he'd satisfied himself who was local, who was from out of town, Wilkins took a small notebook from a suit pocket and clicked his ballpoint. "Just tying up some loose ends from the accident last night." Steffie's mouth gave a little twitch as the rest of us leaned forward, ready for news about the accident.

But no. Wilkins wasn't here to give information, he was here to get information. "When did you last see Mr. Jonker?"

"Last night." Dad nominated himself to be the group's spokesman. "At his house."

"All of you?" asked Wilkins.

"I saw him yesterday," Steffie said, quickly amending it to, "Here. At the store."

"We were at his house last night," said Dad, circling with his hand to indicate the rest of us. "We had a meeting about the business."

Wilkins made a note, then pointed at Dan in his green service technician's uniform pants and shirt, looking as if he'd driven straight from his shop. Dan was the quiet one. He'd come out of the service side of the business, had not gone to college, and deferred to those who had. He was the only one who seemed genuinely interested in the rec room's bar sink (something to do with a "below grade drain") and the TV set's hookup. He'd spent much of Otto's meet-and-greet-and-product-demonstration time standing silently at the side of the room, sipping at his beer and observing. Wilkins asked, "What time did you leave?"

Dan said the meeting broke up a little after 11:30 and we'd left to return to the hotel. As he spoke, the rest of us nodded in agreement.

"How did he seem? Mr. Jonker."

After a few seconds, three people spoke at once: "Nervous." "Excited." "Keyed up." Wilkins pointed at Nick, who'd been silent. "What about you?"

"I'd say he was . . . anxious." Nick spoke slowly, choosing his words carefully. He'd driven up to the Berkshires from Pennsylvania and was probably Dad's closest business friend. Closer than Otto. They talked a couple times a month. Nick had been a bomber pilot during Vietnam, so they had flying in common in addition to appliance-TV retailing. Nick was an Air Force Academy graduate, divorced ("Married too young," Mom diagnosed), and had a long-time girlfriend who was a flight attendant. At the moment she was somewhere over the Pacific. Nick, gray at the temples, still wore his hair in a military cut. I wondered why someone with his education and background would be content to be an appliance dealer, but what did I know? Nick added, "He was worried about the business . . . about the business climate here in town . . . and he . . . he was perspiring."

Detective Wilkins had a technique of listening carefully to whoever spoke while observing others for their reactions. Noticing Dad paying close attention, Wilkins asked, "Did he seem depressed? Desperate?"

Dad shook his head. "No, not depressed. He was excited to have us here. Happy to show off his house. But I don't understand. Are you asking if Otto was suicidal?"

Wilkins neatly deflected Dad with the universal palm out "halt" sign, not rudely but not friendly either. "I'll get to that." Then he turned his full attention on me. "And you are?" He glanced at the business cards on the desk.

"Thomas Lovell, Junior. That's my father."

Wilkins' head bobbed slightly to glance at his notes. "You were at the Jonker house last night as well? Did Mr. Jonker seem to you as if . . . he might want to hurt himself?" He was asking me while aware of the others.

I barely knew Otto and Christine but, like Dad, I had an opinion. On everything. I told the detective: "No, not suicidal that

I could see. I thought he might have a heart attack, given the sweat pouring off him and his red face and the jumpy way he was acting." Wilkins waited for more. "He was . . . you know . . . all wound up. Talking a mile a minute. Showing off. Trying to put the best face on things." After a couple seconds I added, "It was like he was trying to sell us on how everything was going to be great now we were in town."

"Was he drinking?" A question for everyone.

We had to think about that. Finally Nick answered, "One beer. Early in the evening. I remember because there were only two St. Pauli Girls. I took one and he took the other. He said he couldn't drink the horse piss Christine usually bought. I don't know if he finished his, because he put it down to show us the stuff in the family room, and then he was talking about the business."

Wilkins looked around at the group, then at the store. He made a little show of rereading his notes, keeping us waiting. "So nobody noticed anything unusual—out of the ordinary—last night." No one could add anything. Wilkins closed the notebook and put it in his jacket pocket. "I guess that's it for now. How long will you people be in town?"

Everyone looked at Dad who said, "I don't know. We only expected to be here for the weekend."

"Some of us have to get back," said Nick.

"I gotta be in my store on Monday morning," said Dan.

"I could stay on a day or two," said Joanne.

There was a silence, and to fill it I said, "I could stay for a week or two." Nobody snickered, but then again, nobody cheered either. Why not stay? After all, what did I have waiting for me in Gloucester? My childhood bedroom. Big whoop.

Dad said, "We're all at the Hilton if you need us," and Wilkins grunted acknowledgment.

Nick finally asked the question we'd avoided for the last half hour: "Any idea how Otto's doing?" Wilkins said nothing for an instant, his face blank, then he looked directly at Nick as he answered. "Still unconscious, still critical." Not the news we'd hoped for, but at least the detective was straight with us instead of talking a line of boilerplate "hope and pray" bullshit.

After shaking hands all around and leaving his business card with Steffie, Wilkins let his eyes wander through the store again with a perceptibly different attitude, something about the way he carried himself, his expression. "You know," he said thoughtfully, "You hear a lot about these video cassette machines lately."

Without missing a beat, Joanne stepped forward, put a hand lightly on Wilkins's arm, and begin urging him toward the VCR display. "They're remarkable machines," she said, in familiar territory at last. "Let me show you what they can do."

8 / Friday morning

"We've asked you to come in early this morning because, as you've all heard, Otto was hurt in an accident last night."

Dad stood with Nick, Dan, Joanne, and me in the bullpen and looked around at fifteen sober employees in the showroom. Steffie Gilberti had phoned everyone and managed to assemble the staff for this all-hands-on-deck meeting.

"He's been operated on and now moved to Intensive Care. He's still in serious condition, but the doctors are hopeful." Dad was trying to be positive, despite what we'd heard from the close-mouthed Detective Wilkins earlier.

The employees—six men, nine women—leaned against almond and white appliances, the TV and stereo consoles in the spacious showroom, staring at Dad and our little group.

"Who are you?" A red-faced older man interrupted, sounding suspicious. Here was Dad, someone the guy had never seen before, acting like he owned the place. "And are we getting our paychecks today?"

A quick panicked look swept over Steffie's face but, after the smallest of nods from Dad, she pulled herself together and said, "I made up the checks, but I don't know if Otto signed them yesterday."

"If he didn't, who else has signing authority?" Dad asked.

"Christine can do it."

He turned back to the red-faced guy. "Okay, we'll make sure everyone gets a check as usual. If Otto hasn't signed them, we'll get Christine's signature." This was Dad's no-nonsense, no back-talk tone, and it worked. The guy leaned back.

One of the younger salesmen, sporting shoulder-length hair and a scruffy Van Dyke, piped up: "Or Brian can sign."

"Not the payroll account," said Steffie. "Only Otto or Christine can sign."

That stopped the conversation for a moment. I flashed to a vision of Otto, bandaged head to toe, attached to a beeping machine, Christine at his bedside. If the staff was thinking what I was thinking, no wonder the place fell silent. But where were the checks? I crossed to Steffie, asked her in a low tone, "Can you put your hands on the checks?" She whispered back, "They're locked in Otto's desk. But he has the key, remember?"

I'd forgotten. One key to the desk, attached to that missing key ring. Now what?

"Steffie, do you know a locksmith who can get over here this morning?" I asked. She lifted an eyebrow, I could almost see the light bulb flick on, and she left the room at a trot.

Meanwhile, Dad was giving Otto's staff a mini-bio by way of explaining his presence: Owner of the two-store Lovell & Son Appliance/TV chain in Gloucester and Beverly (he was the Son, not me; he took it over from Grandad); in business almost twenty-five years; friendly with Otto and Christine for more than ten years. That Otto had asked him to look over the entire Jonker's operation—something I wouldn't have revealed to this bunch, at least not yet—and that Nick, Dan, Joanne, and his son—me—were along for our special expertise. I don't know what special expertise I brought to the party, but it was nice to hear.

"So what are you going to do?" asked one woman, perched

on a dehumidifier carton. From the chip on her shoulder, I had the sense she wouldn't like anything we did.

Before Dad could answer, he was interrupted by a woman resting her ass against a washer. "But what exactly happened to Otto? All I heard is he got hurt."

A voice from the back spoke right up. Her husband was the desk sergeant last night and told her all about the incident over breakfast. The accident happened on the loop road in the state forest, a narrow, one-way road that goes up the mountain to a campground then down to a parking lot and picnic area.

Now that the cop's wife had the floor, she was going to make the most of it. And I have to admit, we were so starved for information, nobody moved a muscle. She stood up. I noticed her nametag said "Lauren" as she spun the story out in slow motion.

A couple of kids were making out at the camp ground at the top of the mountain and they didn't hear anything—no screech of brakes, no crunch of metal—but when they started home, coming down the twisting mountain road, they saw a motorcycle smashed up against the guardrail with no rider. The road's so narrow, they had to squeeze around the crashed bike. They didn't stop. Kids! They expected to see the rider walking down to the parking lot and see if he needed a ride. But they didn't see anyone so they drove back to town. When they passed the first pay phone they began to argue whether they should call 911. The boy wouldn't stop. He didn't want to have anything to do with the police. Neither of them wanted parents asking a lot of questions about exactly where they'd been or what they'd been doing. But when the girl got home, her conscience began to bother her, so at that point she called in the accident.

This delay meant the police didn't dispatch a car to the state forest until two in the morning or so and the officer on the scene didn't call for an ambulance until he'd actually gone into the woods and found Otto's body. It took another half hour or more to get an ambulance to the scene and to carry Otto out of the woods and into the ambulance.

Lauren had been on quite a roll with the story, but suddenly she stopped speaking. I thought she was blabbing a little too freely about police business, and I guess that realization finally caught up with her mouth.

The crowd seemed hungry for all the gory details. "Was he wearing a helmet?" someone asked.

"Hell, no, I bet," said a short guy leaning against a high-end refrigerator. "You know Otto."

"How serious is it?" someone else asked.

Dad cut the speculation short. "Believe me, as soon as we know anything definite, we'll let you know."

"So what are you going to do here?" the dehumidifier sitter asked again.

"Mrs. Jonker asked us to help out until Otto can return to work," said Dad, as easily as if it were true. "We'll be on the premises for the next few days, talking to you individually about the business and what you and the family can do to make Jonker's even stronger."

I heard a woman standing in the stereo console display give a soft sniffle, followed by a muffled moan as two staff members hugged each other in consolation. The rest looked around uncomfortably, not volunteering, not asking questions, nothing. When Gina and I shuttered the restaurant, our newly-unemployed staff gave us more sympathy than this sullen bunch had for their long-time boss.

Dad took this as a sign to start his motivational speech, sounding more like a member of the Chamber of Commerce than an out-of-town entrepreneur who'd flown in to help a friend for the weekend. "This business has been a fixture on North Street for more than fifty years, and many of you have known Otto and Christine far longer than I have. I won't pretend that this is an easy time—or an easy economy—but if we all work together I'm sure Jonker Appliance & TV will be here for another fifty years."

That sounded like bullshit to me, but it wouldn't help the situation to tell the employees the ship was sinking under them. I'm sure Dad believed that if everyone bailed hard enough and fast enough he could keep it afloat.

"I don't know if Otto told you, but my colleagues and I all have our own businesses and so between us we've got—" He paused to make up a number. "—more than a hundred years' combined experience managing businesses very much like this one." He looked around the showroom. "We came to Pittsfield to meet with you all and to give Otto some ideas about improving the business. Obviously the situation has changed. I'd say Jonker's needs your help more than ever during this crisis."

Only a few of the faces appeared remotely friendly, despite Dad's upbeat "we can do this together" manner. Not hostile exactly, but not welcoming. Wary, perhaps. With good reason. Dad explained we would be talking to employees one-on-one throughout the day. If someone could suggest something—anything—that would help Jonker's make money or save money, speak up. It was an opportunity for anyone who'd been nursing a good idea to present it to receptive ears.

Reading the staff's expressions, I figured a third of the salespeople were somewhat enthusiastic, another third silently hostile, the rest indifferent or confused.

I made my escape when Steffie tapped me on the shoulder and pointed to the doorway. A guy in a work shirt with Berkshire Safe and Lock embroidered over the breast pocket was in the hallway. "It's a desk," I said, leading him back to Otto's office while Steffie stayed for the end of Dad's pep talk.

Dad was still talking about this difficult time—difficult for the staff, difficult for the Jonker family. But they were all professionals and would do their best and . . . I closed Otto's office door, shutting him off.

The locksmith worked about two minutes on the desk lock, turned it, and pulled the drawers all slightly ajar to demonstrate everything was open. He found a bunch of keys in the center drawer's utility tray, picked one out, and said I could use it to lock back up. I thanked him for coming out so promptly as he scribbled an invoice. I promised the store would cut a check as soon as possible and figured Dad would take care of it. I sure wasn't going to pay him.

He left, and I sat behind the desk to go through the drawers. In the top center drawer, right where Otto had probably stuck it yesterday afternoon, was a file folder with the unsigned paychecks. Thumbing through the bottom drawers on the two side pedestals, I found a different batch of files, some with neatly typed labels, others handwritten: "Personnel," "First Aggie Bank," "Berkshire Savings," "Pending," "Accounting," "B Eagle," "promotion," "Critique," "ideas," "major app," "electronics," "audio."

Way in the back of the right-hand drawer was a thick, unlabeled folder. Curious, I pulled it out.

It was stuffed with black-and-white and color Polaroid photos, maybe twenty altogether. Full frontal shots of naked women. The photographer (Otto?) focused on the strike zone—boobs and snatch. No faces, no legs below the knee. More than one woman. I guessed five or six, but all similar. All Rubenesque, with voluptuous bellies, thick thighs, lush pubic thatch, heavy breasts. What the hell? I could imagine one of the models was Christine. But who were the others? Steffie Gilberti and friends?

9 / Friday morning

Back in my role as ace collections clerk, I held the phone away from my ear as yet another recorded answering machine message played, watching Steffie bend over one of the desks to speak to a salesman. In my mind's eye, I tried to connect a bawdy Polaroid with the heavy figure in the sweater and skirt in front of me, but my imagination failed. The woman in the picture was flat on her back, her weight making an impression on the mattress. Steffie at the desk was in profile, bent at the waist, bundled up tight. I could see no connection. Just as well. Better to keep my attention on collecting poor Otto's money than on identifying his women.

Steffie happened to look toward the service department and was so startled she dropped the file she was holding, the papers scattering. "Brian! We tried to call you." I craned my neck to watch this Brian guy ambling down the hallway from the service entrance.

As he approached, I noticed how short Brian Jonker was, only a few inches over five feet, smaller than his sister Wendy and surprisingly, not much heavier. I guess neither had inherited their parents' big-frame genes. At first glance, he looked like a younger version of Wendy, with the same light brown hair and brown eyes. But even from a distance, Brian's eyes didn't have

Wendy's liveliness, let alone her exhaustion and concern. As his face came into focus, I thought Brian looked surly, as if resentful he had to show up for work at all.

I picked up an invoice and pretended to read it while Steffie handled what promised to be an ugly conversation. Brian didn't even look around and greet the rest of the store's staff, addressing only the office manager. "Why? What's up?

Steffie gasped, her voice rising in a mix of anxiety and annoyance. "It's your father! He's had an accident! He's in the hospital!"

Leaving my face turned to the invoice, I shifted my eyes enough to catch Brian's change of expression. Now he looked almost shocked, as if she'd struck him—the office manager hitting the boss's son. I could hear him having trouble forming a question. "What . . . what happened?"

Steffie told him the story we'd just heard from the cop's wife. Brian listened with his arms folded across his chest, protecting himself from Steffie's words and growing paler as she spoke. "How serious is it?" he asked when she trailed off. "Is he going to be all right?"

Steffie threw up her hands, a gesture of frustrated helplessness. "We just don't know! After surgery, he was taken to intensive care. Your mother and your sister, they were both with him this morning." Anyone in earshot would get the message: Where were you?

Brian stood uncertain for several seconds as if trying to decide whether to go to the hospital or settle down to work. He looked around the showroom, seeing it for the first time. Two salesmen Nick had trained were at desks making collection calls, just like me. Joanne was having an intense discussion with a saleswoman near the refrigerator displays. Two other salespeople were, like me, trying to invisibly eavesdrop on Brian's exchange with Steffie. "So—so what's going on," he sputtered. "I mean, who's running the store? Who's in charge? You?"

"I . . . I guess Mr. Lovell is."

"Who the fuck is Mr. Lovell?"

She pointed toward Otto's office, her face carefully bland. "He says he talked to your mother."

Brian sure didn't take that well. "Who's Mr. Lovell? Where is he?"

I jumped into this dialogue. "He's in Mr. Jonker's office." Brian was so agitated, he didn't react to my presence as a stranger or to my ever-so-slight emphasis on "Mister."

Brian charged ahead into Otto's office and I followed. He started right in on Dad: "Where'd you get the right to come in here and take over?"

Dad ignored the gruff challenge. "You're Brian? . . . I'm sorry, truly sorry about your father's accident." He stood to greet Brian, his tone calm, conciliatory, his hand extended in friendship. "I'm Tom Lovell. You dad called me a week ago to check over some things here at the store. We arrived last night"—he gestured toward me and swept in the showroom—"and I've spoken to your mother about helping out during this emergency since we didn't know where you were." Brian ignored Dad's hand.

Brian wasn't about to be calmed. "It doesn't make any difference where I was." I expected him to stamp his foot in anger. "You don't have any right to come in here and start . . . start—" Brian couldn't describe what we couldn't do.

"Like I said, we're here at your father's request. I've given my word to Christine that she can count on our help," Dad said in his I'm-the-parent-and-I-know-best voice.

"We don't need your help."

Dad sat back in Otto's big leather chair to look at Brian as though from a height, never mind that Brian was standing, fists balled, on the other side of the desk. I stepped inside the office and closed the office door in case things got louder.

Dad began quietly, "Actually, Brian, you do."

He waited for a moment, then continued. "This is a very sick store. You lost money in the first two quarters, and you probably lost even more in the third quarter." Dad was personalizing; the store was now 'you.'

"You're over-staffed and every time we turn over another rock, we find another problem. If you don't get help—and quickly—you'll be out of business by Christmas."

Brian wasn't sure how to take that. His expression lost some of its defiance, but he snapped back, "You're full of shit."

"I've got the figures." Dad was like a judge pronouncing a sentence.

"I don't believe it," said Brian.

Dad narrowed his eyes. "Have you seen the financial statements?"

Brian couldn't look Dad in the eye. He stared at the window that overlooked the sales floor, now covered by the venetian blind I'd lowered.

Dad went on, "Does your father share them with you?"

I knew where Dad was going with this. He believed in "open book" management. Everyone who worked at Lovell's knew how the business performed every month, all the seasonal fluctuations in sales and profits. They even knew how much everyone earned—including Dad's pay. They knew that if the stores did well, they would do well. Somehow Dad and Mom had managed to minimize the petty jockeying for power and money I'd seen in other businesses. If my restaurant had gotten beyond the startup stage, I'd have opened the books, such as they were.

Brian's "No" was a reluctant no.

"With your mother's permission, I'll show them to you and go over them with you. No secrets. Nothing hidden. But, for now, you'll have to take my word for it. This is a desperately sick business. And until your mother tells us otherwise, we're going to stay here and do what we can to help get it back on track."

Brian wasn't going to let some stranger take over without a fight. "I'm going to talk to her, you wait and see."

Dad nodded his approval, not that Brian needed it, and added, "I think you should. See how she's holding up. Give her some comfort. I know she's worried about you. And your dad." As Brian turned to storm out the door, Dad added, "As long as you're going out to the house, would you take my son Tommy along? We need your mother's signature on the paychecks." He took a folder from the now neat desktop and held it out to me.

Up to now, Brian hadn't even glanced in my direction and now he looked me up and down, as if he didn't quite know what to make of me. To disarm him, I smiled and stuck out my hand and, after a moment's hesitation, Brian gave me a clammy and limp handshake. I was no salesman, but I found it hard to believe that someone with Brian's handshake could sell anything. The point after all was to make an instant, positive impression. How did Brian get customers enthusiastic enough to buy anything in the audio department we'd been told he was running? Maybe Brian came to life when he talked about woofers, tweeters, frequency response, and quadraphonic sound. Maybe.

"What can I do?" I said to him with a conspiratorial shrug and a nod toward Dad. "He's my father." Brian glanced back at Dad, gave his own shrug, and opened the office door. I followed him down the hall, through the service department, and out the rear door.

Did Dad have the fantasy that Brian and I would become fast friends? Yeah, we had so much in common: retailer fathers, store experience, assigned roles in the family business. Dad probably imagined we'd hit it off. Talk as equals. Bitch about our fathers. Because I was seven or so years older than Brian, I was young enough to gain his confidence, old enough to have some perspective. Brian would share his hopes and dreams and I would report back. Tell Dad what I thought of Brian's ability, talent, and potential as a manager in the family business. Dad tended to think everyone had leadership ability until proven otherwise. He always thought I had leadership ability, a belief I'd unthinkingly assumed about myself. With Si Accomodi's failure, I wasn't so sure.

I couldn't guess Brian's first impression of me, but I was put off by his sullen and childish personality. I wondered about Brian's relationship with his father. He didn't seem terribly broken up by Otto's accident. Just thinking about the injuries and the blood, I felt my stomach clench. Did Brian think it wasn't serious? Did he not care? I was upset, and I hardly knew Otto.

Brian's car was a fire-engine red Mazda RX-7. Even parked, it looked as if it were breaking the speed limit. "Nice car." I ran my hand over the buttery leather upholstery as I slid into the seat. A little flattery goes a long way, and the car was impressive.

"Better than the Cougar I was driving." He kept his eyes on the dash, fiddling with the knobs.

"Cougar's a nice car too."

"Not when it's your sister's hand-me-down. They gave it to her when she graduated from high school, but after a while she didn't want the parking hassle around campus, so they gave it to me. Well, screw that." Brian threw the Mazda into gear and peeled out of the lot, the acceleration jamming me against my seat. He didn't pause to check for oncoming traffic at the lot's exit. The little side street probably never had much traffic but Brian's recklessness gave me a nasty jolt. Getting T-boned in a little Mazda sports car would not be a lot of fun.

We entered the Jonker house through the three-car garage. Christine was sitting at the kitchen island, and her face brightened when she spotted Brian in the lead. "Oh, Brian! Brian, honey!" She rose on unsteady legs to greet him with a hug, nodding to me over his shoulder.

"What happened? Is Daddy all right?"

Christine, clinging to Brian, poured out in gulping sobs what Steffie had essentially told him in the store. I stood back to give mother and son a zone of privacy, but in the fragments I overheard, I learned Otto had "severe head trauma . . . spinal fracture . . . uncertain prognosis . . . ." They'd operated on his skull, and now it was a waiting game to see how he felt when—if—he regained consciousness, Maybe hours. Maybe a day. Maybe longer.

Sounded ominous to me, but Brian either didn't appreciate what she was telling him or—I thought in an attempt to be generous—he didn't understand the situation's seriousness, because he barely reacted. He held his mother and muttered something, but his expression of irritation stayed glued to his face.

When Christine had recovered enough to pull away, find a tissue, and blow her nose, Brian launched into his complaint. What right did this Lovell guy have to come into the store and take over? Still motionless in the doorway, I fought the urge to, well, defend Dad, then decided to keep my mouth shut and let them fight it out themselves.

Christine sat back down on the kitchen stool, toyed for a moment with the coffee mug in front of her, then pushed it aside. "Daddy asked him to come. Tom Lovell is the best businessman I know, and that includes every single person in Berkshire County. If Tom is willing to give up his weekend to help our store, I trust him to do the right thing."

"He says the store is sick," persisted Brian.

Christine's shoulders gave a little shudder. "I know it is." Her statement was so unequivocal, I wondered if she knew more than she'd let on at last night's meeting.

"So you're just going to let him take over?" Was there a threat in Brian's voice? Some long-simmering family problem about to boil over?

Christine glanced at me for a split second before looking

Brian squarely in the eye. "He's not 'taking over,' Brian. He and his friends are just helping us out while your father's in the hospital."

"It sure looked like to me like he was taking over."

"Whatever he's doing, I'm sure it's for the best." Her eyes wandered over Brian's shoulder to my direction, saw me clutching the file folder. "Your father and I would trust Tom Lovell with . . . with . . . our bank account."

I took that as my cue to say, "Mrs. Jonker, if you have a minute. My dad asked me to bring some checks for your signature," and held out the folder.

Christine opened the folder, accepted the pen I handed her from my pocket, and began scribbling her signature on the twenty-four checks. I silently counted as she signed, another legacy of watching Dad do this week after week for years on end. Twenty-four people seemed like a lot; our Gloucester business with two stores had only a baker's dozen. But maybe Jonker's had a bigger service business and needed more technicians. What did I know?

Brian watched silently and, as she reached the bottom of the pile, said, "That one's mine," and reached for it.

She gave him the check without comment. He folded and stuffed it into the pocket of his blue polo shirt. As she pushed the folder across the kitchen counter toward me, he tried one last time to get her on his side. "You're not going to do anything?" he asked.

Christine turned the questioning around on him. "Where were you last night? We called the apartment."

For the first time since I'd met him, Brian's face showed an expression other than impatience or irritability. It might have been embarrassment with a flicker of fear. "I . . . I was out." He stared at the counter, not at his mother, and I made a mental note to find out more once we were alone in the car.

- 62 -

Christine was obviously too wrung out to push Brian any further, and I suspected this was a regular routine between them anyway. "I won't ask where. You're a grown man. You have your own life."

Brian didn't seem to know what to make of that and stood to go. Without looking at me, he asked, "You coming?"

"Sure." I picked up the check folder. "I'm truly sorry about Mr. Jonker," I said softly.

"Tell your father I know what he's doing for us. Tell him we appreciate it." I braced for a new flood of tears, but the moment passed and she picked up her mug. "Tell him I'll stop by the store later."

10 / Friday noon

Back in the car, Brian announced, "I'm fucking starving. Let's go to Hancock's."

Good timing: I'd been wondering how to pump Brian for more info. This guy's father is in the hospital, his family's business is going down the toilet, he's out of touch overnight with no explanation—and his top priority is lunch?

I tried not to look too eager when I answered. "Great, but first, let's drop these checks off. You got yours, the others are waiting for theirs, right?"

Brian snorted but put the car in gear, and a few minutes later, he had us parked at the back entrance of Jonker's. I hopped out, found Dad on the phone in Otto's office, and handed him the folder of checks, mouthing "Back soon, going out with Brian." He covered the receiver, whispered "Otto's back in surgery," and went back to his call.

I told Brian his father was in surgery, but he only shook his head as the Mazda roared off to Hancock's. Maybe I should offer to drive? No, Brian needs something to keep himself busy. Sitting in the passenger seat as buildings whipped by, I had the impression of a compact little city in a bowl in the hills, nothing more than ten minutes away from anything else. Especially with Brian at the wheel.

Hancock's Tavern turned out to be a bar and restaurant about three blocks from our hotel, dark and quiet with TV sets mounted on the ceiling at either end of the bar. They were tuned to two different channels and, thankfully, the sound was turned low. As a newly minted member of the ex-restaurant-owner club, I noticed this owner had made a stab at decoration with antique tools fastened to the walls: buck saws, pitch forks, sheep sheers, muck rake, scythes. Two white-haired guys at the bar were nursing beers, and several of the high-backed booths were filled. Not a bad start for the day's lunch business.

Brian and I took one of the booths and the slow-moving waitress greeted Brian by name. "The usual?" she asked. Brian grunted agreement and I ordered a draft Sam Adams.

Our drinks arrived and none too soon, judging by the way Brian gripped his glass. He gave the impression he was letting the Bloody Mary do its job. I sipped and thought about an opening gambit.

"Sorry about your dad," I said. If our situations were reversed, if Dad's plane had crashed and he was in the hospital, that's what Brian would say to me. Well, maybe not Brian, considering what I'd seen so far this morning.

Brian stopped tapping his fingers on the polyurethaned wood tabletop, the rhythm like muffled hoof beats on a trail. "Yeah. Me too." He took another long swallow. "You don't know what to think, you know. Sort of fuckin' numb."

"I can guess." We sat for a time, the flickering television sets barely a distraction for me. The Red Sox stuff was riling up the regulars, but I'd learned early how to tune out. If I watched the twenty or thirty TV sets that were on all day in our stores, I'd never notice a customer.

I'd spent too much time in the store. One of my earliest memories was of playing in the back room of what was then

Grandad's Store. I was about three. Building towers with wooden blocks my grandfather kept around just for me. When I knocked them down, Dad looked in to tell me, with a smile, not to make such a racket. When I was seven, grandfather Lovell sold the store proudly renamed Lovell & Son to my parents and disappeared to a place called Sunny Florida except when he and grandmother Lovell returned to Gloucester for a Good Old-Fashioned Christmas (actually to help with the holiday business crush) and for a week in summer. The store became Dad's other child (something happened when I was born and Mom couldn't have any more children). I loved Dad but he'd spent too many years paying more attention to Lovell's than to my interests for me to forgive him entirely.

My most vivid childhood memories were of rainy, raw, late-fall Saturdays at Lovell's—the store's harshly bright fluorescent light, the stockroom's gloom, the service department's clutter. When I was very young, I watched morning cartoons on what was called 'Tommy's TV,' a high-end Magnavox console at the front of the store. As I grew older, I watched less and worked more. I was told to sweep the floor, unpack the merchandise, make "Sale!" price tags, wash the front windows. Stand at the front to watch cold rain beat on parked cars. Watch passing cars splash through puddles on the road. As confined to the store as a prisoner to his cell, from age seven to seventeen. College was my escape, returning to the prison on holidays.

What would I be feeling if Dad's plane had gone down on the way to Pittsfield? I sure wouldn't be sitting in a bar getting tipsy with a stranger. I was only halfway through my Sam Adams when Brian wiggled his fingers for another Bloody Mary. I nodded that I'd take another draft. Might as well be his drinking buddy.

"So . . . you're not living at home," I said to get the conversation going, since Brian wasn't volunteering anything.

"No . . . Got my own place up in Lanesboro." At my silent question, he added, "North of here. One bedroom, but it's my own."

Feeling I had nothing to lose, I asked right out, "What's with you and your mom and Wendy?"

"Long story," said Brian with a vague wave across his face, as though brushing off cobwebs. He sipped at his second Bloody Mary and I finished my first beer, waiting him out. I was trying Nick's technique: ask a question, then shut up until you get a real answer. "We don't get along too well," Brian added finally.

"Yeah, I got that much." I put on a sympathetic voice to urge him on. No luck.

Brian signaled the waitress again. He told her he wanted three eggs, hash browns, bacon on the side. Although I was feeling my beer, the vodka didn't seem to be having much effect on Brian. Maybe making him a little more mellow. I checked the blackboard and ordered the day's lunch special, pulled pork with fries.

Try a new, neutral subject: "How long you been running the audio department?"

Brian looked puzzled. "Hell, I don't know . . . two years or so." Then, more confidently: "Yeah, a little over two years. I started after I dropped out of UMass."

"You dropped out of UMass?"

Brian became suspicious at my enthusiasm. "What about it?"

At last, a shared experience. "I dropped out of UMass. I was wasting time. And money." Not the whole truth, but the part Brian might identify with.

"I thought you went to Harvard or something."

"No. Big disappointment to the family when I didn't get into Williams or Dartmouth. Then I dropped out of UMass after my second year, only made it worse." Come on, Brian, buddy, you can trust me.

"Yeah. Whatever you do makes it fuckin' worse." Brian gave a wry smile and finished his Bloody Mary.

"You like selling audio?"

"It's okay."

Getting nowhere, I switched the subject midstream. "What are you listening to these days?"

Brian had to close his eyes to think. "I don't know. Klymaxx . . . Billy Ocean . . . The Pet Shop Boys . . . Mr. Mister . . . whatever the hell's popular."

The only music I knew was Billy Ocean's. Music was another conversational dead end, so I said, "Anything you want to ask me?"

Brian had to think for a couple seconds. "Yeah. How long are you people going to be here?"

I didn't see myself as one of "you people," but at least Brian was calmer than he'd been a couple of hours ago. Progress. "I guess we're waiting to see how your dad is doing. Me, I can't go until my dad says it's okay to go." I gave him my you-know-how-it-is laugh, one oppressed son-of-the-owner to another.

The waitress arrived with our food, a bottle of ketchup tucked under one arm. Gina—ever fussy, rearranging garnish till the last second—would never have let these plates out of Si Accomodi's kitchen. That was then, this was now. Brian mumbled his thanks, doused the eggs and potatoes with ketchup, and dug in.

I followed up on the topic of fathers as I picked at my pork: "How do you get along with your dad?" Brian's behavior all morning had suggested problems with Otto (and Christine): Veiled resentment? Smoldering anger? Disguised nervousness? What?

Fortified by the vodka and his breakfast, Brian flashed a brief, bitter smile. "Not so well. You?"

I gave a similar knowing smile. "About the same." Again,

not the entire truth. But Brian was the one under the microscope, not me.

"He's always on my case, you know? Second guessing what I'm doing. Why don't we add Pioneer? Drop Bang & Olufsen? I mean, if he wants to fucking run the department, why the hell doesn't *he* run it? Know what I mean?"

I nodded that I knew, though Dad did things differently. He belonged to the Toss-Them-in-the-Water-to-Learn-to-Swim School of Management.

Brian wasn't finished. "I mean, long as sales are good, what the fuck does he care if we've got Pioneer or Bang & Olufsen?"

"Sales been good? Even in this market?"

"Fuck yeah, my department's doing fine. Not like the other departments. Sales up every year. Even in this shitty market." If Brian's sales are up, why's the store so sick? I prodded for more.

"So why doesn't he leave you alone?"

Brian used a piece of toast to break an egg yoke and soak up the ooze. Just when I thought he wasn't going to answer, he looked up, eyebrows raised to his hairline, and said, "Beats the shit out of me."

I took another forkful of my pulled pork, but, as I looked at the platter, I suddenly recognized it—the pork spilling out of the sourdough bun, three pickle slices to the side, the mound of fries—as a one of the regular products my food distributor salesman had in his book of four-color spec sheets: "Pulled Pork w/Cottage Fries—A Popular Favorite with a Healthy Gross Margin." Hancock's cook might have added a touch of cumin to cut the overcooked taste of the meat, but the mix was right out of the distributor's institutional five-pound plastic sack. Not Si Accomodi's style at all. We'd served pork, of course, and I felt a stab of sadness. One of our specials was a dish I'd never taste again, Gina's fantastic Italian breaded pork chops.

To push that memory away, I asked, "So what do you think's

going to happen? If he's out for six months, say." Brian shook his head to deny the possibility. "Can your mom run things?"

"Oh, he'll be back." Brian spoke with certainty. "It'd take a hell of a lot more than getting thrown from his bike to kill him."

"But if . . . ." I broke off and waited.

Brian chewed thoughtfully for a minute. "My mother and Wendy'll take over." He reached for the empty Bloody Mary glass, then stopped. "The two of 'em are just aching to run things. Wendy's the good girl who stayed in college and went for the MBA. I'm the big disappointment."

"Think they can handle it?"

A sneer spread over Brian's face. "A hell of a lot more to running a store than standing around waiting for customers to walk in. Wendy's no salesman. She can't sell shit. She's more like a fuckin' strategic thinker, you know? Full of ideas how we can expand, improve processes, stick her nose in where it doesn't belong." His tone made him sound like a cranky seven-year-old.

"What about your mom? Can she sell?"

A nod. "Used to. When I was little, she worked the floor a couple days a week. But she hasn't been around the store much for four . . . five years. More of a behind-the-scenes person, know what I mean?"

"She and your dad get along okay?" I asked as casually as I could, zeroing in on what I figured was a sore point. Brian looked rattled but tried to hide it. "Sure, why not?"

"Just asking." There'd been a time when I was sure my parents were going to divorce. Dad was always busy with the store, never showed up for parent-teacher conferences, never came with Mom to my football games, never took time off to visit colleges with us—colleges he expected me to attend.

Dad always had an excuse and the excuse was always reasonable—a week before the Dartmouth-Williams-Syracuse college research trip a fire destroyed much of our warehouse, you name it—but by the time I went to UMass, Mom's feelings were clear to me. I couldn't imagine what, other than wanting to give me a two-parent home, had kept them together. I wanted to tell them: Look, you don't have to stay together for me. At least you wouldn't be fighting all the time.

Now, after a few weeks at home, I was surprised and pleased to find my parents much closer, much better friends than they'd ever been. Lovers almost. I wondered if my moving out had actually brought them closer. Maybe I'd had it backwards all along: They didn't stay together because of me, they almost split up because of me.

Meanwhile, Brian wasn't going to let me into his inner sanctum, so I finished my pork and fries. I considered asking if Brian knew where to score some pot. Then I realized that if Brian knew I was smoking pot, it could come back to bite me. I didn't know how it might bite me, but I wasn't jonesing enough to take the risk. Not letting Brian into my inner sanctum, either.

When Brian picked up his Bloody Mary glass and shook the ice to attract the waitress, I said, "Why don't we head back and find out what's happening with your dad." I didn't make it much of a question.

For a moment, it looked as if Brian was going to argue, then he shrugged. "Yeah, I guess." We both reached for our wallets, but, to my surprise, Brian waved me away. "I'll get this."

Without thinking, I said, "You don't have to do that." Once I spoke, I let it go. I had less than sixty bucks, and didn't want to spend if I didn't have to. Especially not on a food distributor's pulled pork special.

Brian made a show of pulling out his wad of bills. "Yeah . . . well. It's no big deal. I come here all the time." Lot of money for a guy who seemed to need his paycheck so badly, I couldn't help noticing. Maybe too much. But what do I know?

Here's what I did know: Brian, like Nick, was another big

tipper. If Si Accomodi had had more Brians and Nicks as customers, we could have survived.

11 / Friday afternoon

When Brian let me out at the store, Joanne was deep in conversation with an animated employee in one corner of the sales bullpen. No sign of Dan, but Nick was at the keyboard of an IBM PC, pecking out a spreadsheet, Steffie sitting beside him. Otto had bought the computer months ago, but no one knew how to use it. Nick was teaching her VisiCalc and making up a budget at the same time. "Save, always save your work," I heard him say as I passed. Good luck with that, I thought.

    I wasn't surprised to see Dad hunched over ledger sheets on Otto's desk, fingers hovering over the adding machine, ignoring my arrival. For a split-second, I felt my gut twist with an old resentment. Seeing my parents so lovey-dovey in recent weeks, I'd hoped my business-comes-ahead-of-everything Dad was history, but maybe Otto's sick store triggered his old reflexes. And Otto's family sure needed all the help they could get.

    I pushed the feeling aside, closed the door, took a guest chair and said, to lighten the mood, "Smells like pizza in here." That got me a smile, followed by a questioning look. "Brian with you?"

    I shook my head. "Maybe headed to the hospital." I didn't bother to hide my skepticism.

Dad put down the printout to ask, "How's Christine?"

"Tired. Worried." Knowing Dad really cared, I tried to put into words what I'd seen at the Jonker house. "She feels helpless, wants to do something but doesn't know what to do. She looked better than she did at the hospital, but that's not saying much. But she did say she'll try to stop by later. And she told Brian you were in charge."

He leaned forward. "How'd Brian take that?"

I'd been dreading this part of the conversation, wishing I'd been able to worm more out of Brian. "Not well. But what's he going to say? He never did tell her where he was last night."

"What's your impression of him?"

I sat up straighter. I didn't want to slouch like Brian. "Professionally? He's got to be the world's best salesman to overcome that attitude and handshake." Dad nodded. "But he claims audio department sales are growing. Maybe he's different in front of a customer. Maybe the others are carrying it. He tells me he doesn't get along with Otto. Says Otto tries to micromanage."

Dad pursed his lips. "That all?"

I had to organize my jumble of impressions. "I think . . . I think Otto disapproves of Brian's lifestyle. Whatever that is. Brian knows it and resents it. He's defensive about where and how he lives. So I didn't push him about where he was last night."

"Drugs?"

I shrugged. "Could be. Judging by our lunch together, the guy's self-medicating with vodka. He resents Wendy—her place in the family. Her college success." I looked away. "He thinks Christine will run things until Otto gets back and then Wendy'll come in and push him out."

Dad jotted notes on a pad as I talked, then looked up. "What about Brian as a manager? Would you have hired him for the restaurant?"

It was an obvious question, yet I would never have expected to hear it coming out of Dad's mouth. Here was Dad asking me, one adult to another, for my considered opinion on something to do with business. A first.

I knew what I wanted to say, but still I took a moment to gather my thoughts. "Hell no. Not with his attitude. He'd drive the staff crazy, and I don't think you can tell him anything. Suggest something and he'll see it as interfering with his . . . autonomy, I guess. His independence. Maybe Otto does micromanage the audio department, but maybe he's just trying to be helpful. So . . . no, I wouldn't have hired him."

Dad was jotting another note when Joanne knocked and, without waiting for an answer, stuck her hand inside, waving a couple of papers. She stepped all the way in, pulled up the other guest chair, shot me a smile, and handed Dad a typed list of the employees and two sheets of typed notes. "Hey, Tom, Tommy, I picked up this employee roster from the appliance department manager. Names, titles, date hired. Plus my notes from Hannah Nicosia, the appliance department manager. Is this the kind of thing you want?" She gave the notes to Dad, who tilted them my way so we could read together.

The employee roster was an impressive lineup. A lot of names and titles to keep straight. It would have been more impressive if I'd thought Jonker's needed all twenty-four employees with all these titles. Separate managers for the audio, appliance, electronics, and service departments? What did they manage? I noticed the list didn't include Christine who, Otto had told us, was on the books as General Manager. Catching Joanne's eye, I mouthed "wow." She mouthed it back. Otto's store must have sky-high payroll expenses.

Dad passed me Joanne's notes from the morning's interview in her neat handwriting on the legal paper. It answered my question about who managed what:.

—Hannah Nicosia, late 40s, at Jonker's for 11 years. On paper, manager of appliance department but says she doesn't manage anything or anyone. Store has a total of five appliance salespeople, but says three would be sufficient.

—If there's not enough sales, how do the salespeople live? Hannah says they're paid salary plus commission, so take-home pay is enough to live on. Commission: the same percentage on all sales—no special inducement to sell high-end, high-margin products. Hannah thinks incentive a good idea, otherwise, "they just sell easiest thing." Says tries to step customers up—"products are better value" and closing a high-end sale gives her sense of accomplishment.

—Otto handles appliance buying. She thinks he sometimes buys more than he needs to win a trip from the supplier. Says the warehouse has lots of outdated products—"we're never going to sell them. Should give them away."

—Who runs the store when Otto's away? Not clear. Hannah takes care of major appliances, David Gendron TVs and stereos, Brian—"when he's around"—audio, Steffie takes care of the office. Hannah has nothing to do with service department or its manager.

—Ideas for improvement? Didn't want to say anything to hurt anybody—I think she was afraid criticism would get back to Otto. Her husband had a good-paying job at GE transformer works here in town, was laid off, now works part time and she needs job. Assured her again this all confidential, and she said if she was in charge she'd cut staff. "Too many people, not enough work." Anyone in particular? Yes, Megan Mattner, who schedules service calls and deliveries, but there's not much to it. Store could get by with half the sales staff. Pressed for more about staff issues, Hannah became nervous, suggested Otto and Steffie were "too friendly." Why? A few months back, she passed the store after hours, and saw Otto's and Steffie's cars in the parking lot.

The image of all those nude photos rose back into my mind. Was Hannah one of them? Which salesperson was Hannah Nicosia? Maybe Joanne could point her out. For now, until I could talk to Dad in private, I didn't want to mention the photos. But something was clearly going on. Rattling the pages to get their attention, I raised an eyebrow. "Otto screwing the staff?" Dad gave me a wry smile. "It's the capitalist system." Joanne hit him lightly with the back of her hand.

Dad would have worked on and on, I knew from experience. But by six forty-five I was tired, hungry, and feeling grouchy after hours of interviewing employees and scribbling notes. I had to believe that Nick, Dan, and Joanne were with me on this one. If Dad wanted to stay until the store closed, that was his choice. I poked my head into Otto's office and announced we were ready to pack it in. He looked at his watch and shook his wrist as if it were lying. "Yeah, okay. I'm coming." He began stuffing documents into a Kelvinator tote bag.

Back in the hotel room, he asked me to read over more notes from Joanne and Dan while he showered. Treating me, again, like an equal member of the team. "Just look at the notes about Minoyan, Mattner, Gamwell, and Gendron," he shouted from behind the bathroom door.

I started with Joanne's notes of her interview with James Minoyan, the appliance salesmen who sort of worked for Hannah Nicosia:

—*Proud of being with Otto more than 25 years. Knows sales are off . . . blames the local economy, says other businesses on North Street struggling.*

—*His comments about Otto: "He's okay." Christine? "Nice lady."*

—*Ideas to improve the business? "Move to a town that's not* dying."

—Reaction to Steffie? "Only thing holding this place together." Says she handles all the little details Otto doesn't have time for.

—Minoyan turns 60 next year. Says if he can hold out two more years he'll take his Social Security, take his savings and his wife, and move to Florida.

Joanne's comment at the top of the Megan Mattner interview read, "Listed in the roster as the business's secretary, hired two years ago."

—Late 20s, early 30s. Schedules service calls and deliveries. Likes her job, easy pace. Does odd jobs Steffie asks her to do—bank deposits, opens the mail, orders office supplies.

—Used to be a waitress in a local restaurant where Otto was a regular. He told her if she didn't like working in the restaurant she could come work for him—so she did.

—Seems concerned she doesn't have a heavy work load—"but, then, no one around here does."

—Has no idea what would help the store. "More advertising?"

Dad came out of the bathroom, a snowy Hilton towel wrapped around his waist. He rummaged in his suitcase for underwear and I looked away, embarrassed to see my father's naked ass, the scar on his hip from a high school car accident. "This is hot stuff," I said.

He laughed. "Almost too much to absorb." As he fished for socks, he asked, "How far did you get?"

"Just finished Joanne's notes on somebody Mattner."

"We'll talk at dinner."

Dad was standing at the desk, collecting papers, when the phone rang. He picked it up, and I could tell from his face that the news wasn't good.

The hotel's restaurant, Melville's, was all dark wood and polished brass, subdued lighting, and waitresses dressed in neat black pants and black shirts. If I were an undercover food critic, I'd give it four stars for Ambiance, three for Presentation, one for Value.

Dan and Nick had already claimed a corner table and their drinks rested on the white tablecloth. Dad and I joined them, followed almost immediately by Joanne. "Any word on Otto?" asked Nick by way of greeting.

Dad said Christine had just phoned: Otto had taken a turn for the worse. Grim as it sounded, he still hoped Christine could spare a few minutes in the morning to discuss staff changes. "Staff changes?" said Nick. "You mean house cleaning."

"I told her she's going to have to make some immediate decisions. She seems okay with that." I thought she was probably numb.

"How could Otto let things get so out of hand?" asked Joanne. My thought exactly.

The waitress, who'd been waiting for Joanne, Dad, and me to get settled, came over and asked for drink orders. Because Dad had his eye on me, I ordered club soda.

After the waitress left, Dad said, "What can I say? We all know the store is going down the tubes. Unless we can get it back on track." Said in Dad's circle-the-wagons rah-rah tone. "And that means some pretty drastic housecleaning."

"Well, you want to keep Angelina Gamwell," said Joanne. "She's capable, motivated. The store would suffer if she left!"

"Okay," said Dad. "Tell us more."

Joanne said Angelina was a former Sears TV salesperson, had worked for Otto almost ten years. Divorced, mother of two teen-age boys. "She says she can sell 'every major appliance made'—including some Otto doesn't carry—like trash compactors." Angelina had enjoyed the store's family atmosphere when she moved from Sears to Jonker's in the mid-70s and business was booming. With Otto adding staff and GE closing down its factory though, no one's making as much money and employees don't trust each other. Her take on Brian: "A real snake. I've seen him lie to his father, sell merchandise below cost to friends, pocket customer cash." Would she be willing to tell Otto? "My word against Brian's? Who's Otto going to believe?" Her take on Steffie: "Ms. Indispensible. Husband's out of work, so she thinks she has to do anything, everything to keep such a good-paying job."

"Including relations with Otto?" Dad asked.

"There's talk, and where there's smoke, there's fire."

Joanne said Angelina had all kinds of ideas to improve the business. "Move out to the new mall being built in next town. Get rid of the dead wood on staff. Change commissions to push high-end products and clear the warehouse. Cross train so everybody can sell everything."

Dan said that, other than Vernon Claridge and three of the five technicians (one didn't show up and one was on vacation), he'd only been able to interview David Gendron, the manager of the electronics department. Dave was outgoing, eager to help. He said that Otto had reorganized the staff after he came back from a management seminar two or three years ago, making Dave electronics sales manager, Hannah appliance sales manager, Vernon service department manager. Everyone was going to have a job description and a box on an organization chart, but somebody dropped the ball and the project petered out. The titles didn't make any difference in the work or the authority, only "more impressive business cards."

"This guy Dave has a few ideas to improve," said Dan "More advertising, more promotions. Better displays. Add some of the newer Japanese electronics lines, Hitachi, Toshiba, models no one else carries." There were nods of approval around the table.

Nick said ruefully, "You guys talked to people who at least had some ideas. I caught Mike Tarabocchia."

Michael was the store's oldest employee. He'd started in 1947 when Otto's father was still running things. Nick said Mike was hostile. "For some reason, he associates our presence with Otto's accident. He wouldn't comment on coworkers, or Otto, or Christine. He did say Brian is 'a little wet behind the ears' to be running the audio department."

Dan asked, "Any idea who should be running the audio department?"

Nick gave him an are-you-kidding look. "No. No ideas. I got the impression our Mr. Tarabocchia is just going through the motions. He didn't have much to say, doesn't want to see any changes."

"Well, that's a big difference from Lauren Davidson," I said. Lauren was another electronics salesperson. "She told me Jonker's used to be a 'nice place to work' but no more. She's thinking of quitting and doesn't care who knows. She thinks the store should get rid of the 'shitty' advertising. It has the best service in town, but it's not properly promoted. She—"

Dan interrupted to volunteer, "That's what I've seen about the service department as well. Needs more promotion."

"Lauren says that Stephanie Gilberti acts bossy—high and mighty. Sales are down, everybody's worried. Otto's away too much, not paying attention to business. Gossipy, selfish employees. And there are too many employees, they come and go as they please. No clear lines of authority, no controls. On paper, she reports to Dave, but actually takes orders from Otto, who corners female staff and makes crude comments."

That was Joanne's cue. "Angelina called Otto an 'okay' businessman, but—" She leaned into the table and dropped her voice. "—she says he's really a lady's man. He hires as many women as he can. Says he's hit on her but she turned him down. She thinks he's had, or is having, 'a thing' with Steffie and Megan Mattner, who's 'too young and dumb to know what's going on,' and with Hannah, which is why she's 'manager' of appliance sales, probably others. Not sure whether Christine knows or cares about Otto's adventures."

Dad shook his head, a gesture of disbelief. "All right, so what you're telling me is Angelina Gamwell and Lauren Davidson seem to have the most ideas of what to do about the store."

I said, "Angelina certainly doesn't give a damn what anyone thinks. She's got her opinions and you're welcome to them whether you want them or not."

"Everyone agrees the store is overstaffed," Joanne added. "And I thought Angelina had a decent recommendation for deciding who goes, who stays."

We discussed individual sales performances and terminating the least productive salespeople, if we could get our hands on more detailed records. Dad had the brainstorm of analyzing salespeople according to commissions earned. "Rank them from highest commissions to lowest commissions and give the poor performers notice tomorrow."

I couldn't believe what he was saying. "Tomorrow! Isn't that a little quick?"

"We'll give them two weeks pay in lieu of notice. We don't want disgruntled ex-employees hanging around the store. Start Monday with a whole new organization . . . if Christine approves, of course."

I tried again. "Dad. Isn't tomorrow a little soon to chop heads? You don't even know these people and you're going to start firing them?"

Dad gave me a long look. I wondered if he was embarrassed

to be questioned in front of his friends, but when he spoke his tone was mild. "Ordinarily, I'd agree with you—but Jonker's is on the brink. We don't have any time." He dropped his voice and leaned in to the table. The mindless background music now didn't seem loud enough to keep the conversation private. "I met with the accountant this afternoon. He came over with the third-quarter and year-to-date figures, and they're ugly. We got out the bank statements and did some quick back-of-the-envelope calculating, and with the current cash flow projections, Jonker's has only about six weeks left."

Nobody said anything for an instant. And that was lucky because the waitress arrived and began serving our meals. As she put down his entrée, Nick asked her, "Do you ever shop at Jonker's?"

"Jonker's?" She'd been focusing on who ordered what and didn't make the connection.

"The appliance/TV business up the street. Across from the department store."

"Oh . . . Jonker's." She set my prime rib in front of me. "Yeah, sure. I bought my washing machine there."

"Did you have a good experience?"

She looked at him uncomprehendingly. "It's a washing machine. A Whirlpool."

"But the experience of buying it—was that good? Would you buy something else there?"

"I guess." I decided the woman, her straw-blond hair pulled tightly back, was trying to decide what answer Nick wanted. "If I needed something."

When she'd picked up her tray and returned to the kitchen, Nick commented, "Not exactly a ringing endorsement." I thought so too, but what did I know?

While we ate, we compared notes on the store's problems. Dad asked me to tell them about my conversations with the two audio salespeople who worked for Brian.

Ross Hubler was young, but enthusiastic and knowledgeable about high fidelity. Ross could not talk about Brian as a manager because he had no real basis of comparison. He'd never worked for anyone before. He did say that when he had problems closing a sale, he'd call Brian over, introduce him as the boss's son, and Brian would negotiate the price. The price tags were for people who didn't know enough to negotiate. Ross had no idea whether the department was profitable or not.

Ashley Strong was an attractive redhead who'd been Brian's baby sitter when she was sixteen and he was eleven. Selling audio gear at Jonker's was the best job she could find when she graduated from community college. She wouldn't provide any specifics about Brian as a manager, but she did say that Otto himself had hired her three years ago.

She told me that shortly after Brian came into the business two years ago and Otto gave him the audio department, she and Brian had a loud, bitter, and public argument in the store. A furious Brian had fired her. But she'd been working in the store longer than Brian and went over his head to Otto. She doesn't know what Otto told Brian, but she wasn't fired any more, and she's stayed in audio sales. Brian has as little contact with her as he can manage. She said she was the department's top sales producer.

"You think Otto's been coming on to her?" Dad asked me.

"I . . . I don't think so." I fumbled around for a reason. "I mean, she's wearing a wedding ring." Also, she was slender and young and the women in Otto's photos were neither. But I wasn't ready to talk about what I'd found hidden in Otto's desk.

Dan, who looked embarrassed, said, "You think Otto's been . . . ?" His voice trailed off.

For a moment, no one spoke. Then Dad said, "It sounds like Otto's been—" He hesitated. "—been making improper suggestions to female staff." Nick rolled his eyes and Dan shook his head.

I wondered whether I should mention the pictures. They certainly supported the gossip. But I was embarrassed for the man. And the whole reason for coming here was to save the store, not to poke around in Otto's private life.

Except, maybe we couldn't save the store without poking around in Otto's private life.

12 / Friday evening

Before the waitress brought dessert menus, I pushed back from the table. "You going up to the room?" Dad asked.

I heard a note of parental disapproval and I answered more belligerently than I intended. "Why? What do you care?"

Dad seemed startled. "Only, I want to do some paperwork, make a couple calls, get ready for tomorrow. If you want to watch TV in the room, I'll work in the business center."

I looked away. "No, you don't have to do that." I had planned to go to the room and watch TV, but, feeling like a petulant child, I improvised. "I'm going out for a walk."

I'd been trapped in Jonker's most of the day. Dad and the others wanted to sit around the table and continue debating how Otto could have let his store get so sick. Me, I could imagine all kinds of reasons—and how it felt in the pit of your stomach to try desperately to turn things around, clutching at hope even when it was clear the business was sinking.

I needed to get outside alone, shake off the stink of failure, breathe some of this fresh fall Berkshire air for which leaf-peeping tourists paid good money. I headed out as Dad and the others turned to dessert decisions and making plans for the next day.

The hotel's revolving door spun me out into the night. Even

with the buildings blocking the wind, the October night seemed cooler than it had been two hours earlier as we'd walked from Otto's store. I hesitated, trying to decide whether my windbreaker was enough, whether to return to the room for my sweater, or to forget about a walk. I told myself I'd take just a quick walk around the block and set off.

At the sidewalk, I turned left to start downhill. Almost no traffic on what I took to be one of the town's main streets. An impressive five-story sandstone building rose across the street, something that looked as if it had been constructed in the 19th century when Pittsfield was a booming mill town and the bank commissioning its headquarters (I assumed it was a bank) expected to spend money on cornices and decorative carved pillars, architectural details designed to impress patrons. I looked back at the hotel with its parking garage and squat office block—poured concrete and brick veneer. Although newer by probably a hundred years and certainly far more expensive, the structures looked shabby by comparison. Purely utilitarian and done on the cheap. Progress.

Why was I annoyed? What did I care? I didn't. Striding through the chilly night air helped clear my thoughts. I felt I could be, should be doing something more productive. I ought to take the Buick and drive over to Otto's house to see if I could help, talk to Christine, Wendy. I ought to go back to the room to ask Dad what I could do to help him. I ought to think about everything Brian and the others had told me today and come up with practical, effective ideas to aid the business. I ought to stop whining and get a life.

At the corner I turned left again to avoid crossing the street and wandered further away from the hotel. Another deserted street, the parking garage on my left, an empty lot across the street. Somebody had said this had been a busy commercial area with an impressive train station across the street through the

1960s, then everything had been torn down in the 1970s for urban renewal. So far, not a lot of renewal or street life. I'd be lucky if a patrolling cop didn't stop me to ask what I was doing. Just walking, officer. Walking where? Nowhere special, just walking; you got a problem with that, officer? My free-floating irritation began to shade into irrational anger at the imaginary cop.

I found myself at a corner I recognized. I'd passed it at noon with Brian. Passed it twice in fact. Going to and coming from Hancock's Tavern. I could cross the street, walk another block, and I'd be at the restaurant. Why not go to Hancock's? I touched my wallet to confirm it was safe. I had money for a drink. At the hotel's bar, of course, I could charge drinks to the room. But then Dad would see how much I'd spent, and that made me uncomfortable. Less stressful to have an off-duty drink at Hancock's.

What could I do for Otto that Dad couldn't do? Dad was the ultimate professional. His friends admired him and he gave orders so naturally, without bossing, that people accepted them. One of my (many) nagging fears had always been that my employees at Si Accomodi—even my own wife—had seen my orders as a joke. I wasn't comfortable telling—asking—someone to do something. I might have been the owner, but I never settled into my authority the way Dad apparently had, and it showed.

I was pleased (one restaurateur to another) to see that Hancock's was enjoying much more business than it had at lunch. The booths were filled and a Friday night crowd gathered around the bar, mostly 20- and 30-year-olds getting a start on the weekend. Women outnumbered men. I noticed a few guys in suits and loosened ties, but most of the men looked fresh from a construction site, garage, or factory—a bar scene not much different from my old Gloucester haunts. As at lunch, the bar TVs showed talking heads excited about the Red Sox going all the way to the World Series. I squeezed into a space at the bar and ordered Jim

Beam on the rocks. Drink in hand, the first sip warming my throat, I surveyed the crowd.

Five young women—who did not look old enough to drink—formed a tight group at the far end of the bar. They swigged beer from green bottles, as if to show they could drink like anyone. They wore jeans and jackets, denim, leather. The girl in a gray fleece that had to be too warm for the bar looked kind of familiar. Straight blond hair, thin lips, round young face. How many people did I know in Pittsfield? Then I made the connection, which gave me a shiver of excitement.

I pushed my way over to the group of women and addressed the blond with a smile. "Hey, Brandi."

She looked blankly at me, but didn't seem put off. "Hi, yourself. Do I know you?" she asked with what I took to be mild curiosity.

"Sure, we met this morning. You're Brandi from Dunkin' Donuts and I'm Tommy Lovell from Gloucester."

Brandi's eyes showed the hint of a smile. "Oh, yeah. The big tipper."

"Gloucester?" said one of the other women. "Are you a fisherman?"

I shook my head, wishing I had a snappy comeback. "No . . . I don't know what I am these days." Go for the sympathy vote.

"Welcome to the club," said Brandi. She had light brown eyes, a small nose, and her lips were a glossy cherry red. Her gray fleece jacket was embroidered "PHS Pom Squad" in purple and white above her left breast. Out of her coffee-shop uniform and name tag, standing a few inches from me, she was a different person. There was something about the set of her mouth, the skin around her eyes that made her look less like the coltish high school girl her mannerisms suggested. Close up, I guessed she was really in her mid-twenties, still a bit of a cheerleader in spirit if not in fact.

We went through a round of introductions—but I was too focused on Brandi to catch the other names and too embarrassed for a repeat. The friend in denim asked me, "So what are you doing in town?"

I had to think for a few seconds. I tried to look sincere and mature. "I'm sort of a management consultant." Even to me, it sounded a little evasive, but Dad had reminded once again as we were going down to Melville's for dinner that our role and what we learned at Jonker's was confidential. ("I know I don't have to tell you this," he'd said, telling me anyway.)

Luckily, the girls didn't care all that much about the details of my work life. "So how long you in town?" asked Brandi.

"Probably until Sunday." As I sipped at my Beam and Brandi companionably tipped up her beer bottle, I tried to think of something—anything—to say that would make me attractive and appealing. It was an odd, unfamiliar sensation to feel a tinge of loneliness in the middle of a noisy bar.

Brandi had a tiny silver softball-shaped earring dangling from one ear, a miniature silver baseball bat from the other. Her shell-shaped, pink earlobes seemed unimaginably alluring in the dim bar light. How would she react if I brushed them gently with my lips? But I only asked, "Brandi, can I buy you another beer?"

She gave me a look of appraisal. I'd been away from the bar scene except as an observer and owner for so long, I was unsure of the nuances. I was offering her a beer. I wanted company and Brandi was company. Tonight, I wasn't looking for more. Or not much more. (If I were standing at the bar with a carefree, untroubled Wendy Jonker, that would be a different story.) By the way she leaned in and tilted her face, I had the impression Brandi was more interested in me than the others were. I wondered what might develop.

Brandi threw her friends a look that—I assumed—indicated she was abandoning them for me. "Sure," she said. "That'd be nice." She turned to give me her full attention and I signaled the bartender.

Returning to Brandi, I asked in my clumsy way, "Why is someone as good looking as you out with the girls on a Friday night?"

"Yeah. Well, you know . . ."

I didn't know. Did she have a boyfriend who was somewhere else tonight?

"Yeah, I know," I said. The bartender brought another bottle and I went into my wallet's inner pocket and took out the folded fifty-dollar bill, my emergency cash. This was an emergency. I put the bill on the counter. I made no move to pick up my change. Nick wasn't the only one who could play Mr. Moneybag. "So what do you like to do when you're not working?"

Brandi looked thoughtful. "Play softball in the summer. Go Sox," she laughed, tinkling her earrings. "Ski in the winter. Make jewelry in between." She put down her beer to pull up one sleeve of her jacket. She exposed an elaborate beaded bracelet that must have taken hours to assemble. "This is one of my designs. Nothing special." When I told her truthfully I thought the bracelet was beautiful, her face flushed with the compliment and she immediately turned the questioning around. "What about you?"

I closed my eyes. I tried to think of activities that might impress her, but all I could picture was myself standing at the cash register in Si Accomodi. Did I want to open that can of worms? "Honestly, work. Just work. I had a restaurant, and all I did was work."

"A restaurant, that sounds really interesting." She in fact sounded interested. "I worked in a restaurant for a while. But the manager wouldn't give me any of the good tables, so I said, 'Screw you' and walked out."

I nodded sagely. "Only thing to do in a situation like that."

On the TV sets over the bar, the shortstop fielded a mean

grounder, then overthrew first, allowing the Sox runner to scamper to second. Even though this was a clip from yesterday's game which the Sox lost, the crowd cheered as enthusiastically as if it were live from Fenway. The guy beside me gave me a hard look to ensure I was another enthusiastic Sox fan. His glance slid off me onto Brandi. "Hey, Brandi, how's it going?"

"Going good, Andy."

Was Andy nearby when I first approached Brandi or had he walked in while she and I were talking? And how well did they know each other? Andy had long blond hair, a wispy blond mustache, and a ruddy face--the face of someone who worked outside all day. Paint-stained T-shirt, jeans, and a denim jacket, one hand holding a beer stein. Because I was the outsider here, I offered my hand. "Tommy Lovell."

"Andy Panetta." Andy did not put down his stein, but reached out with his left for a cursory shake. He shifted his position to include Brandi and me, creating a clump of four. The fourth, the guy beside Andy, also greeted Brandi with the attitude of an old friend and introduced himself as Craig Figlar. Craig wore white painter's pants, a faded T-shirt, and a leather jacket.

As we chatted, I felt older by the minute. Andy and Craig were at least five years younger than me, former high school football stars, and seemed to be interested exclusively in sports, cars, and women (indicated by their comments on the "broads" in the car commercials that ran between Sox replays). I had trouble splitting my attention between the two guys and Brandi, but she seemed perfectly comfortable chatting with them and me simultaneously.

Andy asked where I was from, and I told him. Andy said that's why he hadn't seen me around and asked what I was doing in town. I said, "Spending a fun-filled weekend at Jonker Appliance & TV . . . the store up on North Street."

"The store where that guy got hurt?"

"You heard about it?"

"Local radio. Big story. It's a tiny-assed town so it's a big deal when a North Street retail executive—that's what they called him, 'a North Street retail executive'—has an accident on his bike."

"Front page news in the *Eagle* tomorrow," remarked Craig.

I perked up my ears and asked, as casually as I could, "You know Jonker's?" I flashed on a vision of Otto hooked up to tubes and wires in his hospital bed.

"Yeah, we bought our TV there. He gave us a deal."

They drank and watched the replays. I wanted to talk to Brandi, but she wasn't sharing her thoughts—or asking mine—in front of Andy and Craig. For a few minutes, the guys analyzed the Sox's chances of going all the way to win the Series, which looked very good.

I used more of my fifty on a second Jim Beam and enjoyed the alcohol's warm, agreeable sensation. It felt liberating to be away from the crisis at Jonker's, away from Dad, away from Dad's friends, accepted by new people.

So I was sipping Beam at the edge of the foursome when Ashley and Caitlin, two lady friends of Andy and Craig arrived. It was hard to tell them apart at first, with their twin striped spandex outfits, middles cinched with matching belts, and haloes of puffy black hair. Ashley (the willowy, chatty one) was Craig's sister and Andy's girl friend. "Andy and Ashley, even the names go together," Brandi explained helpfully. Ashley gave a happy squeal as Andy gave her ass a proprietary squeeze.

Caitlin, who even with her high hair only came up to my shoulder, was Craig's girl and Ashley's best friend. They both knew Brandi ("We were all on the pom-pom team"). They worked at a hair salon further up North Street from Jonker's, and had just gotten off work. Brandi introduced me by saying, "He's a management consultant, working at Jonker's."

"Oh, we know someone who works there," said Ashley. "Steffie Gilberti? Brown hair with auburn highlights? Thinning? But a nice wave?"

I said I'd met her.

"Tommy's from Gloucester," Andy announced.

"Are you a fisherman?" asked Caitlin. Not an unusual question, and ordinarily, I had a snappy answer. Not tonight.

I repeated my earlier answer, "No. These days I don't know what I am, but I'll get back to you on it." Said with a smile, just enough to ward off more inquiry.

"I know what I am," said Ashley. "Hungry." One of the booths was just clearing and she bulled her way through the crowd to claim it.

Caitlin and Brandi slid into the seat beside Ashley. Because Andy and Craig filled their side of the booth, I pulled over a chair to sit at the end of the table, close enough to Brandi to sense the faint coffee-and-donut scent in her hair. We ordered two pizzas and the three women checked me out as the newcomer while Andy and Craig drank their beer, ate pizza, and half-listened to the table conversation while watching the TV, which was now showing a basketball game.

How long would I be in town?

Two more days, then headed back to Gloucester.

"I wish I could get out of this shithole in two days," said Brandi.

I stared her curiously. "What's stopping you?"

She met my eyes and gave a resigned shrug. "Nowhere to go."

"No one to go with," Caitlin amended.

"That too," said Brandi with a tap of her ragged fingernail on the bottle. Encouragement?

"You married?" asked Ashley.

I hesitated for a moment. "Separated."

"I wondered, 'cause you used to wear a ring." Ashley pointed to the pale skin on the ring finger of my left hand.

"That's what they teach you," said Andy, dropping momentarily into the conversation. "Take your wedding ring off when you come into a strange town. Otherwise it makes chicks nervous."

"Is that what you'd do?" Ashley reached across the pizza platter to gave Andy a slap on the arm.

"Who? Me?" He assumed a look of innocence, took a long pull at his beer, and returned his attention to the TV.

As the only married (well, soon to be previously married) person at the table, I suddenly felt old. These kids had their entire twenties ahead of them; my life was more than a third over. "Let's just say the marriage didn't work out. I took the ring off a month ago. We're just waiting for the lawyers to work things out."

"Unattached," Caitlin confirmed to Brandi.

"Any kids?" Ashley followed up.

"No. Working too damn hard." It slipped out before I could strip the self-pity out of my tone.

It was almost true. I thought Gina and I'd agreed to wait to start a family. Get the restaurant up and running smoothly, become independent so we could give our children a secure life. That's what I thought, anyway.

Apparently, Gina hadn't totally agreed. In the past year or so, she'd begun hinting she was tired of the restaurant. "You know what I really want?" she'd asked one midnight as we were closing up after yet another slow dinner period. "I'd like to burn this fucking place down." Her sweeping gesture took in Si Accomodi and the entire strip mall. "Move to the country and have a baby."

I blinked myself back into Friday night and Brandi's situation. "Why can't you leave town? Go some place interesting.

Boston...New York...Las Vegas. Anywhere. What holds you back?"

The spandex twins turned to hear Brandi's answer. "I don't know. Money." She finished her beer and paused, sitting back in the booth, not taking my question seriously. "I don't know anybody in Las Vegas."

"Don't give up on yourself. You can get out if you really want to," I insisted. I sucked the last of the Jim Beam from the ice. "Goals. Write it down as one of your goals." Oh, no, was I turning into my Dad? Time for another drink.

"Do you have goals?" asked Caitlin.

I was just tipsy enough to give them an honest answer. "Once upon a time I had three goals: Get married, have my own business, own my own plane. I got married and started my own business, so two out of three. Now my goals are to get unmarried, start another business, and have my own plane." I waved my glass impatiently at the waitress, who ignored me.

Andy must have had his ears in our conversation even though his eyes were on the TV because he asked, without looking away from the screen, "You fly?"

"Yeah, I fly. We have our own plane. My dad flew it up here yesterday afternoon. It's parked out at the airport right now. A Cessna Skyhawk."

In the weeks I'd been home, I'd managed (with Dad's considerable help, of course) to renew my student ticket. I'd brushed up on FAA rules and the ins and outs of our Skyhawk, taken the written test. Now I was again licensed to fly alone.

At the mention of flying, Brandi's attitude, which I'd taken as friendly but reserved, changed noticeably. "What's it like?" She seemed impressed that she was sitting with her knee jammed against the knee of someone who had access to the sky. "To fly? Up in the clouds. By yourself."

Maybe this wasn't the time to mention I had only a student

license and could not fly with a passenger. "Up there, you see the world, all the familiar landmarks, from a different perspective." I moved my hand to suggest a plane in flight. "You're free in a way you're never free on the ground. Go anywhere you want."

"Awesome!" Brandi's face was glowing. "Take me for a ride?"

"Sure." Sure was the drink talking, but I was ready to take her out to the airport right now and set myself in cockpit, Brandi at my right. Take off and show her Pittsfield's lights from the air. Give her a thrill she'd never forget.

But I was sober enough to realize that was truly crazy thinking. Aside from the simple mechanics—I'd have to get the key from Dad, which would be impossible, and was the Pittsfield airport even open at this hour?—I was too far gone to fly. "But not tonight," I told her. "You want your pilot to be stone cold sober." (Did she want me at all?)

Brandi's face showed her disappointment, but she took it well. "Promise?" She put out her right hand, pinky extended.

I clasped her pinky finger with mine and gave her a soulful look. "Promise."

No one wanted the last slice of mushroom pizza. I stopped myself from taking it. Another drink? No, it would only push me over an edge I didn't want to go over. I was nicely mellow. More alcohol and I could see myself puking into the hotel room toilet, me aware of Dad aware of my retching, physical agony compounded by mortification.

Andy leaned across the table to Ashley. "Another round, or you want to go?"

Ashley shook her head. "Go. We work tomorrow morning. Even if you don't." This seemed a familiar pattern; they sounded like old-married couples. The way she said "Go" made me wonder what it included.

The three women slid out of the booth and walked toward

the restrooms. Watching Brandi in her jeans, I looked for but couldn't see a panty line. Andy and Craig pulled crumpled bills from their pockets and put them on the table. I added a couple of bills for my share. Standing too quickly, I felt the room rocking, and I had to hold the table's edge until it stopped. "I should get back," I said to Andy.

"You got something waiting for you back at the hotel?"

"Nothing special." Just Dad working away at the room's desk.

"Then don't go. Brandi likes you." How could Andy tell? "Come with us. Maybe you'll get lucky." He gave an incongruous wink.

"Where we going?" I asked as we began to shuffle toward the front door. I had to focus to read my watch. Almost midnight.

The cold night air smacked me in the face and helped clear my head. I shivered and wished I'd gone back for my sweater. We headed toward an old Chrysler four-door, a boat of a car with rust scabs and a dented fender. Andy opened the driver's door and pointed me to the back seat.

I stopped moving, uneasy. Who was this guy? What did he want? Where was he going to take me? Had he seen me break the fifty at the bar? Did they think I had more? (Wouldn't they be surprised!) "Where are we going?" I asked again.

"State forest. Brandi's cool." Craig spotted the three women coming around Hancock's corner and waved to them. "Everything come out all right?" he asked as they approached.

"It did in the end," said Ashley, sticking her tongue out at him. She climbed into the front seat and slid over to Andy. Craig held one of the back doors open.

Brandi got right in. "See you," she said to Caitlin.

"Yeah, tomorrow," said Caitlin. She turned toward another car.

"Don't do anything I wouldn't do," Craig called to Brandi,

closing the door and following Caitlin across the lot.

Leaving me with just Andy, Ashley, and Brandi. Relieved, I clambered in beside Brandi, who leaned against me. She smelled of a flowery perfume, something added in the ladies room. By the Chrysler's dome light, I could tell she and Ashley had repaired their lipstick and fixed their hair.

Andy backed out of the parking spot, and swung onto the street. I couldn't see where we were going because Brandi was playing with my face, running her fingers lightly over my nose and lips and chin, around my ear and down my jaw. Looking ahead, I could see Ashley doing her best to distract Andy as well. She was licking his neck and ear, but he kept both hands on the wheel.

As my anxiety ebbed, I used a free hand to pull Brandi closer and kiss her. She tasted of pizza and beer. It was a friendly kiss, a kiss promising more to come. She settled comfortably against my arm.

I explored Brandi's adorable ear with my lips and felt her tremble. The skin of her cheek and jaw was as smooth as polished granite, but warm with a faint hint of flowers. She let me survey the territory, turning her head to give me better access. I kissed her again.

The car's tires crunching to a halt on gravel roused me from exploration. Andy killed the lights and turned off the engine. Wherever we were was solid dark, no light anywhere. "Where are we?" I whispered into Brandi's ear.

"The state forest. The picnic area parking lot," she whispered back. "They come out here all the time."

Andy and Ashley wordlessly opened their doors. I moved to follow, but Brandi pulled my hand from the door handle. Andy popped the trunk, removed something, and slammed it shut, an explosion in the silent dark. "Blanket," Brandi whispered. In the starlight I could barely make out the two shadows moving away from the car. "They come out here all the time. They've got a regular spot."

"Seems . . . rough." Especially in October's cold.

"Sometimes the cops check out cars."

In the silence, I heard the cooling engine's ping. Uncertain what she expected—or would permit—I asked, "Come here often?"

She began to giggle. "That's what you're supposed to ask back at Hancock's."

"No. Back at Hancock's I should have asked, 'What's your sign?'"

She giggled harder and could barely whisper, "Slippery When Wet."

"Not, 'Bridge Freezes Before Road Surface'?"

Why whisper? There's nobody around. But it felt right.

"The worst pickup line a guy ever used on me was last summer. At softball. He looks me over and says, 'I'm an umpire—give me your number so I can make the call.'"

I groaned. "God, that's terrible. Hope you didn't . . ."

She shook her head. "Not as bad as the guy who came into Dunkin' and said, 'Hi there. I'm a thief, and I'm here to steal your heart.' I told him we had him on the surveillance camera." Her laugh gave me little wingies.

I wanted to keep her laughing. "One time in college . . . I can't believe I actually said this." I paused, uncertain whether to admit my callowness, then plunged ahead. "One time I told a girl, 'When I look into your eyes, it's like a gateway into a far-away galaxy I want to be part of.' She thought I was a dork."

"Aww, that's sweet."

"I got it out of a book."

I reached to kiss her, a prelude to something more serious. When she returned the kiss, I found the pull tab at her throat and unzipped her pom-pom jacket. She let me run my hand underneath until I began trying to find my way onto bare skin. With a gasp ("Cold!") she pushed my hand away, but kept her face near mine.

For some reason—Jim Beam screwing up my coordination?—I couldn't deal with her bra hooks through her shirt. I also couldn't tell—and it seemed important to know—whether Brandi enjoyed what I was doing or if she simply tolerated my fumbling. There were times of the month when Gina's breasts had been so tender she would slap my hand if I tried to touch her. Other times, she'd bring my hand to them. I never knew what to expect and felt too awkward to ask outright.

More aroused than I'd been in months, I had to break away to adjust my shorts. Just how far would things progress, out here in the state forest, parked in somebody else's junker? I was a teenager, thinking of the old baseball metaphor. Had I even made it to first base? Any chance of a home run? No way. Not tonight.

She leaned back just out of reach and tried to draw me out. "Tommy, can I ask you—How did you meet your wife?"

Uh-oh, a serious conversation. "We were at UMass together," I said cautiously.

"How long were you married?"

"Well, strictly speaking—" I hesitated. "—we still are." I had to think. "We got married January of eighty-two . . . so about four years." To derail this train of thought, I gently pulled her closer, kissed her while caressing her breast through two layers of fabric.

What was I? A high school boy? I was an experienced man, a thoughtful lover (I hoped), taking time to make love slowly and properly to women I cared for. And in the case of Gina, to do it legally with the blessing of church and state. Not making out in the back seat of a car with a girl I'd barely met. It was undignified. Unworthy of who I considered myself to be.

A thump on the hood announced the return of Andy and

Ashley. Andy dropped the blanket in the trunk as Ashley took her seat in front. "You guys all right?" she asked, giving us privacy by not turning around.

"You know me," said Brandi.

"No vans tonight," Ashley announced as Andy joined her in the front seat.

That seemed like an odd comment. "No vans?" I said.

"Yeah, last night," said Andy. "We couldn't believe it. There we are, snug like bugs in our rug when this van comes whipping into the parking lot, does a one-eighty, and starts backing up the loop road. Like it's not hard enough to drive that fucker the right way. Ten minutes later he comes shooting right back down and right out past the gate house. Lucky for him the ranger's off at sundown or he'd of had cops all over him." Andy started the engine and ran the heater full blast to clear the windshield's mist. "Back to the Hilton?"

"Where else?" I put my mouth close to Brandi's ear to ask softly. "Do you have a phone number?"

She nodded and ripped a corner off an envelope from her purse, and plucked the pen from my shirt pocket. "I'll call you," I mouthed as she scribbled.

Andy pulled into the Hilton's turning circle and stopped in front of the lobby door, waiting for me to climb out of the Chrysler. It hit me: What if someone from Dad's group saw Brandi giving me a passionate, sensual, French-kiss goodnight?

Well, what if?

Rather than a passionate, sensual, French-kiss however, Brandi gave me a quick peck on the lips, then leaned back into the seat. I stuck my head into the car to thank Andy for the adventure. Brandi grinned when I repeated, "I'll call you." I patted the pocket where she'd tucked in her phone number, and gave a little salute when the Chrysler pulled away.

As I stood in the empty lobby waiting for the elevator, no

desk clerk in sight, the restaurant dark, feeling entirely sober, I abruptly connected Andy's van to Otto's motorcycle.

What if Otto, racing down the mountain road, had met that van backing up? No room to pass, no time to stop, so into the guardrail and into the trees like a rag doll.

Maybe Otto's accident wasn't an accident.

13 / Friday night

I tried to make as little noise as possible entering our hotel room, but there was no need. Dad was sitting at the desk, deep in conversation with Nick, who had pulled up the room's easy chair. Catching sight of Dad's expression, I knew bad news was on the way. Really bad news.

"Christine called after you left." He hesitated. "About Otto . . . I'm afraid." Another pause. "Well, he never came out of the coma. He died this evening."

It felt like a punch. "Oh, jeez! I didn't know. That's awful. How's Christine? Wendy?" I leaned against the wall to stare at Dad's face, tired and elderly in the shadows. It didn't seem possible that while I was trying to impress Brandi at the bar, nuzzling her neck in the forest, Otto was passing out of life a mile or so away.

As if anything I might have done would have made any difference.

Nick said, "We don't know much yet. She kept it short, had more calls to make."

I couldn't let it go. "But what was it? I thought he was doing better after the surgery."

Dad shrugged and sighed, his voice soft. "You know what I

know. Christine called. Otto died. She didn't give any details, and I didn't push for them."

"Shit. I guess that changes everything," I was thinking out loud, trying to make some sense of things.

Dad and Nick exchanged a look. "There's still the store," said Nick. "That hasn't changed."

"The store? What about the store?" How could they worry about appliances and inventory and all that crap when their friend had just died? I glanced at the papers on the desk. Payroll records. Apparently Dad and Nick had been working all evening even though Otto was dead.

"We're going back in tomorrow, make this weekend count," said Dad. "If there's no business, I don't know what'll happen to Christine and the others."

"The store? The goddamn store? It's more important than the man's death?" Why was I so infuriated?

"Look, Tommy, Nick and I feel terrible about Otto." Dad's tone was mild. "We're all in shock, we all want to help. We can't do anything about his death. We *can* do something about his business."

"Yeah? Really? You really think you can save it?"

He wasn't going to fight me. "I hope so," he said. "It's going to be close." He looked down at his papers and began tapping them into order. "But we can do it." It sounded hollow to me.

"Take a lot of work," Nick added. "You in?"

I waffled, "I thought with the receivables . . ." I didn't know what I thought.

"Money coming in will help," said Dad.

Nick stood, stretched, and massaged the back of his neck. "It's late. I'm heading back to my room. See you two in the morning." Guess I was in.

"Another full day tomorrow," said Dad.

Once Nick shut the door, I waited for Dad to ask where I'd

been—and wondered which version of the truth to tell. Instead he asked, "You want to hear what Nick and I decided about the employees?"

That took a second to sink in, but I felt relieved he wasn't going to question me, and flattered he'd make the offer. I made myself comfortable in the easy chair. "Of course. Sure."

He began with the blindingly obvious: "Jonker's lives on sales, so we want to keep the best salespeople. The ones who sell the most may be picking the low-hanging fruit, selling whatever they can sell. We want salespeople who think about the customers and the store's profits." Dad said that while Otto's records sucked, he and Nick did a lot of flipping back and forth through the paperwork to chart pay versus performance.

He showed me a couple of outliers. Jonker's had paid James Minoyan $200 every week as his draw, whether he sold anything or not. Most weeks, his commissions were two or three times that. So Minoyan was making money for himself and the store.

For some reason, the store's oldest employee, Mike Tarabocchia, was drawing $300 every week, but his commissions rarely equaled it. Dad and Nick went back to the beginning of the year. This guy's performance was consistently weak. A tally showed that Mike had actually been paid $9,000 more than he'd earned in commissions so far this year, making him a charity case Jonker's could no longer afford.

I looked from the figures, to the window, and back to the figures. They didn't compute. "Dad, does this sound like the Otto you know? I mean, knew—I mean—oh, God, you know . . ."

Dad cupped his hand over his mouth. An unthinkable death, an unanswerable question. After a moment, he turned back to the figures and lists. He said he and Nick identified eight names of people to let go, seven salespeople and Megan Mattner, the secretary who didn't seem to have much to do. One of the salespeople was Dave Gendron, manager of the electronics department, but with a performance worse than Mike's.

I said, "I wonder if Gendron thinks because he's got the 'manager' title he doesn't actually have to talk to a customer."

Dad and Nick didn't want to touch the service department without talking to Dan, the expert in that area. "If the techs are completing their calls—and assuming the store has enough service business to keep all five working full time—they should be pulling their weight. The only way Jonker's is going to survive is with better service than the chains."

I had nothing to add and with a yawn, began to undress for bed. Dad put his papers in order, finished in the bathroom, let me have a turn, and clicked off the desk lamp. No questions about where I'd been or what I'd been doing. Whew.

After Dad turned out the lights, the drapes admitted a slit of light. He clamped them shut with a clothespin from his shaving kit. The tiny red eye of the smoke detector on the ceiling watched unblinking. As I listened to Dad's breathing become deep and regular, my thoughts simmered. I couldn't stop thinking about Andy and the van and Otto.

Why in the world would a van be backing up the forest road?

The loop road where Otto had his accident. Was it the same road? But how many loop roads were there? (I should check.)

What time had the van backed up the road?

It had to be late. But not too late because Andy and Ashley had to get to work this Friday morning. Also, it was a weeknight, so they'd probably driven out after Hancock's closed at eleven. That is, assuming they'd gone to Hancock's, then to the state forest for their regular tryst after the bar closed. (I should check.)

What time had Otto driven up the loop road? Had Andy heard his motorcycle? (I should check.)

My best guess was that Otto was up there around eleven forty-five or so, since the meeting at the house broke up after eleven. Christine said Otto rode off right after the meeting.

Assume for a moment Otto headed up the loop road one way and a few minutes later the van backed up the loop road from the other way.

What if Otto had met the van while he was roaring down off the mountain?

From the flicker of landscape I'd seen in the Chrysler's headlights from the back seat, the loop road was a narrow, one-way strip of asphalt. Not a whole lot of room to pass. Nowhere to go. Come around a curve on that road and meet a van blocking your way and you were shit out of luck.

But why would someone back up the loop road in the first place? Some idiot showing off to his girlfriend just as Otto was ripping down the mountain? Was Otto simply in the wrong place at the wrong time?

Or was someone deliberately blocking the road? Was Otto's accident really an accident?

But how would someone know Otto was on the road?

First assumption: a van had something to do with Otto's accident. Although I had to wonder. Here's Otto thrown from his motorcycle on the loop road and two people see a van driven strangely on the same road around the same time. But suppose the van driver *did* want to force Otto off the road, how did he (she?) know Otto would be coming down the road just then?

Second assumption: Andy and Ashley actually *had* seen a van backing up the road. They weren't imagining things. I'd asked what kind of van. Andy thought it was white. Ashley volunteered it was a service truck. "Like for flowers. Writing on the side."

"Appliance service?"

"It was dark, you know?"

"And we weren't paying a lot of attention to the road," said Andy, sounding self-satisfied. "If you know what I mean."

What were the odds that some florist or electrician was backing up the Pittsfield state forest loop road at midnight? Somewhere between slim and impossible, I'd bet, but it gave me something to look into. My gut was telling me this whole thing felt off somehow. Everybody else seemed to be working their asses off to save Jonker's. Before I said anything to Dad, I was going to double- and triple-check the van thing and the timing.

Starting with what time Andy and Ashley had seen the van. If I could put the van on the loop road at the same time as the motorcycle . . . then what?

I rolled onto my side and pulled the bed's second pillow against my ear to muffle Dad's snores so I could concentrate. Jonker's had service vans. There'd been two or three in the parking lot behind the store when Nick and I had returned with the coffee. If Jonker's had the same system as Lovell & Son, Otto would try to schedule the last service call of the day close to the technician's home so he could keep the van overnight. The technicians didn't have to use their own cars to get to and from work, they could respond to the rare midnight emergency, and the vans were secure. Everyone wins.

Why assume the van was from Jonker's? There had to be a couple hundred white vans in a city the size of Pittsfield.

Dad's snoring penetrated my pillow, gave a loud rattle, and stopped. I raised my head to listen. No sound from the other bed. For several seconds I wondered if he'd died, then his regular breathing resumed softly.

My last conscious thoughts were a confused mixture of Otto's broken body on the forest's leaves, ear plugs, Jonker vans, Brandi's mouth, and the flower fragrance of her perfume.

14 / Saturday morning

We were a somber group at breakfast the next morning, gathered around the same corner table where we'd had dinner. I was tangled in my own thoughts about Otto's death, what the van on the road might mean. Nobody was in a chatty mood, there was none of the usual banter and small talk.

Dad repeated to the others what he'd said to me as we dressed for the day. "I think we should stay for the funeral or whatever Christine wants."

That was okay with me, there was no place I had to be. But what about with the others? They had businesses, families, real lives.

Joanne didn't hesitate. "Sure thing."

Nick nodded. Only Dan had reservations. "I'm not sure. Any idea when that's going to be?"

Dad said he'd find out more when he and Joanne went to the house to meet with Christine a little later. "I know it's a bad time for her, but if we don't start making changes at the store immediately, it's going to be worse. Much worse." He wanted a power of attorney that would give him the authority to terminate staff and make other business decisions. Joanne asked how he and Nick decided who to fire, and Nick explained their rationale.

Dad said he expected to begin talking to the employees as soon as he returned from the house. He didn't sound happy about it. A dirty job but somebody had to do it. One of the drawbacks of being in charge. One of the things that haunted me about the ugly end of my restaurant business.

Dan suggested: "Have someone from the family with you when you're talking to the people. Send the message the family knows what we're doing."

"And approves," Joanne added.

Dad pointed his fork at Joanne. "Good thought, but I can't ask Christine to come in this morning. She's got so much on her plate already . . . maybe an hour this afternoon." Nods all around.

Dad asked for a quick sketch of the day's plans. Dan was going to continue analyzing the service department, since it didn't seem as profitable as it ought to be. He still had questions about the number of technicians and the types of repairs they were doing.

Nick was building the VisiCalc cash flow budget and bringing Steffie Gilberti up to speed on the program. Entering the figures gave him a natural way to ask her about some of the expenses that seemed out of whack.

Joanne said she planned to work with Angelina Gamwell, the former Sears salesperson, to organize sales training sessions for the staff.

When heads turned in my direction, I said I'd work on collection calls. Not my favorite thing, but at least it would be productive—and let me look busy while making calls to follow up on the van sighting.

Dad had a better idea: "Train the sales people to make those calls when they're not actually selling. Tell anyone who's more than ninety days past due if they aren't in here Monday with some money, we're turning them over to a collection agency."

"Heck, tell them that if they're more than sixty days late," said Nick. "No more Mr. Nice Guy Otto Jonker." The others nodded agreement.

No more Otto at all, I thought, and again flashed on a vision of a shattered and bloody body lying in the dark woods.

Because Otto had scheduled a full-page sale ad in Saturday morning's *Berkshire Eagle*, we expected the store to be busy most of the day. When we arrived at the loading dock a little before eight, the service door was unlocked. The lights were on in the service department, the break room, and Otto's office, but not in the showroom. Following the aroma of fresh coffee, I stopped in the doorway of the break room to pour a mugful and plucked a glazed donut from the box open on the table.

Walking down the hall, I heard Dad say: "You're here early." Steffie was bent over her desk file drawer, fingers walking through folders, searching for something Dad wanted. "I think we have one." She pulled a folder free, opened it on her desk, and flipped through the papers. "Here. I don't know the last time we needed one. Or what for." She was going through the motions of being a good manager, but it was clear she was almost as distressed as she'd been yesterday morning.

Dad scanned the sheet, reading in an undertone: ". . . made and appointed . . . true and lawful attorney for him/her and in his/her name, place, and stead, giving . . . general, full and unlimited power and authority to do and perform all and every act and thing whatsoever requisite necessary to be done in and about the premises as fully . . ."

He thanked Steffie, whose eyes were about to overflow with more tears. "What's going to happen? Now that Otto's—" She hesitated. "—gone." I caught Dad's eye. I thought he was urging me forward to console her. I hung back, a little ashamed not to know how to go about it.

Dad stepped closer and gave Steffie's shoulder a brief comforting squeeze. "I know, I know. So sudden. It's a terrible shock." She gripped her tissue tighter, then her shoulders relaxed a minute later as she appeared to regain control. Finally she looked up at Dad and gave him a nod. She was ready to carry on.

"Listen, this store needs you, more than ever," he said. "And we need you. We have to move ahead without Otto. It's the best thing we can do for Christine and the family right now." Once he was sure she was all right, he turned and went back to Otto's office. I saw him drop the blinds in the window overlooking the sales floor. Good move, Dad: No one in the showroom should be able to witness the trauma of someone being fired.

I began, "Excuse me, Mrs. Gilberti—"

She looked at me with red-rimmed eyes to interrupt. "Steffie. Call me Steffie. Everybody does."

Because I was uncomfortable calling a woman of Dad's age (or older) "Steffie," I sidestepped this and went right to my question. "How many vans does Jonker's have? Service vans, I mean." I clicked my pen to make myself look official.

She gave me a why-do-you-want-to-know look, thought a moment, and said, "Six. Five technicians. They each drive one, of course. And Vernon has one because he sometimes goes out on calls when one of the techs can't fix something."

I wondered why the service manager couldn't use his car. Vernon didn't need a van full of parts and tools; he could use the tools in the van at the scene. Made a note: A question for Vernon.

"What do the technicians do when a van breaks down or needs repairs?" I didn't care but I didn't want Steffie to think I had a special interest in the vans. I was just part of the group, poking my nose into all kinds of corners to improve the business. She told me the store had a contract with a local garage. I jotted another note, then asked casually, "Do you know who was driving a van Thursday evening?"

She gave me another curious look. "Why, the technicians, of course."

"What happens at the end of the day?"

"They drive them home after their last call."

"All six?" Steffie nodded, her brown curls shaking. "So they all had them this week?"

She began to nod again, then stopped. "Well . . . not every one. Jason, that's Jason Durso, he's on vacation. He's visiting his sister in Pittsburgh and our Ford's in the shop, so my husband's been using Jason's van." She paused, a flicker of worry in her eyes. "Otto said it was okay. We've been keeping it in our garage. You don't want something like a service van sitting out on the street or in the parking lot out back. Not the way things have been going here in town."

"A lot of crime?"

She nodded. "Just read the *Eagle*. Burglaries. Cars broken into, right in front of your house . . . in your driveway. It's horrible."

I considered saying something about a bad economy making people desperate but Steffie didn't need to hear my opinion about crime. She had far worse things on her mind. Like Otto. Like maybe an affair with Otto.

Not sure how else to say it, I told her straight out, in the gentlest voice, "I'm really sorry about Mr. Jonker."

It was as if I'd punched an aching bruise. Her eyes began to tear, and she fumbled with a desk drawer to find a fresh tissue. Her bosom heaved and she had trouble breathing. I muttered something like, "You must have been close to him," and asked aloud, "Can I get you something? Coffee? Water?"

Her face buried in a handful of tissues, she mumbled something I took to mean, "No, no, I'll be all right." I echoed Dad's gesture, giving her arm a quick pat, and gave her privacy while I made my escape.

In search of more coffee, I found Dan alone in the break room. "Mind if I sit?"

"You can help," he said.

Dan was leafing through a thick sheaf of old service tickets. He would read off a number, and I had to find it in a log—which was nothing more than a school composition book—and read out a technician's name, "Sokolich... Mount... Durso... Kieffer... Mount... Telesca... Kieffer..." Apparently it was not always obvious from the completed ticket who'd done the job, but every so often Dan put a ticket aside, so he had a handle on what was going on. Once we got to the bottom of the pile of tickets, Dan asked me to bring Steffie back to the break room.

She seemed to have recovered from her wave of grief, but she didn't want to sit in the chair Dan indicated. She said she had important things to do before the store opened. Just when I thought she was going to tell him off, Dan told me to close the break room door, and complimented her on her organizational skills. That's why he was asking for her help in understanding exactly how the service department operated.

Dan said we were trying to understand how the technicians collected for their work, how the service tickets were reconciled, what happened to the money. He'd spent time going through the service department records and called a number of service customers. He wanted to make sure he understood the system.

Steffie calmed down and explained that Megan Mattner, the secretary, made up a service ticket when a customer called. Depending on the product—major appliance or consumer electronics—Megan assigned the call to a technician, alternating names so every tech had the same number of calls. She didn't try to determine whether it was a big job or small, whether it would take thirty minutes or two hours. "Otto says—said—it all worked out about even at the end of the day."

Steffie said the technicians looked over their tickets every morning and they decided the order they'd make their calls. "No sense driving from one end of town and back if you've got two calls in the same neighborhood. Also, they can usually guess from what the customer says how big a job it'll be." They scheduled the last call as close to home as they could.

"What if it's an emergency?" asked Dan. "It's July and my refrigerator just stopped."

"They all carry pagers," said Steffie. Megan would call the next technician on the list to send him to the customer's house.

What happened to the money they collected? Steffie said it was accounted for every morning when the technicians came in to pick up the day's calls. They turned in their service tickets and the checks and cash for the calls they'd completed the day before. The store extended no credit to individual service customers, only to a few commercial accounts. "I make sure the money matches the service tickets, enter it in the books, and add it to the day's bank deposit."

"No problems with discrepancies between what the technician charges a customer and what he turns in?" Dan had a way of asking a question that made it sound casual, but I could tell this one was loaded.

A frown of thought lines creased Steffie's forehead for a moment. "Once in a while," she said reluctantly, as if unwilling to criticize. "Sometimes they'll be a few dollars under. Sometimes they'll be a little over. Everyone makes mistakes. Never more than a couple dollars. Except Glen . . . Glen Kieffer. He's always exact. And anyway it's never more than five dollars or so in a whole week. Anyway, it all works out in the end. It'd be more expensive to try to correct than it's worth. That's what Otto always said, don't make a federal case out of a couple of bucks."

I sure didn't agree with Otto on that. I wondered if customers who'd been overcharged would think a refund—even a two-dollar refund—was worth the store's trouble.

Dan had one more question: Does the store phone customers after a service call to be sure they're satisfied? No, they've never done that. Steffie thought it might be a good idea, but immediately assumed she'd have to make the calls. Her hands fluttered. She said she was working as hard as she could right now; she couldn't possibly do anything more. Dan said he could see that, thanked her for all her help, and she left.

I waited until she was out of earshot. "What do you think?"

"I think we have to talk to Glen Kieffer."

Dan and I walked back to the service department. Vernon sat at his desk in his neatly pressed uniform shirt studying a Whirlpool service manual. "Where's Glen Kieffer? He due in this morning?" Dan asked. They were questions, but they sounded like orders.

"Glen?" Vernon examined our faces as if he'd never seen us before.

"He didn't come in for his interview last night after his last call," said Dan.

"Last night?"

"We had an appointment. We were going to talk after work."

Vernon didn't want to return anyone's stare. "Glen's pretty independent."

"Aren't you his boss?" Dan's tone carried an edge.

Vernon's expression shifted from bland cooperation to crossly irritated, a certain tightness around his eyes and mouth. "Oh, yes. That I am."

"Then get him in here."

"I can't just—" He broke off to let us finish the sentence.

In my head, I tried to fill it for him: —interrupt Glen's breakfast? —reach him on the road? —give him a direct order?

"Why not?" asked Dan. "You're his boss. Today's a work day, isn't it?"

Vernon seemed to be fumbling around for a reason not to

call Glen. Dan cut him off. "Tell him if he isn't here by . . ." He glanced at his watch. "If he isn't here by nine-thirty, he doesn't have to come in again. Ever. We'll have someone pick up his truck."

Vernon looked as if Dan had kicked him. "Are you kidding? I can't tell him that."

"Why not?" Dan asked again.

"You guys are just here to look over the business. You can't just go around threatening to fire people."

You don't know the half of what we're going to do, I thought. I felt a smidgen of sympathy for Vernon. Here was a guy who in all probability was more comfortable taking a washing machine apart than dealing with people and he's being asked—no, being told—to be a manager, something he didn't sign up for. Dan said nothing, waiting for Vernon to pick up the phone.

Vernon looked irritated for a few seconds, maybe weighing his options, then he caved. "Okay, okay, I'll call him."

Dan headed back to the break room, leaving me to hover over Vernon's desk. He gave me a sour look. "Look, I said I'd call."

"I know. I want to ask about something else."

"Is that all you people do? Ask questions?" Without waiting for an answer, he picked up the phone, pushed a button for an outside line, and punched out a number so hard I thought the phone would crack. "Glen? This is Vern down at the store. Listen, you gotta come in right now . . . These people Otto brought in, they want to talk to you. You didn't stop by last night . . ." Pause.

"Glen, listen to me. This is serious . . . I know. It's on the radio . . . I know, I know, but you gotta come in. Right now. I mean it . . ." He listened for another few seconds. "Glen, listen to me. Listen. These people, they're really serious. I don't care what she says, they want you down here at the store right now. Don't screw around or I can't guarantee what'll happen. You understand? This is really serious."

I don't know what the other guy said, but Vernon appeared to relax slightly. Maybe he thought we'd fire *him* if he didn't get Glen into the store. "Okay, good," he said finally. "Fifteen minutes." He hung up and glared at me, "You satisfied?"

"Actually, I don't care whether he comes in or not. That's Dan's call. I have questions of my own. I want to know why you're driving one of the service vans."

"What the hell do you care?" Vernon rubbed his forehead as if fending off a headache. "Because I need one. For my job."

"But you're the service slash parts manager. You're in the store all day. What do you need a van for?"

"If one of the guys can't handle a job, or they need a part, I can take it out to them. Saves a second call. Keeps customers happy."

"You could use a car for that. You don't need a van."

"Did you see the piece of crap van I'm driving?"

I shook my head. I hadn't inspected any of the vans. Something I ought to do. If one of Jonker's vans had been blocking the road, maybe Otto's Harley dinged it in the accident.

But Vernon was picking up steam with his rationalization. "When Otto bought Glen a new van, he got a deal from the dealer—two new vans for the price of one and a half. The dealer wouldn't give him anything for the old van, and Otto said it was a rolling billboard, so I got it."

"You take it home every evening?"

"You're obviously not from around here, or you'd know better than to leave anything worth anything sitting behind the store all night. "

"What about the delivery truck? It's parked out there."

"A lot harder to get into, all kinds of locks and alarms. Touch it and it goes off like a fire engine. And the police station's only a block away."

Glen Kieffer swaggered into the break room wearing jeans, plaid flannel shirt, denim jacket and an attitude. I remembered him from yesterday morning's meeting as the oldest technician, a lined face with a bushy gray mustache. He reeked of tobacco smoke. His look took us in and, I suspected, dismissed Dan and me equally.

Taking a donut, he said, "Mind if I have coffee and a donut? Haven't had a chance to have breakfast." He hadn't shaved either.

Dan got right down to business. "Doesn't the service department work on Saturdays?" The three other technicians had checked in earlier, bringing their completed service tickets and customer payments to Steffie, picking up the day's calls, and pulling parts from stock. I knew from our store Saturday was a busy day for a service department because customers were home from work.

Glen poured himself a mug of coffee. "The department does. I don't."

"Why is that?" Dan sounded genuinely curious.

"Not enough work. Even with Jason on vacation, we don't have enough calls for me to work on Saturday."

Dan leaned toward Glen. "If you're only working four days a week, is that enough for you to get by?"

Glen ignored Dan. He appeared fascinated by the Zenith TV poster on the wall. Finally he plunked himself down at the table facing us. "I get by okay."

"We've been looking at your tickets," said Dan. "You seem to have a number of no-charge calls."

"Well, you know, if it's just plugging the set back in, it doesn't seem right to charge the customer for the call." He spoke as if explaining basic business principles to people who knew nothing about them. "I tell them there's no charge, so it's an n/c.

Builds good will for the store."

I leaned forward to ask, "That happen often? Nothing more than a plug out of the wall?"

He stared at me, his blue eyes guileless. "Or a fuse. Something really simple. Five minutes. In and out."

"We've been calling the n/c's," said Dan. "You had six in September. Six more than any other tech."

Glen's face hardened, his eyes suddenly wary. "Yeah?"

"The customers tell us they did pay you. Twenty-five bucks for the call, plus fifteen for the half hour you worked."

"That's bullshit."

"Mrs....Mrs.—" Dan flipped through the top five or six service tickets to find the name. "Mrs. De Pasquale. Her ticket says n/c. But she says she's got the canceled check to prove she paid." His tone was sharp. "You used Mrs. De Pasquale's check to replace the forty bucks in cash you pocketed. Make everything come out correctly. Mrs. Gilberti just checks the total amount you turn in against the service tickets, not the checks against the names."

"You can't prove anything." Glen sat back in his chair, arms across his chest, mouth tight.

Dan pulled another ticket from his small pile. "How long does it take to replace a picture tube and adjust color balance?"

I wondered why the sudden change in direction, but kept my question to myself. Glen looked slightly relieved. He answered easily. "Depends on the brand."

"Say a Magnavox."

"I don't know. Maybe an hour. Maybe more. Depends on how old the set was."

"That's about right," said Dan thoughtfully. "That's about what it would take one of my guys, and my guys are good." Dan's confirmation didn't appear to help Glen's disposition. "Yet, here's one of your tickets from just last Tuesday. It said you replaced the Magnavox picture tube and adjusted the color in less than half an hour. That's fast work."

Glen wasn't pleased by the compliment. "So?"

"The customer told me on the phone yesterday you were in her living room over an hour and a half. She remembers, because you got there at four o'clock and she was afraid her husband was going to miss the six o'clock news. She paid you for the tube, the call, and forty-five bucks for the labor, but you only turned in fifteen bucks for the labor."

I worried for a moment, the way Glen's neck muscles tightened, he was going to reach across the table, snatch the service ticket from Dan's hand, and . . . do what? Whack Dan across the face with it? Worse? I caught my breath. The more rocks we turned over, the more snakes crawled out.

But Glen crossed his arms and leaned back defiantly in his chair. "Yeah? So what are you going to do about it?"

"We're thinking of pressing charges."

"For what?" Glen was dismissing him.

"Theft," said Dan. He patted the stack of service tickets. "It'd take some work, but we could probably go back far enough to make the amount you've stolen from Jonker's into a felony charge."

The "felony" part got Glen's attention, all right. He licked his lips. "You think I'm the only one ripping off the store?"

Dan shook the tickets at him. "I think you're the one we've caught."

"Well, I think you ought to look a little closer. Like maybe you should look at the parts in Vernon's truck. Bet you never thought of that. The boxes may say 'Genuine RCA Color Tube' or "Genuine Whirlpool Compressor' but that ain't what's inside."

Dan understood immediately. "So you've been charging brand-name prices for no-name parts." Dan shook his head, as if profoundly disappointed at what Glen was telling him.

"Or reconditioned," he added. "Check out the tickets."

I did some mental figuring. How much could Vernon Claridge make by selling generic or reconditioned parts in place of brand-name stuff? For a refrigerator compressor or a washing machine motor or a picture tube, possibly a lot. And who'd ever know? Who ever opened up the back of a TV or fridge to read the fine print on the parts? I had to admire their ingenuity—for ripping off the store and the customers.

Dan began making notes on a yellow legal pad. "Thank you, Mr. Kieffer." To keep my hands busy, I leafed slowly through the service tickets as if following up on the information. How many crooks could one appliance store have?

Glen didn't move for a moment. He sounded a little uncertain when he asked, "That's it?"

Dan looked up. "That's it. Leave the van keys here. We'll take care of it. Tommy will go out with you so you can take any personal articles you've left in it. You'll have to get a ride home."

Glen jerked his head up. "Hey, I need that van for work."

"You don't need the van any more, Mr. Kieffer. You don't work for Jonker's any more."

Glen shot up out of his seat, shaking. "What the fuck? You think you're firing me? You can't fire me. Who the fuck you think are, you think you can fire me?"

Dan didn't budge, but I braced myself. Glen looked wiry. Strong. As tall as me, but smaller than Dan, and he looked angry enough to start swinging. Fear spiked through me. Would this guy kick over a chair, or pick one up and start swinging?

After a minute, while everything stopped in the break room, Glen slowly reached into a jeans pocket, took out a set of keys, and threw them down hard in front of Dan. I picked them up and followed Glen, careful to stay a few steps behind. He made a point of marching out the back service door without a word to Vernon, who watched us curiously as we passed his desk.

As I unlocked and opened the van door for him, Glen muttered, "You fuckers think you can get away with this?" He took out a pair of sunglasses, two unopened packs of cigarettes, and a small leather portfolio. "This is my own." He showed it to me but didn't open it. "Bought with my own money, shithead."

"Sounds good to me," I said, waving it away. Glen finished fishing around in the glove box. I relocked the driver's door and checked the van's rear doors to be sure they were secure.

Glen still looked as if he wanted to punch someone—and I was the closest. "You shits ain't going to get away with this. We're not finished here, understand?"

Don't call us, I thought, we'll call you. But I admit, I breathed easier when he stomped away and rounded the corner out of sight.

Back in the break room, the door closed for privacy, I looked at Dan. "What are you going to do about Glen?"

"We'll have to talk to Tom. And Christine."

"Not to Vernon," I said. "Not if his truck is full of no-name parts—if Glen's telling the truth." A thought: Had Dad ever caught someone stealing time or money? Probably. Any company in business long enough will hire one thief, but I couldn't recall my parents ever discussing a dishonest employee, at least not over the dining room table.

I'd never caught an employee stealing from the restaurant—but then we were only in business four years. My employees gave me every other problem: lateness, missed work, confused orders, a tray of food dropped, and more. Much more. But not theft.

I told Dan I wanted to follow up on Vernon. "Let me check out his truck. Maybe the office manager has another set of keys. I assume the truck is locked, out in the back." With Dan's nod, I went to the bullpen at the back of the store, handed Glen's keys to Steffie ("He won't be needing them any more,"), and said I needed to borrow the keys to Vernon's van. Without asking why I needed to open Vernon's van and didn't ask Vernon himself—my mood must have been obvious—she took a gray steel key safe from a desk drawer, unlocked it, and pawed through several sets of keys. "That's strange." She again ran her hand over the keys, setting off a tinkle of metal. "They're not here." She looked one more time. "They should be, but they're not."

"You're sure?"

She looked at all the tags. "No. I don't know . . ."

I said thanks, I'd ask Vernon for his set. As I started back to the service area, I thought, I need a story. Something better than: Vernon, we want to see if you're substituting knockoffs for brand name parts. And if he asked me about Glen? You'll have to talk to Dan and my father.

Vernon was working on a disassembled washer control panel. "Listen," I began. "They want me to take something out to Otto's house. I need to borrow your van." I waited to see what Vernon would say.

Vernon looked up at me. I searched for a hint of suspicion in his expression, but all I could detect was irritation at being interrupted. "Yeah, sure, I guess." He unclipped a carabiner from a belt loop and slid off a ring holding two keys. He tossed them to me. "Square one's the ignition." He turned his attention back to the control panel.

"Great. Thanks." Out in the parking lot, Dan and I had no problem telling Vernon's van from Glen's. Glen's needed a wash, but it looked new; Vernon's had rust scabs, dents in one bumper, and a cracked tail light held in place with red tape. I inspected the back. Was this the van that Otto hit on the mountain road?

Running my hands over the bumper and dings on the back panel, it looked as if someone had backed smartly into a loading dock some time in the past—not recently. None looked as if a motorcycle made them. (But how would I be able to tell?) Too bad. It would have been satisfying to find some evidence this van was involved in Otto's death.

I handed Dan the keys, he unlocked the back doors, and we stuck our heads in. Parts cartons lined both sides with an aisle down the middle. While a few carried brand names—Zenith, GE, RCA, Whirlpool, Kelvinator, Frigidaire—most were nondescript cardboard boxes from Japan, China, Taiwan, with only model numbers and symbols to identify the contents. Unbelievable. It was all in plain sight, if anybody bothered to check the van.

"Looks like Glen was telling the truth," I said.

"Looks like it," agreed Dan. He climbed into the van and opened a few of the unbranded cartons. "Looks like it," he repeated.

"But how much profit margin is there on parts?" I asked. "How much could he be making?" Were the other technicians part of the scheme? They got their parts from Vernon and they had to know the difference between the real thing and a cheap knock-off. If they knew customers were being overcharged, did Vernon have to kick back part of his profit to keep them quiet? Was it worth the paperwork—and the risk? Any technician from a competing store who happened to work on an appliance Jonker had serviced would know immediately a part wasn't from the original manufacturer. It seemed like a lot of risk for very little return.

Dan stepped down out of van and locked the back doors. "We'll have to look at the records. In the meantime, you want to give these back to Vernon?" He handed me the keys.

As we walked through Jonker's service entrance, the unexpected sense of danger and uncertainty made me shudder.

15 / Saturday morning

Dad and Joanne returned from the Jonker house with the signed power of attorney a good half hour before the store opened for the day's business and we all went into Otto's office for a quick update. By the look on Dad's face, I figured things weren't going well at Jonker's and asked about the mood at the house.

Dad shook his head, mouth set in a grim line. He said everyone had been there, Christine, Wendy, Brian, and Christine's sister. "We offered our condolences, but they're in shock. They don't know what to think. They can't even plan Otto's funeral because the police want an autopsy so the hospital can't release the body. A hell of a situation."

He looked at Joanne, who picked up the story. "Christine is so overwhelmed by the accident, the death, she can't focus on the store. She didn't flat-out say so, but it's clear she wants and needs us to keep the store going. Wendy said she thought we were doing all the right things. They weren't second-guessing us, and said they'd try to answer any questions we might have."

"What about Brian?" I figured he'd be the biggest obstacle.

Dad snorted. "Brian, well, he was a lot more skeptical; with everything that's going on, his big concern was how much longer we were going to be in the store. I told him, 'As long as it takes to turn it around.' Then Joanne and I explained about the staff changes."

"How'd that go over?" I asked.

Another snort from Dad. To bring the family up to speed, he and Joanne had summarized all we'd learned except the part about the thefts. It was obvious to everyone the store was overstaffed. Without immediate changes, Jonker's would have a serious cash flow problem within weeks—it was hemorrhaging money. True, we'd begun calling delinquent customers to bring in cash, would continue that effort, and Dad planned to talk to a collection agency about selling the older receivables. But even if Jonker's could collect every single dollar outstanding, the business couldn't cover payroll and the other monthly expenses past Christmas.

"Wendy was under the impression that salespeople were on commission only, but Christine knew about Otto's policy of allowing a generous weekly draw against commissions," Dad continued. "Nothing wrong with that—except when half the salespeople haven't made enough sales to cover their draw for months. It took a little persuading, but Joanne and I got Christine to agree to let us fire the least productive employees for the good of the store."

Joanne said, "I told them it's never easy to let someone go—particularly in a situation like this when it's not really the employee's fault. Tom and I made it clear that there's no other way to stabilize Jonker's quickly. In the end, they said they trust our judgment and we should go ahead." I didn't think it would go smoothly, but I wanted to be a team player and remained silent.

Dan said the store was already down one body, and explained Glen's time thefts and the used parts scam. Dad supported Dan's firing of Glen and asked what Dan recommended about Vernon and the parts. Dan said he needed more information. One problem was that Vernon appeared to be a terrific service manager in terms of training and supporting the technicians and repairing appliances and electronics. Jonker's was lucky to have him.

We delayed opening the store a few minutes so Dad could talk with the staff. Everyone showed up promptly, aware of Otto's death, anxious about the future. Looking at their faces, I remembered the day I had to fire people and close the restaurant. A day I'd never forget, a day I'd never thought would come. What had Otto been thinking? He wouldn't need this many people to take orders for a going-out-of-business/every-thing-must-go sale with customers fighting to get in the door. A lot of people were going to be upset. Would things get ugly?

Soberly and gently, his voice low and serious, Dad told the staff what they already knew. Otto had died from his injuries. People glanced at each other as if to confirm what they'd heard. He said he knew they were all distressed because of Otto's accident and death, and he and we grieved with them. "Otto was a close friend. I know I'll miss him—his laugh, his jokes, his high spirits."

The employees murmured their own condolences, but they also kept their eyes on Dad. When things quieted down, he went on: "To help the Jonker family, Nick and Joanne and Dan and I have resolved to do whatever we can to perpetuate the business. We plan to begin making changes immediately. For example, Jonker's isn't going to offer any more credit. If the credit company won't accept a customer's application, and the customer can't borrow from a bank or credit union, we're just going to have to pass on the sale."

No point in increasing the store's receivables. Especially, as Nick pointed out, if customers begin to think the store would go under because of Otto's accident and they'd never have to pay—

leaving the business in even worse financial shape.

"Lose the sale?" A heavy-set salesman in a blue dress shirt and navy blazer sounded incredulous. "Otto wouldn't want us to lose sales."

He apparently had not noticed that Otto wasn't going to be around any more.

"I know it's not easy," Dad agreed. "You spend all kinds of time qualifying, answering questions, and finally get the customer to make a decision—and then you have to tell them their credit's no good. You don't want to say it, and they don't want to hear it. But that's the way it's got to be. Eventually, Christine may change the policy. But for now, Jonker Appliance and TV is out of the credit business."

I noticed a few heads nodding, while the sullen faces saw only lost sales and commissions.

Dad checked his watch and looked up. "Does anybody have any questions?"

The uncomfortable silence lasted for several seconds. Then a short, black-haired woman, one of the sullen faces, asked, "What if someone asks about Otto?"

"Tell them the truth. He passed away last night in the hospital."

"When's the funeral?"

"Arrangements are being made. We should know something soon."

"Who's running the store?" This was from the salesman who was unhappy about giving up sales.

"I am," said Dad in a voice he must have used as an Army officer. "Christine has given me the authority." He paused to let this sink in, then continued somewhat more gently, "The Jonker family needs our help—needs your help. You're all professionals, you know the store, and you know what needs to be done. Otto counted on you to make every customer contact count. To help customers buy the products they want and need. To make every sale this store needs."

Megan Mattner, the secretary, was sitting at one of the bullpen desks when I asked her to please come back to Otto's office. She didn't put out her cigarette, so Dad found a crude ceramic ashtray (a Wendy or Brian school craft project?) on the credenza behind Otto's desk and put it where Megan could reach it. Dad in Otto's big leather chair, me in a chair beside the desk faced Megan like judges (which, I guess, in a sense we were). I was going to leave, but Dad asked me to sit with him and keep notes.

Dad had cleaned the desktop so a neat pile of documents sat in one of the letter trays, the pen and pencil set was handy, and the clock/thermometer said it was 10:19. I was tempted to rotate the clock to have it show the temperature—the room seemed warm—but I kept my hands still.

Dad used his friendly but no-nonsense tone as he told Megan that unfortunately it was necessary to trim the staff. The decision had nothing to do with the quality of her work or with Otto's accident. There would have been staff reductions even if Otto had never had his accident. The family thanked her for her work, and the store was giving her a week's salary in lieu of notice. She would definitely get a positive recommendation from Jonker's. But she was free to leave now and of course she didn't have to come to work on Monday.

Megan, who wore high brown leather boots and a wide silver bracelet, listened to the speech without a change in expression. She took one long drag on her cigarette, then ground it out in the ash tray. She gave the impression she'd expected this the moment I'd asked her to step into Otto's office.

"Do you have any questions?" Dad asked.

"No." She shook her head. "When can I get my check?"

Check? I didn't know what she was talking about. We'd paid everyone yesterday afternoon.

"We'll have the final checks available for people to pick up at—" Dad gave me a questioning look, then made up an answer. "—the end of day Monday?" As if I knew.

"Right," I said. "Monday afternoon." I pulled my pad over and scribbled one more note: "Severance checks! Monday!"

Dad stood to indicate the meeting was over. Megan also stood to go. As she reached for the office door, I said, "Good luck."

Megan looked back at me with an unfriendly expression (what did I expect? thanks?) and left without a word.

Clare Brock, an appliance salesperson who'd been with the store since 1970, seemed to have no personality. She had a weary, lined face, light brown eyes, entirely white hair. She nodded agreement when Dad told her we were going to have to reduce the staff. She smiled a thin, tight smile when he said this had nothing to do with her performance, which was not true because Clare was one of the salespeople who'd barely earned her draw.

She could understand why it was necessary to trim the staff. She murmured, "Of course," She made me feel we were the ones who needed assurance that everything would be all right. When Dad mentioned the severance check, she shook her head decisively. "I haven't earned anything this month. It's only the fourth. I don't have anything coming."

I'd prepared myself for a variety of reactions, but not this one. Dad asked, "Will . . . will you be all right?"

"Oh yes," said Clare, "I know you don't like doing this, but sometimes we've got to do things we don't want to do."

When she'd left the office, I shook my head. "You never know how someone will react, do you?"

Dad agreed and said, "Of course, we'll get her a check."

Ross Huber was one of the two audio department salespeople, and someone had to go. Ashley Strong had better sales numbers, so Ross was it.

As Dad made his this-has-nothing-to-do-with-your-performance speech, Ross's face reddened and he grew visibly angry. "What?" he snapped finally. "Brian didn't have the balls to do this himself?"

Dad hesitated. Brian was part of the family and—on paper—Ross's immediate superior, but Ross could hardly blame Brian. "This wasn't Brian's decision."

"Oh no?" Ross's voice squeaked. "He's wanted to get rid of me ever since I caught on."

I leaned forward. "Caught on to what?" I asked.

Ross, who'd been quick to attack, became unresponsive. "Nothing."

"No, what?" I pressed him.

Ross's face—so young I wondered if he had to shave—was closed. "Nothing."

Dad heard the same thing I heard in this guy's voice. "What did you catch on to?"

"It's nothing. You fired me. I'm out of here, okay? Make Brian's day."

Dad put both hands flat on the desk, a gesture of sincere interest. "Ross, Brian really had nothing whatever to do with this decision to reduce the staff. Why do you think he'd want you fired?"

"Because he hates my guts." Ross sounded bitter—and ready to spill his guts to us.

I gave him an opening: "Why does he hate your guts?"

Ross had to think about his answer for several seconds, blinking rapidly. Finally, he said, "Because he knows I know he's been stealing."

"Brian? Stealing?" I guess I shouldn't have been surprised at one more viper in this snake pit, but I never guessed Brian.

Ross nodded.

Now it was Dad's turn: "How do you know that?"

Ross sat back in the chair, his posture a bit more open, loose. His tone was confident, certain. "I caught on six, nine months ago. He sells something for cash—a receiver, a cassette deck, a CD player—and pockets the money."

"You've seen him do this?" I asked, keeping my voice level.

"I've seen him put the money in his pocket, yeah."

"But there has to be a record," Dad insisted. "A piece of merchandise comes out of inventory, there's a record where it went."

I could easily imagine Brian—any salesperson—putting cash temporarily into a pocket in the process of helping the customer inspect and understand the merchandise and take it out of the store, then ring up the sale later. Not the best way to handle the transaction, but inefficiency wasn't theft. Much as I found Brian unlikeable, it was hard to imagine him stealing from his father's business.

Ross's voice dropped. "He's got some deal with Vernon. They're responsible for the cage. I don't know how it works, but they're the only ones who've got a key, and Vernon's the one who keeps the cage records."

"Anything else you can tell us?" Dad spread his hands wide on the desk.

Ross frowned in thought. After several seconds he gave his head a negative shake. "No. I don't think so."

"We'll keep your name and phone number on file in case there's any change in circumstances," said Dad. I'd have said nothing. No point in giving Ross hope he'd be selling audio equipment again soon. After being reassured about severance and a recommendation, Ross couldn't get out of Otto's office fast enough.

When he'd left, I asked Dad, "The cage?"

"We don't have one, for good reason." He explained that a store would have a locked room or cage for damaged products or merchandise that failed right out of the box for safekeeping while waiting for a "Return Authorization" from manufacturers. "The way cage theft usually works is that a dishonest employee puts the stuff he wants to steal in the cage with a note 'Waiting for RA.' There's so much junk waiting for RAs nobody gives the extra stuff a second glance, and nobody thinks the stuff in the cage is worth stealing because presumably the items are broken or scratched or some other problem. And because one employee handles the paperwork, nobody tracks what's going in and out of the cage."

I whistled. "And given the state of Otto's paperwork, no one ever checks inventory against sales records."

"Brian's probably been using the system to hide the missing merchandise." Dad's expression was thoughtful.

"While pocketing the cash."

"Tommy, you think Brian is capable of stealing from the store? From Otto?"

"Could be." I didn't have a solid reason to think Brian was a thief, just a gut feeling. "Why would Ross bother to make up this kind of story?"

"That's going to be a real problem for Christine."

"Just what she needs," I said. "An in-house thief she can't fire so easily."

When Dad said he needed a pit stop and more coffee, I went out into the showroom. Nick sat at one of the bullpen desks talking on the phone. Three customers were talking to salespeople: a couple opening and closing refrigerator doors; a young couple with a child in a stroller asking Hannah, the appliance department manager, about a washing machine; and a man inspecting console television sets. When Nick wound up his call, I asked in a low voice, "How's it going?"

"Traffic's been steady all morning. The ad may look like crap—" Nick gestured at the full-page FALL PREVIEW SALE! newspaper page pinned to the bulletin board. "But it's pulling them in. How's it going back in HR hell?"

"About as well as can be expected." I leaned down to speak privately. "Something's come up. In the audio department. We think there's a problem."

"Problem?" Nick echoed softly.

"Maybe." I sketched out the situation, and Nick said he'd look into it. I straightened up and crossed to the office manager. "Steffie, can you point out David Gendron?"

Her tone told me that she, at least, wasn't blaming the messenger. "He stepped out for a minute." At my expression, she added, "Since you people are using the break room, there's no place for coffee, so they've gone down to the cafe."

"And that's Michael Tarabocchia?" I indicated the stooped, balding man in the flannel shirt and vest at the end of the line of TV sets. She nodded, and I asked Mike to come back to Otto's office.

Mike didn't want to take the indicated chair in front of Otto's desk, so we all stood while Dad gave his speech, which was becoming smooth with practice. We recognized Mr. Tarabocchia's long and devoted service to the store, but, as he was no doubt aware, sales were not what Otto might have wished, and so blah, blah, blah.

Mike said in a tone of wonder, "You're firing me? Me?" Dad began to say something, but the old man went on, "You know I started working here in nineteen forty-seven? When the old man was running things. Now *there* was a businessman! Didn't let any grass grow under *his* feet! Not like his boy, may he rest in peace." He automatically (and unconsciously?) crossed himself. "I sold Dumont television sets—you know that? We were the first store in the Berkshires to show TV. The old man put an antenna up on October Mountain and run a wire all the way down to the store just so we could receive something here in this bowl in the mountains. We couldn't get a signal even from Albany until we had that antenna. Of course all that's changed now. Cable. Get channels from all over. Hartford. Springfield. New York City even."

Dad waited until Mike paused to take a breath, then jumped in. "The family appreciates your loyalty and your many years of service. Nobody questions your performance, but you have to understand that cuts must be made. You can take the rest of the day off, and of course you don't have to come in on Monday."

"You're actually letting me go?" He seemed confused.

"We have to let a number of people go."

"I should have seen it coming." He sounded resigned. "When the old man turned things over to Otto. Now there was a businessman! The son just didn't have it." He crossed himself again.

"Let me walk you out the back." I came around the desk. "Do you have a jacket or a cap or something?"

When I returned to the office, I said to Dad, "You didn't mention a final check."

"That's one I want to finesse. Mike's into the business for at least $12,000 this year and I don't even want to think about last year or further back."

When LeighAnn Spafford was seated in front of the desk, Dad gave the termination speech. She didn't even blink. She got a little aggressive, inquiring about a severance package (her husband had worked for GE and received a healthy severance), vacation pay, unemployment. For her finale, she said she was one of the lucky ones. She was getting out before the whole business collapsed.

David Gendron, the electronics department manager, turned out to be the salesman who was unhappy about giving up sales to people who flunked the credit application. Dad gave his speech to David's stony face. When he stopped, David said, "What makes you think you can just come in here and take over?"

Dad explained that the family knew exactly what we planned to do. "They understood and gave their agreement."

"Because they're not thinking straight," said David. "Otto just died. His wife's in shock. She doesn't know what she's doing."

"Be that as it may, Otto—and now Christine—asked us to do what's necessary to put this business on a more solid footing."

"You think firing me is going to make a difference?"

I almost said that, at the very least, it would take one more unproductive employee off the payroll.

Dad was more diplomatic. "Mr. Gendron, I can understand your feelings, but—"

"Bullshit!" David had a menacing look on his face, forehead beaded with sweat. He reached out and gripped the front edge of the desk. "You don't understand my feelings! Don't hand me that crap!"

Dad didn't flinch. I held my breath as he told David in a steady voice, "I know this is a shock, Otto's accident, the store in difficulty, it's a lot to deal with. But Otto would have wanted the store to continue, to help his family."

David, his eyes bulging slightly, stared at Dad, then looked at me. I sure wasn't going to give him any support, and after a moment he stood unsteadily. "Okay, you sons of bitches, I'll go. But I'm not going to forget this. I've been working in this store since nineteen seventy-nine."

Dad stood as well. "We'll have a final check ready on Monday afternoon."

"Screw you," said David and marched out of the office.

Dad followed David to close the door behind him. He turned to me with a wry smile. "I thought that went well."

"At least he didn't try to push the desk over onto you. I thought for a minute there he might try, the way he was holding onto the edge."

He returned to Otto's chair and looked at his list. "Two more to go. Let's hope that was the worst."

16 / Saturday morning

My thoughts were jumbled as I walked back to the bullpen after we finished the termination interviews. I sat down at a desk, opened the collection file, and pressed the phone to my ear, but all I could think about was Glen Kieffer, Vernon, Otto's accident, the file of obscene pictures, and that van on the state forest road.

What had Andy really seen? Did Vernon know that Glen was playing games with his labor charges? Glen knew Vernon was playing games with the parts. Had Glen challenged Vernon? Glen stuck me as the kind of guy who would challenge his boss. Was Glen getting a cut on the parts' profit?

Or was it the other way? Had Vernon challenged Glen? Was Glen paying Vernon a piece of his labor overcharges for his cooperation? Did any of this have anything to do with Otto's accident?

On the one hand, I thought I should tell Dad what I'd heard last night. On the other, I didn't want to explain how I'd happened to hear it. But I should tell someone, especially now that Otto had died. I owed it to him, to Wendy, to Christine.

Nick was staring at the computer screen when I stood up and pulled on my jacket. "I'm going out for a few minutes," I called to him. "I'll be back before lunch." He grunted, but I don't think my message registered.

As I walked through the showroom, I wondered about the effect of the morning's firings. The staff had to know Jonker's was over-staffed. The remaining salespeople had to realize they now had more opportunities to sell. If I were still standing after a massacre like this morning's I'd be relieved I'd dodged the bullet and work harder. Or start looking for a job in a more stable organization.

Outside, I pulled up my collar to cut the bite of the wind as I headed to the police station. A few minutes later, I was staring at the desk sergeant, who stared back without interest.

"Is Detective Wilkins around?"

"Who wants to know?"

"I'm Tommy Lovell. I'm with the group at Jonker Appliances. I met Detective Wilkins yesterday morning when he came by the store. I've got some information about Otto Jonker's accident." Looking across the counter at the official face, I was back in high school, looking across the counter at the principal. Neither one intimidated me.

The officer's eyes narrowed. "What kind of information?"

"I should talk to Detective Wilkins."

He considered me for a long moment, then said, "Okay. Sit over there and I'll see if I can find him. Your name again?"

I repeated my name and sat on a wooden bench so scarred it could have been left over from Colonial days. I could see the sergeant on the phone. Then I waited. And waited.

The clock on the sergeant's wall said I'd been waiting almost twenty minutes. I was about to tell the officer I'd come back later—and never come back—when a door opened and Wilkins came out. "Mr. Lovell?"

Pretty good deduction since I was the only person in the lobby. I stood and held out my hand. Wilkins hesitated, then shook it. "You have some information?"

I glanced at the desk sergeant and spoke softly. "I don't think Otto Jonker's accident was an accident." Wilkins' face, which had shown polite interest, seemed to close up so I added, "That is, I mean, I think someone caused it."

"Yes?" I was stuck by how little curiosity Wilkins could convey by a single word. But I couldn't stop now.

"I met a couple last night who said they saw a van backing up the loop road in the state forest. If Otto ran into the van coming down the mountain, he could have been run off the road and into the woods."

This got his attention. "What time did they see this van backing up the loop road?"

Damn, they hadn't said—and I didn't ask. "I don't know. Late."

"And who were these people who saw this van?"

I hesitated, unsure whether to get them involved. "Uh, Andy and Ashley. I think he's a painter and she works in a beauty parlor on North Street. I met them at Hancock's Tavern on the street that goes out toward the state forest."

"Last names?"

I caught Wilkins glance over at the desk sergeant. I was certain the sergeant was rolling his eyes at this nuisance off the street.

Had I heard Andy's name last night? I didn't think so. But even if I'd heard it, I didn't retain it because Andy was just a guy I met in a bar, someone I never expected to see again. "Sorry, I don't know."

Wilkins gave a little shrug. "Well…thanks for stopping by. We'll look into it." That had to be a total lie. His tone of voice made it clear what he thought about my playing detective. I'd read too many Hardy Boys books. My "information" was useless.

As Wilkins turned to go back into the inner offices, I said, out of desperation, "Hey, how's the new VCR player?"

Wilkins now gave me a small, knowing grin. "Remarkable piece of technology. No more missing a show because you've got to work. Zip right through the commercials." It sounded as if he was parroting Joanne's sales pitch. I got the message: End of conversation.

Back outside, I realized I was only a block or so from Dunkin' Donuts. If Brandi was working, I could say hello--and ask her about Andy. I hurried to the next corner, turned right, and there, a block away, right where it was supposed to be, was the Dunkin' Donuts. It reassured me to know exactly where I was and to have a sense of a purpose and direction.

The shop, fragrant with coffee and sugary stuff, was empty of customers, but Brandi was right behind the counter where I'd hoped she'd be. "Hi, there," I said.

"Hi, yourself." Brandi's smile told me she was surprised and pleased to see me, and she gave her head a cautionary twitch to indicate a fluffy-haired woman just behind her, fiddling with the coffee machine. The manager? "Can I help you, sir?"

"Yes. I'd like a...." I looked up at the menu board. I didn't know what I'd like. No more donuts and I was sloshing with coffee. The manager turned away. "Small coffee, cream and sugar. And some information."

As Brandi poured the coffee, she lowered her voice. "What?"

"What's Andy's phone number?"

"Andy? From last night?"

"Or Ashley's."

"You came to ask me for Ashley's number?" From the look on her face, I could see I'd stepped in it. Ask one girl for another girl's number? I put my hands up in surrender. "No, nothing like that. I want to find Andy, and I thought Ashley could help."

Now Brandi looked even more suspicious. "Listen, I don't know their phone numbers right off the top of my head. They're just guys I hang out with at the bar."

"How about names? What's Andy's last name? You know where he lives?"

"Who cares? What's so important?"

"Didn't you hear? Otto Jonker died." I waited to see her expression change. "The appliance dealer on North Street."

She frowned. "Oh, that's a shame."

"I think the van Andy and Ashley saw might have been involved."

Her frown became deeper. "You think?"

"I don't know. That's why I need to talk to Andy. Or Ashley."

She thought for a moment. "It's Panetta. Andy Panetta. On Linden Street somewhere." The manager was inching closer, so Brandi handed me my coffee and took my bill.

"Thanks." That didn't seem adequate, considering what she may have expected when she saw me come through the front door, so I added, "If you're not doing anything special tonight, I could come by when you get off work." Even as the words left my mouth, my brain was shouting, Don't do this! Don't do it!

"No. I'm not doing anything." The full smile she gave me, her eyes wide, was warm and genuine. "I get off at five."

"Okay, then. See you then." I gave her a friendly wave with my free hand, a gesture to seal our date.

Back at the parking lot, I used the public phone to get the number of a Panetta on Linden Street. I dropped another quarter into the slot and waited through a dozen rings.

I was about to hang up, when Andy answered. He sounded barely awake. "Hullo?"

"Andy? Listen, I'm really sorry to call so early, but I needed to catch you. This is Tommy from last night. Tommy Lovell." I paused to let my words sink in.

"Oh, yeah. Last night."

"Listen, I've got a question." Another pause. "About that van you saw the other night. You know what time that was? Approximately."

Andy's turn to pause. As the silence stretched toward a full minute, I began to fear he wasn't going to respond. Then he said, "Yeah. Maybe twelve. Ashley's old lady wanted her home by midnight like as if she's like still sixteen years old. But it's easier to go along to get along, if you know what I mean. So we made it back by ten after twelve, so she wouldn't have a cow."

"Yeah, I know what you mean." I remembered girlfriends with curfews and overbearing moms waiting at the door. "Thanks. That helps a lot. That really helps. I'll see you around."

"Yeah, man. You know where."

I hung up, listened to my quarter drop, then automatically checked the coin return. Nothing, but you never know. Then I picked up my still unopened coffee, holding it away so I wouldn't spill any on my good khaki pants, and headed back to the police station.

It felt like the Twilight Zone, the same desk sergeant giving me the same vacant look when I asked, "Is Detective Wilkins still around?"

He didn't even pretend to help. "No. He's out."

For a minute, I considered telling the cop he was full of shit, but instead I said, "When he comes back, could you tell him the van was backing up the loop road between eleven-thirty and midnight? He'll know what I mean. Tell him the witness's name is Andy Panetta on Linden Street. He can check it out." I gave him the phone number.

"I'll tell him." The cop made a note. Progress, I thought.

I held up the coffee container. "Would you like this? Cream and sugar. I haven't touched it." The sergeant looked at me warily. What was I up to? Had I pissed in it? Laced it with something? At the same time, I could see his craving. "Take it," I said with a wink, and put it on the counter. "If you don't want it, toss it." I turned to walk away, content that I'd made the gesture.

"Yeah, well . . . thanks." Then I was out the door to walk back to the store.

17 / Saturday noon

The crisp air helped clear my thoughts as I walked back to Jonker's. Tagging along on a routine business checkup, I'd stumbled into a weekend of tragedy, plus the rampant theft going on under Otto's oblivious nose. Not to mention the photos in Otto's desk, which I hadn't mentioned to anyone. And it was only Saturday morning. What next?

The store. It all revolved around the store. And it occurred to me that if Dad could get Jonker's looking good enough, maybe Christine could find an investor or sell the business. Maybe even sell it to the employees—the honest ones, anyway. Being Dad, he'd probably considered these possibilities, but I went into Otto's office to suggest them anyhow.

We were on the same page as it turned out. "I think we have to have a serious heart-to-heart with Steffie. She knows where the bodies are buried." No irony in Dad's voice.

"Any particular bodies you want to dig up?"

"First, what happened to Otto. Why'd he let the store get away from him? He used to say he was a hands-off manager, but this store's falling apart at the seams. And we need to know more about all the relationships. Between Christine and the staff—if she's going to be running things. Between Brian and the staff—if he's going to be the second in command. If they can't run it—or don't want to run it—selling it might be for the best."

"What about Wendy?" Don't leave out Wendy.

Dad waved her off. "She's got to finish her degree. She's not going to be around."

"Come on, Dad! She's only two hours away." I hesitated. "Okay, maybe she's not going to be in the store all day every day, but she's got to be involved. She's part of this."

He held up a hand. "You're right, you're right. So let's find out what Steffie says about Wendy, about the whole situation. Get her away from the store for a little bit and have a private chat."

But Steffie didn't want to leave the store to have lunch with us. It had been an exceptionally busy sales morning, "The busiest we've had in months!" She sounded pleasantly frazzled. The ad had brought in people, but so had the collection calls. "You can't believe how many people have come in with money," she said in a tone of wonder. She also thought the story about Otto's accident on page three of the *Eagle*, printed before his death last night, had attracted some traffic.

When Dad mentioned lunch, Steffie seemed apprehensive, protesting that she'd brought a sandwich from home to eat at her desk and was juggling the service calls in addition to everything else now that Megan Mattner was gone. "Not that you did wrong by letting her go, of course." Her hands fluttered as she assured us. "She never really did fit in, but . . . "

I switched into persuasive mode, the way I'd seen Dad do it. "But . . . Steffie, you are really the beating heart of this store—and that's why we need your help. Let us take you to lunch, half an hour. An hour at most. The faster we work out a plan, the better it'll be for the employees and the family."

Steffie glanced in Nick's direction, at the next desk. "I guess . . . if he could take the service calls while we're out . . ." I caught Nick's eye, and he nodded, scooting his chair closer to look at the blank service forms she had ready.

After reassuring herself that Nick could cover the desk for an hour, Steffie reluctantly abandoned the safety of her duties, found her purse and jacket, and led the way through the showroom. On the way out, I had a thought—could Joanne join us? Dad agreed, and I sprinted back through the store to find her.

Once the four of us stood on the sidewalk, I turned to Steffie to ask about a restaurant nearby. She concentrated for several seconds, squinting into the overcast October distance, then named an Italian restaurant she said was a block or so away.

The place looked like a long-time local fixture: antique photos on the paneled walls, worn parquet floor, old-fashioned stainless coffee urn behind the lunch counter. The irresistible aroma of oregano and rosemary and thyme in sauce simmering just beyond the kitchen door. We took a corner booth. The table had been scrubbed so often that the Formica's abstract pattern was worn away in spots. Joanne and Dad sat with their backs to the wall, Steffie and I sat across from them.

"I can't tell you how very sorry I am about Otto," Dad began. "As I said this morning, he was my good friend and I'll do whatever I can to help the family and everyone at the store."

"Thank you," said Steffie, not raising her face from the menu. She gave a little sniffle.

The waitress arrived, recited the day's specials, and we ordered. That out of the way, I eased into our conversation. "It's great to see the store so busy." Dad and Joanne nodded, let me take the lead. "How long have you worked there?"

That was an easy question because Steffie responded immediately. "I started in seventy-one." I calculated mentally: fifteen years.

She'd been a bookkeeper in an insurance office but when a friend told her Otto was looking for a bookkeeper/office manager she applied. Otto was a wonderful boss, so different from the insurance agent. Warm, understanding, considerate. A wonderful man. Her eyes filled with tears and she looked about to break down in sobs again.

"So Brian was about eight years old when you started?" said Dad. Steffie thought a second and nodded. "And Wendy was about ten?" She nodded again. "Did you see much of them?"

Steffie took a breath to compose herself and said they both worked in the store during the summers, doing whatever they could to help out—sweeping the floor, changing price tags, filing, running errands. It sounded all too familiar.

For a long time, Christine worked in the store as well. "It was a real family business. The employees—most of us anyway—we felt like we were all part of a family."

The flow of Steffie's words slowed. She became hesitant when she whispered that something must have happened three or four years ago between Otto and Christine because Christine stopped working regularly in the store. "She'd come in for a few hours at a time. She'd help with the ads. Or if he was off by himself at a conference or something, she'd come in to watch things while he was gone."

"Not full time?" I asked.

Steffie grew thoughtful. "Not like before. They never argued in front of the employees, but I could hear them raise their voices at each other in his office. No matter what, he never complained about her in public. He was too much a gentleman for that. But anyone with half an eye could tell he wasn't happy. The store was doing well, though, well enough that"—her voice cracked a little, as if she couldn't quite bring herself to say Otto's name—"he could buy that motorcycle, buy all the gadgets he loved."

Joanne leaned forward. "Do you have any idea what the problem might have been?"

Steffie became evasive, looking around at the worn woodwork. "I don't think I should say. It's none of my business."

"A woman's change of life?" Joanne's voice was light.

Steffie, apparently pleased she didn't have to spell everything out, nodded.

I wanted to hear more about Otto and Christine, but Dad changed the subject. "Who do you think should be running the store? Now that Otto's . . . passed." Steffie flinched at Otto's name.

Steffie was unconsciously twisting her wedding ring, which seemed tight on her puffy finger. "I . . . I have no idea."

Joanne reached across the table and put her hand on Steffie's. She asked so quietly I wasn't sure I heard clearly above the restaurant clatter. "Steffie, were you having an affair with Otto?" I'd read the comments in the employee interviews, so this wasn't totally out of left field, but the question seemed unnecessarily blunt. It also made me wonder which of the nudes in Otto's desk was Steffie.

She began to tear up and started to fumble for her purse. Joanne was ready for her; she had a tissue out and was handing it across the table before Steffie could open her bag.

The waitress arrived with our meals, gave a disapproving look at the sight of the sobbing woman who was apparently being tormented by three out-of-towners, and returned to the kitchen without a word.

Joanne patted Steffie's arm while murmuring soothing sounds: "It's all right . . . it's gonna be all right. Just let it out. It's okay . . . "

When Steffie could talk in full sentences, she whispered she *had* been having an affair with Otto. She seemed relieved to talk about it, share her story with three sympathetic strangers who would listen without judging, and Joanne encouraged her. "You'll feel better."

The affair had started after her husband Lou's accident at the GE factory. He'd slipped, fallen against a machine, and hurt his back. He'd been in a cast for months, a wheelchair for more months, and now received a monthly disability check. Even if he could work (and Steffie suggested he could work even with his disability; he just didn't want to), the GE Transformer works had closed down and there were no local jobs for a union lathe operator in this economy.

Listening, I got the impression that Steffie's relationship with her husband had not been close even before the accident made him angry and bitter.

"He depends on me, you know?" Steffie was speaking only to Joanne. Dad and I kept our mouths shut. "But nothing's ever good enough. He needs me to take care of him—he'd be eating cold beans out of the can if I didn't cook his meals—but something's always wrong. There's not enough salt, or too much, or something else—always something. And you can forget any kind of . . ." She hesitated, then plunged ahead. ". . . marital relations. Those went away before the accident and the accident just gave him an excuse. I don't think he ever forgave me for not getting pregnant." She looked thoughtful for a moment, then added, "Maybe it's just as well. I can't imagine him as a very loving father. Not like Otto." She looked at her forkful of ziti and dropped it back on the plate.

"A loving father . . . ?" asked Joanne, encouraging her to continue.

"You could see it, the way he treated Wendy and Brian. The way he was in the store. Never a harsh word. Ready to help someone any time they were in trouble. Advice. Time. Money. Whatever they needed. And people loved him. Although I do have to say—" She hesitated, then continued, "Wendy was more her father's daughter than Brian was his father's son."

"Brian was a troublemaker?" asked Joanne.

"I wouldn't go that far, but I will say he was, well, a handful." Steffie shook her head, a gesture of ruefulness. "Always looking for a way to avoid work. Looking for a shortcut. When he was a teenager, he had no respect. Not for his father. Not for anything. He almost lost his license in a DWI check. I don't know what Otto did to fix that, but he really worried about Brian."

I had to ask: "Why'd Otto put him in charge of the audio department?"

"Brian really likes stereo equipment. And after he dropped out of college he didn't seem to know what he wanted to do, so Otto put him in charge. But I noticed Otto checking up on Brian from time to time."

Dad and I looked at each other, thinking about the merchandise scam Brian was pulling, but we didn't dare interrupt. Joanne lowered her voice and asked, "Steffie, do you think Christine knows about you and Otto?"

Steffie took up another forkful of pasta to delay answering. She finally said, "She might have known, but, in my opinion, even if she suspected, she didn't care. Married to a man like Otto, she had to know he was a man who needed a woman. He said as much. He had appetites. She had to know that. I'm sure I wasn't Otto's first woman on the side."

As long as Otto (or Steffie) didn't rub Christine's nose in what he was doing, Christine didn't seem like the type to raise a fuss or ask a lot of questions.

"What about your husband?" asked Joanne. "Does he know?"

"No!" Steffie was emphatic, her eyes frightened. "Lord, no! Lou'd kill me if he suspected anything. That's after he killed Otto. Lou's no use in bed any more, but he's vicious as a Doberman. What's his is his, and you better not fool with it."

Joanne licked her lips. "Weren't you worried? That your husband would find out?"

Steffie's mouth tightened. "Yeah, a little. But we were careful."

"What about the other employees?" Joanne asked. "Did they know . . . about you and . . . ?"

Once again Steffie took her time while she thought about the answer, then slowly shook her head. "Like I said, we were careful. I knew it wouldn't be good if people thought I was getting special . . . favors from Otto. So I wouldn't let him act too friendly around me. There was always lots of kidding, joking around, of course, and some people might have suspected something. I mean, people always suspect something. But everyone knew he was interested in other women in the store." Her eyes hardened.

"Megan?" asked Joanne. I suddenly flashed on the expression Megan had given us as she'd left Otto's office. She'd been furious, but there'd been something else. Regret? Sadness?

Steffie nodded and said she'd never understood what Megan was doing on the payroll in the first place. "I tried to talk to Otto about Megan, what she could be doing to help out some more. But he brushed me off. 'Megan's fine,' he'd say. 'She's learning the ropes,' he'd say. 'She'll make a real contribution some day,' he'd say." I could hear Otto's inflection in Steffie's voice—and her sarcasm in parroting him. "Once Otto hired somebody, he never wanted to let them go."

To let someone go would be to admit he'd made a mistake. Dad had said Otto always had trouble admitting a mistake.

"It hurt his feelings when somebody quit. Like when Patty Sodoski married Vernon and quit to have their baby. You'd think she was going to work for Sears Roebuck and take all our customers with her." She threw up her hands and flashed the first smile we'd seen at lunch.

"Anybody else Otto was involved with?" Joanne prompted. "Hannah Nicosia?"

"That stick?" Steffie scoffed. "Otto liked a woman with some meat on her bones." She gave a faint smile and did a tiny shimmy to make her point. "He might have kidded around with Hannah, but he kidded around with everybody—employees, distributor salespeople, customers. Everybody. It wasn't serious with Otto. Nothing was serious with him, not even the sex. I asked him once, 'Which would you rather have, sex or a big steak dinner?' What do you think he said? He said, 'Can I get back to you on that?' That was Otto. God, I miss him." Her eyes again filled with tears. She took her paper napkin to blot them and blow her nose.

After a minute, Dad asked, "So you're pretty sure no one in the store knew about you and Otto?"

"Oh, no. We were very, very careful. No one in the store—" She broke off abruptly and an odd expression crossed her face. She let out a tiny gasp of pain.

"What?" asked Joanne.

Red spots appeared on Steffie's cheeks and spread to her forehead, chin, and neck. She took another tissue from Joanne to wipe her upper lip. "Forgot—forgot Vernon," she said in a strangled voice. "Vern saw us one time."

"The service manager?" I said, not expecting this guy's name to come up.

"It was late. Way after business hours. The store was all locked up. And we were in Otto's office, working on something, really working. Maybe the advertising. And he suddenly said he couldn't wait. He had an appetite, Otto did. He didn't want to drive all the way over to New York State to the motel. It was late, and Lou expected me home late, but not way after midnight. And, you know, when Otto said he couldn't wait, it started me thinking too. So we used his desk, and Vernon had let himself in the service entrance for some reason. I don't know what he was doing in the store at ten-thirty at night, but he must have seen the lights in Otto's office. God, I don't know what he thought. Maybe somebody left the lights on or maybe he was going to ask Otto a question, but anyway he opened the office door, took one look—I heard the door so I turned my head and saw his face—Otto was busy—I'll never forget Vernon's expression—and he said something like, 'Sorry' and shut the door right away."

We sat without speaking though Joanne looked my way and raised an eyebrow a fraction. I couldn't tell from Steffie's expression or the way she'd told her story whether she was ashamed of what she'd been doing or privately proud that Otto found her so desirable he could not resist. I guessed she was embarrassed they'd been caught, not that they'd been having sex on Otto's desk. Now I was glad I hadn't blabbed to anyone about those photos, even to Dad.

We put the conversation on pause while Joanne gave Steffie a tissue and she blew her nose. Then Dad asked, in a gentle voice, "What happened?"

"Nothing. Otto said something like, 'What's the matter?' He hadn't looked up. I said, 'Vernon was at the door.' 'Oh,' he said and finished what he was doing. 'I'll talk to him,' he said."

"Did he?"

"I suppose so. We never talked about it any more. Vernon never said anything to me or anything. He acted like nothing happened, and I wasn't going to say anything to him."

Joanne asked, "What about gossip in the store? Do you think he said anything to anyone?"

She must have worried over it, since she had a lot to say. "I don't think Vernon said anything. He's not that close to the other employees. He works by himself back in the service area. The technicians are out making calls all day. The salespeople hang around together in the bullpen and in the break room and they talk together when things are slow. But Vernon keeps to himself. You know how it is. You run a store. I don't think he said anything. I'm pretty sure. Nobody acted any different toward me that you'd notice. And you'd think they would if they'd heard gossip."

The waitress stopped by to see if we wanted coffee or dessert. Dad shook his head and asked for the check. Joanne squeezed Steffie's shoulder as they walked ahead of us. At the corner, I came up on Steffie's other side as she was telling Joanne that the employees were on edge this morning, waiting to see who'd be called into the office next. If that was the atmosphere in the store, I was surprised anyone sold anything. Dad assured her that he had no plans to let anyone else go. He said Otto had bragged about Steffie being a key member of the team. Now the business would need her even more in the weeks and months ahead. Christine and Brian and Wendy would be depending on her knowledge and experience.

We left Steffie at her desk and Dad asked Nick and Dan to join Joanne and me in Otto's office for a quick update.

"Reaction on the sales floor to this morning's personnel changes has been, I'd say, positive," said Nick, with a wry wink. "The remaining salespeople have figured out that they'll have more chances to sell. More sales, more money. They're out there, approaching customers, trying to close sales. We're getting a lot of foot traffic, but I don't know how much of it is because of the news about Otto and how much is because of the store's ad in today's paper."

"I do know the collection effort is starting to pay off," he added. "Steffie will have to give us the exact figures, but I'd guess we had a dozen people make payments this morning. They don't want us to come pick up the merchandise and they don't want a collection agency hounding them."

Dad smiled broadly. "Okay. We're slowing the hemorrhage of money. That's a good thing."

Not to burst his bubble, but—"Dad, we've really got to do something about Vernon . . . and Brian if they're in something together," I said. I wondered out loud whether Glen was the one bad apple in the service department.

Dan said he'd spot-checked the service tickets of the other technicians. "They all seem clean."

Dad pulled us in closer and spoke in a low tone. "Christine is coming in this afternoon. I don't know how much she can handle, just one day after Otto's death, but we've got to set up some kind of structure so the business can operate going forward."

We all nodded, then nodded again when Nick commented, "Good luck with that."

18 / Saturday afternoon

If the Pittsfield Police Department didn't think Otto's death was worth investigating further, I wasn't going to wait for them. Steffie said her husband would kill Otto if he knew about their affair. A figure of speech? Didn't sound like it. After all, Steffie and her husband were driving one of the store's vans this week.

Dad and the others had the store under control for the moment so I borrowed the keys to Glen's van and went out to the parking lot where I sat in the cab, cool now that a soft gray overcast hid the sun. Maybe the weather forecast of a storm was accurate. Too bad for the weekend leaf-peepers.

I looked into the big side view mirror and tried to visualize a forest road behind me, a motorcycle's single headlight bearing down. I tried, but all that appeared was the parking lot, shadowless in the flat light. A shiver went through me—I found it creepy to imagine someone deliberately blocking the mountain road to send Otto flying over the guardrail to his death. Why? Who? Was it even a Jonker van?

Maybe I was no Sonny Crocket, but I knew it was time to think about motive, means, and opportunity. I couldn't see that anyone had a strong enough motive to harm big-hearted, fun-loving Otto, not Lou Gilberti or the guy on the phone who threatened to stick the VCR where the sun don't shine, or even the penny-ante thieves on the store payroll.

If I drove to Andy Panetta's house, maybe seeing the Jonker van would trigger a better memory of what he saw Thursday night in the state forest. Is this the van you saw? If I knew it was a Jonker van, that would help.

Another thought: Maybe Andy would know where I could score some pot.

With that cheerful thought, I found a neatly-folded Pittsfield street map in the van's door pocket and located Linden Street.

The Panetta house was a blue clapboard set back from the street. A second-story porch ran across the entire front, the overhang shading the first-floor porch, windows, and front door. Those front rooms had to be gloomy as hell, with no natural light.

Andy answered the doorbell in jeans, t-shirt, and stocking feet. "Oh, hi." He wasn't unfriendly, just mildly surprised at seeing me at his door.

"Hi. Sorry to bother you. Again."

"No biggie."

"After the phone call, and all. I'm just trying to figure something out. Maybe you can help?"

"No problem, man. What'd you need?"

"Listen, I'm trying to figure out what happened to Otto Jonker—the appliance guy who got killed Thursday night. Was that the van you guys saw?" I moved aside to give Andy an unobstructed view of the van parked at the curb.

Andy glanced at it and shook his head. "Look, man, like I told you on the phone, we weren't paying a lot of attention. The only reason we saw anything is because the van pulled a one-eighty with a lot of noise and then started backing up. Seemed like a crazy thing to do."

"You didn't see the writing on the side?"

"It was dark."

I rocked from one foot to the other. I could hear a television playing in the living room behind Andy. "Yeah, well . . . anything else?" I had a sudden thought: "Like a motorcycle going up the loop road? Before the van showed up?"

Andy frowned and pursed his lips, then nodded slowly. "Yeah. Yeah, there was. Didn't make a lot of noise, and the guy didn't stop, but, yeah, like five, ten minutes before the van, there was a motorcycle. Just cruised through and up the loop road. I forgot about it."

Otto was on his bike. It had to be him. "Anything else?" Like the sound of Otto smashing into the guardrail?

Andy did his best, but said finally, "No-o-o. Like I said before, we weren't paying a whole lot of attention to the traffic. The only reason we noticed the van was because he was kicking gravel all over and heading up the wrong way, man."

"That's really great, thanks." I reached out to shake Andy's hand, who hesitated, taken aback, then shook. Continuing to hold Andy's hand, I leaned close and dropped my voice. "Listen, do you know how I could score some pot in this town?"

Andy regarded me closely for several seconds. He might have been wondering if I was a cop. But driving a Jonker Appliance & TV service van? Come on. He glanced up and down the empty residential street. "What do you need? A nickel bag?"

I pulled out my wallet and found a bill. "That's good. Here." I handed him the bill. "Catch you tonight at Hancock's?"

"Yeah, after eight or so."

Back in the van, I thought about returning to the store, but Otto's accident nagged at me. I pulled out the street map and traced the route to the state forest.

Fifteen minutes later I was passing the rustic state sign that identified the park, and then the empty ranger booth. I scanned the parking area where we must have stopped last night and tried to shut out the taste of Brandi's lips, the texture of her cheek. The scattering of picnic benches littered with fallen leaves made me wonder where Andy and Ashley spread their blanket. A single family sat at one of the tables, smoke wafting from a grill. A playground with swings and seesaw nearby.

The road to the top of the mountain was marked with a one-way sign. A second sign warned that the road was closed to all traffic between November 15 and March 15. I shifted into second and began to climb the narrow asphalt strip.

The road hugged the side of the mountain, which probably wouldn't be called a mountain except in the Berkshires. Not more than 2,000 feet or so. On my left, the slope was a steep forested wall. On the passenger side and beyond the wooden guardrail, the bank dropped precipitously into a cleft in the mountain. At the top, the road leveled off for a couple hundred yards. A sign pointed to the Berry Pond campground. I stopped the van to look. At least five groups had set up tents, one with a small RV. A plaid-shirted man and a boy in boots stood at the edge of the pond holding fishing rods. I wondered how many fish they could catch at the top of this little mountain, but maybe that wasn't the point.

Beyond the campground the road began to drop back into the valley. I shifted down to second gear to help slow the van but kept one foot on the brake. Not a good place to lose your brakes. The wooden guardrail might stop a motorcycle but a runaway truck would smash right through.

Creeping down the road, I inspected the guardrail's planks looking for a fresh gash, a splintering—anything that would indicate where Otto had his accident. I came around a bend, and spotted what looked like a single skid mark on the pavement and a fresh scrape on the weathered timber. I stopped short, clicked on the emergency blinkers, pulled the handbrake tightly, waited to see if the van would stir (it didn't), and climbed out gingerly.

If someone comes tearing around that corner, I thought, I'm going to be in deep shit. But the forest was quiet, the only sound the van's idling engine. I ought to hear a vehicle coming. Anyway, who'd be nuts enough to come speeding down this road?

Dried leaves crackled underfoot as I inspected the guardrail's scrape. I couldn't tell whether it was two days old, two weeks old, two months old.

I craned my neck looking down the steep forested hillside for any evidence of Otto's trajectory. Nothing. Leaves and small shrubs had been disturbed, so maybe this was where the paramedics and cops had brought Otto's body back to the road. Maybe. But maybe not. A small shudder ran through me.

Anxious that another vehicle would come down the road, I took a quick look at the pavement. A small stain discolored the asphalt several feet beyond the front of the van. Fresh? I couldn't tell. Oil? Antifreeze? Blood? Something else? I couldn't tell.

And who was I kidding? I should go back to the store and forget about playing detective. And yet, that's what Dad was doing. Playing detective in the store. Looking for clues to figure out what happened to Otto's business. No clues here in the state forest, so far as I could tell.

Back in the driver's seat, I eased down the last stretch of loop road to the picnic area I'd passed on the way up. I waved at a little girl on a swing, drove past the ranger booth and onto the road back to town.

I got back to the store just as Dad was ushering Nick, Joanne, and Dan into the break room for a private meeting with the Jonkers. Christine and Wendy had their chairs pulled together, both looking slightly dazed but clear-eyed. When I slipped into the room, Brian was turning his chair around to straddle it with the back facing forward. I nodded in their direction as I crossed the room to sit next to Dad.

Dad outlined what we'd learned and accomplished in a day

and a half: Interviewed the employees. Reduced the headcount. Begun collecting the receivables. Begun sales training.

Nick said the cash flow budget he was working on with Steffie was almost finished. They'd talked to the accountant, who was available all weekend to answer questions.

Joanne talked about the marketing plan she was formulating to take the store through the holidays—newspaper advertising, radio spots, direct mail. "I know there's co-op money available from the manufacturers to pay for a lot of it. I think Jonker's has been leaving promotional money on the table. My store gets these promo deals, so Jonker's should have access to the same money."

When Dad paused for the family to ask questions, I mentally crossed my fingers that Christine wouldn't start asking questions about Steffie and her role. Clearly Steffie knew more about the business's daily mechanics than anyone—more than Christine, more than Brian—and from what I'd seen, she seemed to be effective, able to put her hand on any document we needed. Firing Steffie out of resentment would cripple the store.

Wendy was the first to speak up. She wanted to know whether the business had enough cash to pay severance to the fired employees.

Dad said it did. She looked relieved and sat back in her chair.

When Brian asked if employee responsibilities had changed, it crossed my mind that maybe he'd heard from a pissed-off Glen. We all turned to Dad for the answer.

"Yes, there are some changes in the works, but it'll take a couple weeks for everything to shake down," he said, keeping his eyes on Christine. Dad went on to say that everyone in the store should be trained to sell everything. And a store the size of Jonker's didn't need separate appliance, electronics, and audio equipment managers. I glanced at Brian for a reaction, waiting for his complaint.

Brian didn't disappoint. In a snooty voice, he told Dad: "I have additional duties. I order the inventory. I go to the distributor meetings. I'm the one who decides what lines we carry. I'm not just a clerk taking orders."

Dad held up his hands, a gesture of appeasement. "I'm sure you're not, and I think you should continue to do just what you've been doing." Brian made a noise I took as agreement. "So I think right now, that's where we are," Dad concluded.

Wendy and Brian looked at their mother, who appeared overwhelmed. She finally broke the prolonged silence. "How bad is it, Tom? Really?"

Dad looked ill at ease, tapping his fingers on the table, his mouth tight. But there was no getting around it. "It's not good."

"How bad?" she asked again.

"I'll have a much clearer picture tomorrow night. By then, Nick will have a good accounting of the receivables still outstanding, we'll have a good estimate of what the inventory is actually worth, the accountant will have updated figures, and Steffie will have the weekend sales totals." I almost cringed when he mentioned Steffie, but luckily, Dad was the center of everyone's attention.

"And if it's too far gone?" Christine's tone carried a note of resignation.

Dad stopped tapping his fingers and looked at her somberly. "In that case, you'll have two choices: liquidate or try to find a buyer." He put on his we'll-cross-that-bridge-when-we-come-to-it reassuring smile. "But Christine, I have to tell you, I doubt it's that far gone. I think there are some real problems, but if we all work together, we can turn this thing around."

Was Dad just trying to be kindhearted, putting the store's condition in the best possible light? Just a day ago, I had the feeling that Jonker's was all but dead and buried—a feeling I knew all too well. It was bad enough that Christine had lost her husband. She didn't need to hear she was going to lose her family's livelihood as well. Christ, maybe even her house. Still, Dad being the straight arrow he was, would he soft-pedal something this serious?

Christine and Wendy gave each other a long look, then Christine said, "Tom, this has turned into a lot more than you bargained for. I know all of you expected to go home tomorrow evening, but . . ." Her voice trailed off without completing the thought.

Dad turned to Joanne, who gave a little shrug. "We all want to be here for—" He hesitated. "—for the funeral. And I know—"

Brian interrupted, "We don't even know when the funeral is."

His mother shot him an annoyed look. "Not until Monday, anyway, since I can't get—can't get—"

Wendy finished Christine's thought in a trembly voice: "The police aren't going to release Pop's body until Monday, at the earliest, they said."

There was an awkward pause, then Joanne jumped in. "We're not going to abandon you. We'll work something out."

I smiled at Wendy. "I guess I could probably stay on for a while." Even I didn't know this was going to pop out of my mouth, but I glanced at Dad for confirmation. "You don't need me back in Gloucester right away, do you?"

"No, no. You could stay on for a while."

Christine would need help for weeks, if not months. After six weeks of hiding out in my old bedroom and going through the motions of work at the store, however, being part of the turnaround at Jonker's could be a nice change. I wouldn't let myself think of anything beyond that.

Christine had herself under control by this time. She told Dad, "I want to talk to the employees. Tell them how much I appreciate what they're doing for us. For the store."

Joanne, Nick, and Dan watched the store while the staff filed in to meet with Christine and Dad in the break room. Only two technicians and the two deliverymen were missing. The mood was grim. It's a wake, I thought; they're here to mourn—maybe for the store as much as for Otto?

Christine stood behind one of the metal folding chairs and began by announcing what everyone knew, her voice ragged: "I'm sorry to say that Otto died last night. Peacefully. At the hospital. His injuries were just too serious. The police are still investigating the accident, so—" Her words choked her. "—so we don't know . . . when the funeral will be. Later this week."

She took a deep breath and started again. "I know many of you, all of you, have been shocked by the events of the past couple days. Otto's accident and the staff changes we had to make here in the store. We had to make changes. Pittsfield is changing. Jonker's could not continue doing business as usual. There'd have been drastic changes even if Otto had never had his accident, but my friend Tom Lovell—" She gestured at him. "—assures me we won't have to reduce the staff any further."

Good luck with that. If sales didn't pick up, I could imagine laying off one or two more people. Then again, with the holidays just around the corner . . .

"Jonker's has been in business for more than fifty years," continued Christine, "and given the ability and knowledge of the people in this room, there's no reason why we won't be in business for the next fifty years."

She paused. She was gripping the back of her chair so tightly I could see the tendons on the backs of her hands. "I know in recent months I've been away from the store more than I liked. But I promise you I will be here and available from now on."

She began to tear up, and somebody, noticing, ripped a paper towel from the roll beside the sink and gave it to her. "Thank you," she said, patting her eyes. "Thank you all for your patience and flexibility during this very difficult time. Wendy and Brian and I, we all appreciate what you're doing."

I expected a flurry of questions about the changes, but the employees kept their mouths shut, their expressions unreadable. After thirty seconds or so as Christine recovered, she turned to Dad and asked if he wanted to add anything.

"Only, again, to thank everyone in this room for your patience and professionalism. I know this morning's changes came as a shock, but my friends and I are here to make sure Jonker's thrives." He stopped to look around the room.

An uncomfortable moment passed while everyone waited for one confident person to make the first move. "So how long are you going to be around?" asked a woman in high leather boots, standing in the far corner.

"One of us will be here as long as necessary," Dad answered with a glance at Christine, who nodded, as did Wendy. Not Brian—of course, not Brian.

A dandyish salesman leaning against a Zenith poster asked, "You really think this store has a future? The way the town is going?" I wondered if he was the one who thought Jonker's should move to the new shopping center.

Dad raised his shoulders and spread his hands, palms up. He wasn't going to lie to these people. "I think it's going to take a lot of work."

The understatement of the decade. More silence, then one of the service techs said, "Let's go back to work," and everyone began shuffling toward the door.

Once the employees had cleared out, I pulled Wendy aside. "Can we talk for a second? What are your plans?" At her expression, I added, "I mean, how much more have you got to go at school?"

"I'm supposed to finish next May. Another semester and a half. But I don't have to, if you think—"

Christine was close enough to overhear my question, and her tone was sharp. "Of course you do. No matter what happens here, you need your degree."

Wendy opened her mouth but I spoke before she could respond. "It seems to me that you'd be more valuable to the business with an MBA next year, rather than leaving school to start working here right away." That didn't sound very diplomatic and I immediately back-tracked: "I mean, I'm sure your dad would have wanted to see you graduate."

"Definitely," said Christine.

Wendy looked disappointed or maybe just doubtful, I couldn't decide which. But she held out her hand to Christine. "I guess so." They held tight for an instant, then Christine said she needed to get home and asked Wendy and Brian to come with her.

"It's Saturday afternoon." Brian sounded defiant. "I have to be in the audio department."

"You're right," said Dad. "And the store needs every sale you can make. But we can cover for you this afternoon. Family comes first."

What could Brian say? No snappy comeback as he reluctantly followed his mother and sister out the back entrance to the parking lot.

Joanne, Dan, and Nick scattered to their posts as I cornered Dad. "Do you think I should start checking the inventory?" A dirty job, but somebody had to do it—and I had my suspicions about this sick store. "You know, figure out how much outdated merchandise Jonker's is holding onto?" Dad gave me the OK sign.

But that wasn't all I wanted to say. I cleared my throat. "Not that I think there's a problem, but sitting in the bullpen and seeing the way the business handles the money coming in and the bank deposits, things are very loosey-goosey. I'm sure Steffie is honest and is doing her best, but the system is wide open to—" I hesitated until I could find the right word. "—abuse."

"You think she's stealing?"

"No, but it'd be easy enough. Nick says she makes up the deposits, writes the checks, keeps the books, and reconciles the bank statements." Now I put on my Dad voice and recited his sage advice: "It's the story you read about in the paper all the time: Faithful Bookkeeper Embezzles Two Hundred Thousand Dollars Over Five Years."

We both laughed, breaking the tension. "You're right. Let's deal with it before it's a problem," said Dad. It felt good to sense Dad's respect. "We could set up a system with Steffie and Christine and the bank and probably one other person internally. Wendy?"

"Let me check with Nick," I said and then asked, "What are you going to do about Brian? And Vernon? I noticed no one brought them up in front of Christine."

"Everyone says Vernon is a heck of a service manager."

"But Dad, he's a crook." Ordinarily, Dad had no patience with crooks.

He thought for several seconds. "We'll talk to Dan. He's interviewed all the technicians. See if any of them have potential to take over the department."

"What would happen if we leave everything as is for the time being? Don't say anything to Vernon or Brian." He stared at me. "Jonker's has to have a service department, right?" Yes. "We've fired the one tech we know was a crook. We tell Vernon that Jonker's new policy is to sell only certified parts. We don't say anything about his scam to sell knock-offs—and that way Jonker's doesn't lose a valuable employee." I had to pause. "Although that doesn't do anything about the deal between Vernon and Brian."

Dad shook his head. "We need more information. That audio

guy Ross could have been exaggerating. Or mistaken." He dropped his head in thought, then said slowly, "See if you can figure out exactly what's been going on with the inventory and the cage, and if there's been funny business going on, how long. When we know more we can talk about Brian."

Before 5:00, I went into Otto's office (when would I stop thinking of it as Otto's office?) where Dad was working. I dropped three sheets of yellow legal-size paper on the corner of the desk. "I didn't get to the cage, but here's everything in the store and back room. Apparently there's a self-storage unit on the edge of town Otto used for overflow inventory, but Steffie doesn't know what's in it."

"We'll check it out tomorrow." He flipped through the clipped sheets. "This is good work. Really good. Broken out by manufacturer and product. Exactly the level of detail we need."

"Doing it that way seemed to make sense." I shifted from one foot to the other, unsure how to bring up what I really wanted to say. "Look, Dad, if you don't need me for anything special, I was going to have dinner with a friend."

His eyebrows did a little dance. I had friends in town? "No, sure, that's fine."

"Could I borrow twenty bucks? I want to be able to pay my own way. And I was going to use the car, if you don't need it."

He was reaching for his wallet before I stopped talking. "Here's a hundred. Gas up the car while you're at it." As he handed me the bills, he tossed me his key ring.

"Thanks, Dad. I really appreciate this."

"Don't mention it. You're really being a terrific help."

19 / Saturday evening

I waited in the idling Buick, cranking the heat higher as I watched for Brandi near the donut shop's employee entrance. So I'd have something to chat about other than a death in a family business, an appliance store full of crooks, and missing merchandise, I caught the tail end of a radio newscast. The Red Sox blew their home game to the Yankees. Well, that wouldn't make happy dinner conversation. On the other hand, Brandi was a skier, not a baseball fan so maybe I should mention the storm headed our way—rain this time, but future storms would be good news for snow-lovers.

Brandi appeared silhouetted in the lighted doorway, looking over the parked cars. I flashed the headlights, and got out of the car to greet her. "Hi there."

"Hi yourself." She looked me over, smiling but with a doubtful expression. "I really didn't think you'd be here." She was wearing jeans and the same Pittsfield HS Pom Squad jacket she'd worn last night. As she came closer, I leaned in for a hello kiss, but she backed away and stood with her arms across her chest. "Look, I don't know what you had in mind for tonight, but I got my goddamn period this afternoon."

It took me a moment to understand. Gina would have locked

herself in a closet before she'd have admitted she had her period. If she absolutely had to mention her period, she'd say only that she was feeling "delicate."

"I . . . I didn't . . ." I fumbled around for some words because in my jacket pocket I could finger the package of condoms I'd bought at the pharmacy on the way, just in case. "Hey, I invited you for dinner. Dinner it is."

Brandi's pose softened slightly. "You sure?"

I smiled and spread my hands, palms up. "You pick the place."

"Okay, then. As long as we understand each other. Dinner."

I opened the passenger door for her. "A gentleman," she murmured as she slipped into the seat.

"I'm working on it." I eased the door closed. Behind the wheel, I turned to her. "So, where to? This is your town." Oh, man, I sounded like my Dad.

Brandi frowned in thought for several seconds, long enough for me to wonder (even as I recognized and despised my condescension) how often she'd eaten in a restaurant more deluxe than Hancock's. She finally said there was a nice place out by Lake Pontoosuc.

"Lake what?"

She laughed, a tinkling musical laugh, and said it was an old Indian name. Snapping her fingers, she tried to remember the name of the restaurant but finally just told me to drive north on Route 7 and she'd recognize the building. I asked, "Is it Italian?"

She looked puzzled. "I don't think so. Why?"

"I'm off Italian for a while." Today's lunch was the exception; I had no say in the decision.

The Riverside Restaurant, a modest building beside a small river, promoted its "Fine American Cuisine." The dining room was dim, the tables lit by votive candles in jelly glasses, the napkins good quality paper. The room was only half filled on a Saturday evening during this peak leaf-peeping weekend. What was business like when there were no tourists? Was the entire area wasting away? The hostess led us to a corner table, gathered up the extra settings, and said a waitress would be right over.

I snuck a glance to admire Brandi as she pulled off her Pom jacket. Too bad about her period. We ordered a beer for Brandi, a glass of merlot for me. I was relieved to see the prices were moderate and was not surprised to see the dishes were mostly family favorites: meat loaf with mashed potatoes and house gravy, chicken fried steak with roasted root vegetables, ham steak with a pineapple glaze.

Tonight's special was shepherd's pie, something Brandi said she'd never had but would try. When she gave the waitress her order, I said, "Make that two," and leaned back to sip the wine and butter a warm dinner roll.

Brandi mock-toasted me with her beer. "I didn't think you were serious. About tonight."

"Yet, here we are." I toasted back.

"Yeah, here we are." She looked around the room. We were the youngest diners. By a lot.

Before I could think of an innocuous open-ended question to break the ice, she launched into a funny story about a customer seeing a famous face in the wrinkles of a glazed donut. Her high-pitched imitation of the customer made us both crack up.

My small-talk skills kicked in, finally. "Brandi, did you grow up here?"

"Yeah, my old man worked for GE."

"Didn't everybody?"

Brandi gave a wry smile. "Just about."

"I guess it was good while it lasted."

"I guess. It sure paid more than Dunkin' Donuts."

"What happened?"

She said GE once had three Pittsfield businesses: the transformer works, the plastics division, and a unit that developed weapons for the Navy. Brandi's father had worked in the transformer division, which died a long, slow, and painful death after the oil embargo in the early 1970s. Brandi's father was one of hundreds laid off, and he and her mother began to fight over money, over his drinking, over her housekeeping, "over the smallest thing. Like she made his coffee too dark. Or he left the top off the toothpaste. He began knocking her around." I winced, thinking of Steffi Gilberti getting the same treatment.

"Sounds grim." I thought about the people Dad had fired that morning. How many lives had *he* ruined?

"Grim ain't the word." She hesitated and looked away. "Mama finally threw him out. Actually, the cops came and got him." From Brandi's tone, I had a feeling she wasn't too sorry to see him go. She took a roll and a butter pat. "He moved to Georgia. Got a job in a factory that makes chopsticks, if you can believe it. He sends me birthday cards." While she tore the roll open, she looked at me as if expecting my judgment.

I wasn't sure how much further down that particular road I wanted to travel so I simply nodded. Another sip, and I asked, "So why's a nice pretty girl like you without a steady boyfriend?"

Brandi sighed and her shoulders slumped. She stirred the melting cubes in her water glass with her straw, seemingly fascinated by the way the ice reflected the candlelight. Her tone was thoughtful. "I don't know. I've had boyfriends. But most of the guys in this town are jerks. They don't want to do more than have a few beers and a pizza and fuck. It gets boring, you know what I mean?"

I said I knew, although back in the day, my friends and I never thought a beer and pizza was enough to get a girl to put out. We believed you needed dinner and a movie or a concert—and more than one. Go to a club in Boston or to a dance somewhere. Maybe options were so limited in Pittsfield the guys did what they could with what they had.

Brandi added, "They don't want to talk, you know what I mean? I mean, you and I have already talked more in—what?—twenty-four hours than some of the guys I dated for a year, if you don't count sports or TV shows. And I don't."

Now I was out of ideas, probably since I was out of practice dating. "So what should we talk about till our shepherd's pies arrive?"

Brandi looked startled. "I . . . I don't know." She hesitated, then looked me in the eye. "Real things, I guess. Important things. Like what we've been talking about. You know—Pittsfield. Families." She leaned toward me, curious. "Like, can I ask, what happened to your wife?"

Now it was time for me to swallow and look down at my wine glass. For a moment I considered answering with no answer. Something like: Boy met girl, boy got girl, boy lost girl. But I'd never talked openly to anyone about my smashed marriage, not to my friends, not to my parents. Why not to Brandi, whose eyes were filled with sympathy—and who I was never going to see again after this evening?

"Nothing happened to her. She's living in our apartment in Marshfield. She's fine. She'll be all right. She's good looking and an incredible cook. She'll get another job. Another husband." I paused and looked at her. "But that's not what you're asking, is it?" She shook her head. "Really, we just got to the point where we couldn't stand the sight of each other. Or, to really tell the truth, she couldn't stand the sight of me."

I closed my eyes to visualize that final scene: We were standing alone in Si Accomodi's kitchen, the last dinner customer long gone on a night as quiet as any we'd ever had. I was dead on my feet, miserable over money. Gina, her hair loose and wild, her cheeks red with fury, screaming she couldn't take it any more, couldn't take me any more, couldn't stand to see my ugly face any more. I couldn't recall exactly what detonated that final quarrel. It had been so slow, I said it looked like we wouldn't have enough money to pay next month's rent.

Gina had her apron half-off when she returned to an old argument, one we'd had many times before. She told me to ask Dad for a loan, and as always, I dismissed the idea, this time without even pretending to consider it. That was a hot button, but I was too tired and stressed to care, and Gina had exploded, "You sonofabitch! It's not fair! You didn't have any problem asking *my* parents for money—and yours have a lot more money than mine! What's the *matter* with you! Mamma's boy afraid to ask daddy for money!"

I'd tried—God knows I'd tried—to make her understand how I felt about Dad and money. To ask Dad for an emergency loan would be to admit a form of failure that would be a kind of death. It wouldn't be a loan, not the way the restaurant was failing. Dad's money would be a gift we could never repay. Begging Dad for money would be to admit he'd been right all along: I had no talent for business. I was a loser. I was not someone Dad could respect and admire.

We'd never talked openly about what he expected of me. But it had been clear from childhood that the men Dad respected were successful business people. Dad admired the men and women (like Joanne) who'd built businesses and made money doing it. Self-made men, like himself—ignoring the head start his father gave him.

Dad defined himself by what he'd achieved in Lovell & Son once he took over from Grandfather Lovell. It was one reason that closing the Ipswich branch had been so painful. It was one of the few times Dad had to admit to himself and to his family that opening a third store had been a mistake—a business failure.

For me to ask for money in a futile attempt to save Si Accomodi would show Dad I was inadequate. Despite Gina's rage, I'd rather lose the restaurant than go crawling to Dad. If Gina didn't understand how I felt, then she couldn't understand anything.

In the restaurant kitchen that night, however, even I thought my response sounded feeble. "I'm sorry, I just can't."

I thought I'd made her so angry she'd grab one of the knives and come at me. Instead she snatched up our midnight dinner platter of spaghetti with ragu and threw it at my face. The plate clattered to the floor, tomato sauce and strands of spaghetti dripped off my cheeks and restaurant shirt. Shocked, all we could do was stare at each other.

Gina finally turned away. "Get out," she said, her voice low and harsh. "Just get out of my fucking life and don't come back."

I slept that night in the car rather than attempt to drive the two hours back to my parents' place in Gloucester.

Brandi was looking at me strangely. "Did you ever hit her?"

That was a kick in the gut.

But maybe the way I'd been talking about Gina gave Brandi ideas. After all, she'd seen violence at home. "No. Absolutely not." I shook my head in a gesture of resignation. "Oh, believe me, I wanted to lash out a couple times. Maybe if I'd stayed, I would have slapped her or she'd have smacked me with more than a plate of spaghetti. But when I slammed that door behind me, I was gone for good. The only time I went back was to pick up clothes and stuff she'd left outside the front door. The only times I've seen her since are in her lawyer's office, the smug bastard."

The waitress, carrying our meals, halted conversation. Brandi used her hands to waft the shepherd's pie aroma toward her, and comment on how the mashed potato peaks were nicely browned. She took a tentative forkful, blew it cool, tasted, then grinned. "Not bad."

I tasted my own shepherd's pie. "See? Told you." Not as good as Gina's, by far, but good enough—and plenty of it.

I guess Brandi had been replaying our conversation from the other night, because she switched the conversation to flying. How hard was it? How expensive? What did you have to do to get a license? Do your eyes have to be perfect? When did I learn to fly? Could someone like her fly?

I answered as best I could, avoiding the key point that if your father owned a plane it was a whole lot easier to practice and get a license. I didn't tell her I'd only just renewed my student license and had been at the controls only twice in the last six years. Both times were in the past two weeks when I went up with Dad. The way Brandi regarded me and flying, she seemed to see me as dashing Ace Tommy Lovell, a romantic figure in a leather flight jacket, goggles, and flapping white silk scarf.

So, no it wasn't all that hard to fly. Harder than driving a car, of course, but then you didn't have traffic. Flying was expensive. You had to apply for a license, take lessons, take tests—both paper and flight examinations. Your eyes didn't have to be perfect, but an FAA certified doctor had to pass your physical ability. I first began to fly when I was seventeen—the lessons were my high school graduation present. Of course someone like Brandi could learn to fly.

Brandi said, "When I was little—maybe eight . . . nine—my dad would sometimes drive me out to the airport on Saturday afternoon and we'd watch the planes take off and land. He'd been in the Air Force, a mechanic, and he'd always wanted to fly." She paused, a distant look on her face. "That was another one of his big disappointments. He'd flown in planes all over the world and he talked about the clouds and the way the earth looked from the air. It sounded like there was this whole other world."

"Yeah, I think there is." I pushed the giant plate away, too full to take another bite. What the Riverside Restaurant lacked in cosmopolitan cuisine it made up for in volume. "A sense of freedom. Of cutting loose. I don't know how to describe it."

Brandi hesitated over the end of her shepherd's pie and finally made a show of moving her hand from her stomach up to her chin, with another of her melodic laughs. No coffee for her— "I'm sick of it, around it all damn day." But she perked up at the mention of apple pie, which the waitress said was homemade by a local lady. After a glance at Brandi, waiting for her nod, I said we'd split a piece and ordered coffee for myself.

We agreed the pie did taste homemade. After the waitress topped up my coffee and went off to tote up the check, I told Brandi I wanted to go to Hancock's to meet Andy Panetta for a minute and we could have a beer or a nightcap if she wanted to hang out. With a wink, I added: "Or, after I see Andy, we could share a joint somewhere."

She seemed startled, but not put off. "Sure."

Now I needed her help. "You know some place the cops won't interrupt us? Other than the state forest?" The state forest was the last place I'd go right now.

She had to think, then said she knew a place out by the wildlife sanctuary. I settled the bill, we picked up our jackets, and I held her door for her when we got back into the car.

I spotted Andy with Ashley at the bar when we entered Hancock's. Brandi didn't want anything to drink, and after a word she and Ashley headed for the women's room. I didn't have to do more than raise my eyebrows in a questioning look for Andy to signal confirmation. He started for the men's room and, after half a minute, I followed.

Andy locked the door, confirmed the single stall was empty, took a baggie from his jacket pocket, and handed it over. "You got any papers?"

"Good catch. No. You got some?"

Andy took out a half-empty pack of Zig-Zag. "Here, I got more. Compliments of the house."

"Thanks, man." I gave Andy a comradely pat on the arm. "I

really appreciate this."

"Don't do anything I wouldn't do. Give me a minute before you come out."

"Andy? Wait, one more thing. You hear anything else about that bike accident in the state forest?" I couldn't come right out and ask, Did you get a visit from the cops, but I had to know whether the detective followed up on my info.

He didn't even turn around—just made a flicking sign with his fingers, like brushing a bug off his collar. Nothing. What a surprise.

I went into the stall, latched the door, sat on the closed toilet, and rolled a couple joints. It was tempting to light up immediately—test the weed's quality—but the way Andy'd acted made me think the cops watched Hancock's. Patience was a better plan. I gave the toilet an unnecessary flush, and went out to find everyone at the bar.

"You all set?" I asked. Brandi had freshened her makeup and redone her hair, adding a pearly barrette on one side. Lovelier and lovelier, but given her earlier manifesto, I admired her without comment.

"I'm set." She took my arm.

"I guess you don't want a beer," said Andy.

"No, I'm good," she said, squeezing my arm.

Ashley raised one eyebrow, said, "Sure you are," and gave a barking laugh.

In the car, I said, "I have a better idea than the wildlife sanctuary. How do we get out to the airport from here?"

"The airport?" She twisted toward me in her seat.

"We can sit in my dad's plane. I've got the keys and nobody's going to come to check out the Cessna's cockpit. If there's any traffic, we can watch the planes take off and land."

"Oh, yessss!" She said it with such enthusiasm I wondered if this was a good idea. I wasn't planning to do more than share a joint and return her to her house. What could she think?

She directed me to the airport road. On the way, she had me stop at a deli, where she ran in to buy a couple of sodas and potato chips. I parked in the airport lot, not surprised to see it almost empty. We walked into the little terminal building, where the manager was reading a paperback at his desk. He was caught off guard to see anyone this late. I held up Dad's keys, indicating the Cessna key, and said we were just going to check out the plane. "The one that came in Thursday night. On the end of the second row." The manager looked doubtful—after all, what could I be up to?—but said nothing. If you look and sound as if you know what you're doing—as if you belong—you can get away with a lot.

I unlocked the door on the co-pilot's side and helped Brandi up and into the narrow bucket seat. I rolled her window open before I closed the door, went to the pilot's side, opened that door and window, climbed up, and settled in.

Not much to see in the dark. Terminal lights. The planes tied down on either side. The empty taxiway. Brandi swiveled her head but seemed afraid to touch anything, as if she might break it or start something running. "It looks complicated. All those dials."

"Yeah, I guess. Until you know what they are." I lit one of the joints, took a deep lungful of smoke, and held it while I passed the joint to her. I finally exhaled toward the window. Probably not a good idea for the cockpit to reek of marijuana when Dad climbed in to fly home.

We smoked silently and companionably as far down on the roach as we could, using one of the soda bottle screwtops as an ashtray. I added the bit of unburned leaf back in the bag. Between the wine and the weed and the admiration of an attractive young woman, I felt as tranquil, as contented, as euphoric as I'd felt in months. Years maybe.

I put my head back and closed my eyes. I wasn't drunk or

out of control. I was hyperaware of where I was and what I was doing. Brandi was unscrewing the top of the second soda bottle. A snap as the seal broke, an intense pssst! as the pressure released. The sound of Brandi drinking, and the icy touch of the plastic on my hand as she shared. I took a long swallow, conscious of the carbonation pricks in my mouth. Brandi's hand touching my cheek tentatively.

She cleared her throat. "The only problem it's so cramped you can't fool around. Worse than a sports car."

"You're not supposed to fool around in a plane." My voice sounded to myself as if it were coming from another place. "Not when you're flying it." I took another swallow. "They teach you that."

"Yeah, I suppose." She dropped her hand into her lap and sat back in the seat, her voice almost forlorn. "Take me flying some time?"

"Sure. Already said I would. Some time when we can see something and I'm not stoned." As I spoke I was entirely sincere, even knowing that the odds of my ever taking Brandi up in the sky were slim to zero.

We sat quietly for a while. I noticed a light in the sky and pointed it out. "He's going to come around and land." We followed the light until it grew and became an entire corporate jet that settled safely at the end of the runway, rushed passed us, stopped, and taxied back to the terminal.

"Cool." I heard the excitement in her voice.

Back in the Buick, she put a hand on my arm, then let it drift into my lap, brushing below my belt. Bending close, she whispered, "Tommy, we could—you know—fool around…"

It was tempting and her caress was having an effect, but I gently lifted it away. "Not tonight, dear," my voice almost natural. "I have a headache."

I couldn't tell if she was disappointed or relieved. But I

reached across the Buick's center hump, much more manageable than the Cessna's cramped cockpit, and kissed her, felt her respond. "You are," I murmured into her ear, "a very attractive, desirable woman, but tonight isn't the night."

"Another night." She took my left hand and placed it on her breast—well, where it would be if her Pom jacket wasn't in the way.

I let my hand rest on the jacket for several seconds. "Another night," I sighed, nuzzling her ear. Time to head home.

She directed me to her mother's house, half of a duplex that needed paint. I calculated it was no more than five or six blocks from the Dunkin' Donuts, which might explain why she didn't have a car. As we sat in front, I told her I wasn't sure when I'd be going back to Gloucester, but it might be Sunday evening.

"Tomorrow?" she exclaimed.

"Is that tomorrow?" I had to think. "Yeah, I guess it is."

"Well . . ." She hesitated, one hand on the door handle, looking up at me through her lashes. "Tommy, it was a lot of fun. Thank you for dinner . . . and the rest."

"You're very welcome, sweet Brandi." Where did that come from?

She leaned toward me and I met her lips in a passionate kiss. When she pulled back, her voice was husky. "If you come back to town, let me know. I'll be here." I could make out a shy smile in the gleam of the streetlight.

"For sure, sweet Brandi."

I watched her walk up to the front door, fumble for her key, and disappear into the building. Driving back to the hotel, I felt a small glow (pot? Brandi's kiss?) but also a tiny disappointment, that condom burning a hole in my pocket.

I was surprised to find our hotel room dark, empty, the message light on the phone blinking. The digital clock said it was 11:28. Pressing the message button, I heard Nick's voice.

"Tommy, when you get this message, come to the hospital. Your dad's been shot."

20 / Saturday night

I was totally wired. My adrenaline had been pumping all the way from the hotel. I imagined I could overcome the pot's fuzzy buzz by willful effort and driving with the windows wide open. It wasn't working. It was creating a manic high. I stumbled like a drunk as I rushed across the hospital lobby. "My dad!" I croaked. "I got a message he'd been shot!" Still couldn't believe it.

The receptionist on duty, alone in the dim lobby, looked at me with a professional "calm down" expression. "Name?"

I told her, then repeated it, then spelled it, and she finally began to type. I could see the yellow letters appearing slowly, too slowly on the green screen reflected in her glasses. Come on, come on. "Yes," she said after what felt like an eon. "Tom Lovell was admitted two hours ago. He may still be in Operating." She tapped a key and added apologetically, "This hasn't been updated. Go on up to the third floor waiting room. They'll be able to tell you more at the nurse's station. The elevator's down there." She pointed down the dim corridor.

When the stainless elevator doors slid open noiselessly on the third floor, I sprinted to the same room where Joanne and I had met Christine two days earlier. The same institutional settee and chairs, sturdy tables, outdated magazines, but everything felt entirely different with Dad as the patient. (Was it only two days ago? It felt like weeks.)

Nick and Dan, but no Joanne—where was Joanne?—looked haggard and anxious, and they jumped to their feet and spoke over each other as I stuck my head in: "Tommy! Tommy! . . . Where have you been? . . . Your dad . . ."

I overpowered the chorus: "What happened? Just tell me what happened!"

Nick put his hand on my arm, a gesture I found calming and comforting. "Your dad's been shot. In the shoulder. He's in surgery right now."

I shook my head. I could understand the individual words, but none of it made any more sense than Nick's voice on the phone machine. How was it possible that Dad had been shot? "How? When?"

"We were closing the store tonight, going out the service entrance." Nick's voice was gentle, confident. "Somebody must have been waiting, out in the dark. On the other side of the road, maybe beyond the railroad tracks."

"Had to be a rifle," Dan added from where he sat at one of the tables, a coffee container in front of him. "You couldn't even hit the building at that distance with a pistol." Nick nodded, seconding Dan's assessment.

I batted away Dan's words. "But how he's doing?"

"We don't know, yet," said Nick. "Waiting for word from in there." He hitched his thumb toward the inner doors. "It caught him in the shoulder."

"But what happened?"

Nick said they were closing up the store. Dan was holding the service door open for everyone to leave. Nick had just set the alarm and was three or four steps behind Dad. He saw the flash across the way and heard the shot but hadn't realized what it was. "But Tom must have known—thought he was back in Korea."

Nick saw Dad drop to the concrete loading dock. Nick shouted, "Kill the lights!" because they were silhouettes in the doorway. He grabbed Dad's legs, dragged him into safety, and Dan let the steel door slam shut. Cool-headed Joanne was already using the service department phone to call 911, asking for police and an ambulance.

"Two minutes," said Dan. "That's all it took for them to show up."

"We told the ambulance guys to come in the front door in case the guy was still back there," said Nick.

"He was long gone," said Dan in a tone of disgust. "Cops didn't find a thing."

"Who do you think did it?" I was addressing Nick, but I was asking both of them.

"I wouldn't put it past that guy Glen, Glen Kieffer," Dan began. "He struck me as being angry enough and vicious enough."

"That's what I told—" Nick stopped speaking and his expression changed at something he noticed behind me in the doorway. I turned to see Joanne and Detective Wilkins entering.

Joanne squeezed my shoulder and whispered in my ear, "Hang in there! Your dad is gonna make it and he needs you to be strong." I had to believe that.

Wilkins gave me a nod of recognition, the dark circles under his eyes making him look as exhausted as the others. "You're the victim's son, right? Saw you at the station today." His version of a greeting.

I had the irrational notion that if Wilkins had done something about my tip earlier in the day, Dad wouldn't have been shot. I knew that was crazy thinking. My information about the van was useless. Far more likely a disgruntled employee wanted revenge on Dad for canning him—or her.

"Yeah, I'm his son." I didn't sound polite, but I sure didn't care how I sounded to him.

"I wonder if we could have a word." Wilkins wasn't wondering, he was ordering. Out of the corner of my eye, I caught Joanne's "go" gesture.

"Sure." Maybe he could tell me more. I followed as Wilkins led me down a corridor to another waiting room, this one entirely empty. Wilkins took one chair and I sat across from him.

He began, "Listen, we're trying to find out what happened to your father tonight." He'd adopted the attitude that we were just best buddies catching up on gossip. I nodded yes, it's a good idea to find out what happened. "You weren't at the store during the incident." Wilkins had a way of making a statement that could turn it into a question, an order, or a suspicion.

Something about the guy's attitude bothered me. He'd had his chance to take me seriously earlier. Now it was a little late. Not letting my guard down, I answered, "No, I wasn't."

"You want to tell me where you were? Around nine-thirty tonight?"

"Nine-thirty?" I had to concentrate. When had Brandi and I left the restaurant? Before nine-thirty. "I don't know, not exactly. I had dinner with a friend and then we drove out to the airport so I could show her my dad's plane."

I wasn't about to mention the stop at Hancock's. If we'd had a beer—a convenient, reasonable reason to spend time at the bar—it'd be different. But the thin freezer bag of weed in my jacket pocket felt like a giant, incriminating bulge shouting, 'Pat me down! Pat me down!'

"This friend have a name?"

"Brandi. With an 'i.' Brandi Perkins. She lives in a duplex on, I think, Pomeroy. I don't know the number, but she works at Dunkin' Donuts."

Wilkins took a small, wire-bound notebook from an inner jacket pocket, pulled a pen from his shirt pocket, and made a note. I waited for his next question. "So tell me about the evening. Just so I get a picture of what happened."

I took him through the evening, from meeting Brandi at the end of her shift to dropping her at home. I skipped the transaction at Hancock's and getting stoned in the Cessna's cockpit. Wilkins must have sensed my account was a tad incomplete because he looked skeptical. "And that's all you did? Sit in the plane?"

I gave my voice a man-of-the-world tone. "There's not a lot of room, detective, and the bucket seats aren't built for . . . much more than flying." Wilkins didn't change expression, so I added, "Brandi's really interested in flying. I told her what all the instruments were, and we talked about flying lessons. She wanted me to take her up for a ride, but—" I began to sound to myself as if I were protesting too much but I couldn't stop. "—but my student license doesn't allow any passengers. So of course we didn't go anywhere. We just sat and talked. Watched a corporate jet land."

Wilkins nodded as if he could understand the Federal Aviation Authority's logic in its rule against students flying with passengers. "Any idea who shot your father?"

I could answer that question honestly. "Has to be one of the people he fired this morning. Pissed about losing their jobs."

Wilkins gave another nod. "We'll be talking to them. Anybody else?" His eyes never left my face.

I forced myself to think. "We don't know anybody in town. I can't think of . . ."

Other than the employees Dad had personally fired—including the snakepit of service guys who'd been ripping off the store—I couldn't picture anyone else. Best to keep the story of how thieves were bleeding the store to myself for now. I looked back at him with wide-open eyes.

Wilkins looked thoughtful. "Anyone unhappy with the store? With Jonker's in general? Not anyone in particular?"

That was an interesting idea. Maybe whoever shot Dad

wasn't trying to shoot him at all. Maybe Dad was just unlucky, coming through the door when he did. I thought back over the past two days. "There was a credit customer who seemed pretty angry we were calling him about his debt. Threatened to shoot anyone who came onto his property." That wasn't exactly true, but it was true enough to sic the cops on the asshole.

"You got a name?"

Not on the tip of my tongue, no. "Bergman?" I guessed. "Bergdorf? It's in the store, in the files. I can get it for you."

Wilkins made a note on his pad.

I leaned forward to get in his face. "You think there's any connection between this shooting and Otto's accident? I talked to that guy Andy Panetta; didn't your desk sergeant tell you? Andy said the van was backing up the loop road right around the time Otto would have been coming down. And he heard a motorcycle before he saw the van."

My question seemed to surprise Wilkins. He looked interested enough to ask, "Think there's a connection?"

Didn't the man watch TV cop shows? Two suspicious, violent incidents in two days meant a murderer was at work. Of course, whoever caused Otto's death couldn't have known he'd go flying into the woods and die in the hospital. And my father wasn't actually dead . . . only in surgery. Still, the last time I was at this hospital, Otto wasn't actually dead, and the thought of Dad dying on the operating table or in a hospital bed made me shiver with dread.

But now that I'd raised the question and reconsidered the situation, I could see how thin, how tenuous this all might seem to a professional detective. "A connection? I thought so but now—" Wilkins' question scrambled my thoughts. "Now, I really don't know. I assume the others told you what a mess the store is in— management-wise." Ordinarily, I'd never use a word like 'management-wise,' but Wilkins unnerved me. "Bad decisions.

Employees stealing. It just seems there's too much going on for an accident and a shooting days apart to be a coincidence."

"Could be." Not exactly dismissing the idea, but not jumping on it either. Wilkins looked expectant. "Anything else?"

I hesitated for several seconds. "I don't think so," I said slowly. "You know how bad it is? My dad."

"Not yet, but we can go back to find out." Wilkins stood, I followed, and the detective led me back to the waiting room where Dad's friends—our friends—were sitting. "Nothing?" he asked.

"Still waiting," said Nick.

Wilkins looked at his watch. "Okay." He seemed to make a decision. "You people all staying at the Hilton? We can reach you there?"

"We'll be at the hotel or at Jonker's," Nick confirmed. I wondered if the store was safe, but kept that thought to myself.

"If you think of anything, let me know," said Wilkins. "My card's got my pager number." A general murmur of agreement followed the detective as he headed out toward the elevator.

My head was clearing and I tried to think what to do next. Sit and stare into space while we waited for news about Dad's condition? Or call Mom? That was a call I dreaded. Call to say Dad's been shot, he's in the operating room and I don't know how he is. Right. Save that until I know more.

A doctor in surgical scrubs came through the inner door to the operating room. She looked around at the anxious faces. "Are you Mr. Lovell's . . . " She hesitated. ". . . family?"

I was on my feet. "I'm his son. How is he? Is he going to be all right?" We gathered around the surgeon, who didn't look much older than me, as she explained, "He's in recovery. We got the bullet out and patched him up. It missed the subclavian artery, which feeds the brachial artery, the main artery of the arm, and that's a good thing. But it may have touched the brachial plexus, the large nerve bundle that controls arm function. I'm afraid he's not going to be able to use that left arm for a good long time."

"Can I see him?" I asked.

"That's what the policeman asked, but I'm afraid you're going to have to wait until morning. He's pretty heavily sedated right now."

No matter how we rephrased our questions about Dad's condition, the surgeon avoided any concrete, specific statements other than reassuring us that he'd come through the surgery very well and was going to live. She told us the nurse's desk would be able to update us if anything changed during the night, and went back through the inner door.

"Now what?" asked Joanne.

"Regroup at the hotel," said Nick. "I need a drink."

"I should stay," I said, thinking of Dad all alone in the hospital—and me, all alone in the hotel.

"And do what?" asked Dan. "Sit here and read old magazines?"

Joanne touched my arm. "You can't do anything more for him here, not tonight. Let's all get some rest." She urged me out, after leaving her name and room number and my name and room number with the nurse's desk.

As we went out the lobby doors, I said I was driving the Buick and if anybody wanted a ride back to the hotel, I'd welcome the company. Joanne said she'd go with me and followed me out to the parking garage.

"Tommy, are you all right?" she asked as I backed supercautiously out of the parking spot.

She sounded like my mother. She was old enough to be my mother. So I shrugged and answered as if she were my mother. "I'm okay."

"You sure? You looked like hell when you came in upstairs, worse when you came back from talking to the detective."

I tried to focus on the act of driving. Brake pedal. Turn signal. Look both ways. Turn slowly onto the empty street. "I'll be okay." We rode two blocks in silence. "I have to call my mom. They talk almost every night and she'll be worried he didn't call."

"At this point, I'd wait until tomorrow when we know more about his situation, how long it's going to take for him to be out and about."

That sounded reasonable. Why wake Mom at two o'clock in the morning with the frightening news that Dad has been shot? He's in the hospital, but he doesn't want you to worry. Which was certainly true even if Dad were in no shape to tell anybody anything. I'd call her first thing in the morning. She'd be pissed, but at least she'd have a good night's sleep.

We assembled in the hotel's penthouse bar at a corner table. The floor-to-ceiling window looked north. From my seat I could see the hospital's lights at the end of the six-block shopping district. Nick had taken charge. He'd call Christine first thing in the morning to tell her about Tom. We all needed to prepare our notes and recommendations for her. He, Nick, would check with his store manager back in Scranton to see if there were any immediate demands back at the store, but he was sure he could stay in Pittsfield for a couple more days—at least until Otto's funeral. The others agreed they wouldn't leave tomorrow evening as planned, especially with Dad in the hospital.

"You have to tell Christine about Brian," I insisted. That stopped the conversation. "If he's been stealing and anybody knows, it'll infect the whole staff."

"Do we know for sure he's been stealing?" asked Joanne. "All we've got is Ross's word for it."

"I checked the paperwork, and the inventory, and the sales tickets," I said. "Expensive stuff is definitely missing." I couldn't prove Brian was the thief, but it sure looked like somebody was going after the high-ticket audio items.

"Anything else?" Nick asked. Nobody said anything. "It's been a full day. Regroup in the morning, at breakfast. And our first order of business is to check on your dad," he told me.

21 / Sunday morning

I was awake half an hour before the seven o'clock alarm, craving more sleep but unwilling to risk even more bad dreams. I stood at the bathroom sink for at least three minutes, telling myself I had to move, had to wash my face, had to call Gloucester, had to tell Mom that Dad had been shot, my thoughts darting like frightened bugs. I took another few minutes to brew a cup of coffee in the room's little machine, then perched on the side of the bed and reluctantly called home—and somehow reached a wrong number. I apologized and hung up, took another swig of thin coffee, and punched in our phone number again.

When Mom picked up, she could tell something was terribly wrong just from the way I said, "Mom, it's me."

"Tommy! What's the matter?"

"I'm okay, but Dad—"

She cut me off. "Dad? What happened to Dad?"

I tried to soften the news as much as I could. "There was an . . . accident last night. His shoulder. He's in the hospital here, Pittsfield Hospital. The surgeon said Dad'll be all right but his left arm will hurt for a while."

"An accident?" She was instantly wide awake, intense. "What kind of accident?"

This was it. "Mom, Dad was shot. I wasn't there, but Dan thinks there was a sniper waiting outside Jonker's when they were locking up last night."

"Shot?" Mom clearly had trouble getting her mind around the idea. "Oh god, he was shot?"

"He fired a bunch of people at the store yesterday morning, and apparently one of them came back last night with a gun."

"Oh god . . . So the police have the guy?"

"Not yet, but we all spoke with the detective working the case. Mom, the doctor says Dad is going to be okay. They wouldn't let me see him last night after surgery, but I'm going to the hospital in a few minutes. Let me call you back after I see how he's doing this morning."

"Right!" The word was a decisive snap. "I'm packing a bag. Right now. I'll talk to Jerry and Charlene—" Our store managers. "—and let them know. I'll be at the hospital by lunchtime, maybe earlier." She sounded determined rather than frightened or distraught. Maybe her experience as the young bride of an infantry lieutenant during the Korean war had toughened her. If Dad lived through that, he'd get through this.

"Mom—" What could I tell her? Drive safely? "I'll tell Dad you're on the way." I'm sure my relief traveled through the line. This weekend—nothing more than a stupid business analysis for an ailing appliance/TV store—had turned ugly and dangerous. Otto dead. Dad shot.

After I hung up, I looked up the number of the hospital and called to ask about Dad and check on visiting hours. Dad had been moved to a private room and only Mom and I, the immediate family members, could visit him. Time to get going.

Downstairs in the hotel restaurant, Nick, Dan, and Joanne had claimed our usual corner table for breakfast. When I walked in, Nick was saying he'd called Christine, told her about the shooting, and she was coming to the store to meet with the group this morning. I got a chorus of nods when I explained that Dad had been moved to a private room and Mom would be in Pittsfield within a few hours.

Dan said that Albany television was reporting the shooting— "Looks like they're linking it to Otto somehow. Speculation that a disgruntled customer has something against Jonker's Appliance and TV." He looked thoughtful. "Maybe Wilkins has a lead on the shooter?"

I doubted it, but what do I know? Dan added: "You wonder what it's going to do for store traffic."

Joanne shot him a look of distaste. "We'll know tomorrow when we open up for business."

I said, "Yeah, we'll see if anybody shows up—customers or employees."

The sky was a solid gray, the temperature had dropped, and the wind was picking up when we stepped outside the lobby. "Weather Channel says we're getting hammered tonight," Dan observed. "High winds, gusty rain, heavy at times."

Didn't matter to me—my plan was to drive up to the hospital to visit Dad. I offered to drop them all off at the store on the way. Standing under the covered hotel entrance, watching a line of wind-blown leaves scurry along the street, they agreed that was a good idea.

North Street at eight-thirty on a blustery Sunday morning was quiet. The parking lot behind Jonker's was empty. I said I'd be back as soon as I could with any news. Even before Dan shut the car door, I could see Nick fishing for the store key and heard Joanne say something about disabling the alarm.

By the time I got to the hospital, Dad was awake, groggy. His left arm and shoulder looked immobile in a cast that went from his chin to under the covers, an IV needle taped into his right arm. His face had aged since yesterday, eyes murky and dull. Against the white pillow, his skin was gray and dark stubble covered his cheek and chin, which unsettled me more than the cast and IV. Dad was always clean-shaven. Always.

"Hi Dad, how're you feeling?" I wanted to hug him but I was afraid I'd hurt something inside his shoulder. So I settled on a gentle squeeze of his right hand. His return squeeze was weak but reassuring.

He tried to smile, got half of his mouth to turn upward, and observed, "Sixteen months in Korea and not a scratch; three days in Pittsfield and I win a Purple Heart." I couldn't help it—I grinned and his eyes twinkled the littlest bit. We Lovell men love an attentive audience.

"Mom's on her way." His smile held, then faltered.

"I hope she's not worried."

I wasn't sure how to respond to that. "Well . . . maybe a little. I couldn't tell her much." I shifted my weight from one foot to the other. "Do you know when they're going to spring you?"

Dad's good arm gave a tentative wave. "Couple days. They don't want to keep me. I'm a pain in the ass."

I could see Dad had left a lot on his breakfast tray, another unsettling sign, because he was a charter member of The Clean Plate Club. If only I could make things all better. "You okay? You need anything?" I asked.

He hesitated. "Where are the others?"

I told him they were all at Jonker's. The hospital wouldn't allow them to visit.

We stared at each other for several seconds. I knew what I wanted to bring up, but I didn't know if this was the right time. On the other hand, if Nick started going through Otto's desk . . .

"Did you find a folder at the back of Otto's desk drawer? Unlabeled. Dark blue. Some pictures of nude women." He gave his head a negative shake. "Nothing to do with the business really, and it would really hurt Christine and Wendy if they found them."

"Nothing to do with the business?"

"Not really." I hesitated. "I thought maybe I should just quietly get rid of them."

Dad closed his eyes, then said, "If they don't have anything to do with the business, get rid of them."

"Okay, yeah. That's what I thought." I shifted mental gears. "Anything I should tell Nick and the others?"

He thought for several seconds. "Nothing now." The conversation seemed to have tired him. He put his head back on his pillow and closed his eyes.

"Okay, Dad, I'll look in on you later. Mom should be here around lunch time." He gave an almost imperceptible nod, eyes still closed, and I left the room.

As I passed the nurse's station, I stumbled on nothing but the smooth tile floor and the nurse looked up, concerned. I shook my head, trying to drive away the sight of Dad's unshaven face, uneaten breakfast. "Nothing, I'm okay," I lied.

Back at Jonker's, I noticed Dan at Vernon's service department desk, one of the drawers wide open, studying something. I gave him the news that Dad was awake and resting, but didn't know when he'd be discharged. Dan winked and turned back to the drawer.

In the break room, I started a pot of coffee. Nick was working on a yellow legal pad at Otto's desk. I repeated the message I'd given Dan. Nick said that a detective had stopped by earlier to pick up the names and addresses of everyone Tom had fired yesterday, "so they're on the case."

Joanne flashed a relieved smile when I told her about Dad, and I left her sorting notes and papers on the desk she'd commandeered in the empty sales bullpen.

I still had work to do on the inventory, a good thing because I needed to be distracted. I searched filing cabinet drawers for purchase, sales, and other documents. Fortunately, someone

(Steffie?) was having a love affair with a labeling device because folders were neatly and clearly labeled. Also a quick flip through the "audio, sales, 1986" folder suggested someone (Steffie again?) had kept the file up to date; the sales tickets seemed in date order. I carried four folders and a calculator back to the break room to begin analyzing the records.

By the time Christine looked in on me, I'd concluded that the audio department had lots of unexplained losses and a ton of missing merchandise that was supposed to be in the cage awaiting a return authorization.

Christine looked much calmer, more in control than yesterday. She asked for an update on Dad, said she couldn't imagine who might have done such a thing, and told me Dad was welcome to move into her guest room when he left the hospital. More than welcome. She insisted. "No reason to go back to the hotel. Your mother too. It's the least I can do."

The others joined us in the break room. Nick had reconstructed Dad's financial analysis and notes and concluded that if—"and it's If with a capital letter"—the collections continued as well as they'd started on Saturday, and if the store traffic remained strong, and if the salespeople continued to close sales at the rate they had, and if they were able to improve gross margins by a couple of percentage points, "then I think you've got a shot."

I looked around the table. Was I the only one who thought this store might be too sick to survive? Tommy, don't be negative, that's what Dad would tell me. I kept my trap shut for the moment.

"Christine, I don't know how to say this any other way," Nick continued. "There are still a ton of problems."

"Don't I know it," said Christine.

"You've got outdated inventory in the back and in that storage locker. The salespeople need training. The advertising . . ." For a moment, I thought Nick was going to say, ". . . sucks."

Rather he concluded, ". . . could be improved."

Joanne added, "We have a staff that's been traumatized by Otto's accident and yesterday's terminations and God knows what they'll think when they hear about last night's shooting."

Christine nodded, her expression grim.

"And you have a problem in the service department," said Dan.

"And the audio department," I couldn't help putting my two cents in.

Christine turned to me. "Brian?"

I suddenly had qualms about telling Christine what I'd found. Your son's been stealing a couple hundred bucks a month. Nick sensed my feelings. "What exactly did you find?" he asked.

I did what I thought Dad would do: I pushed my sheet of notes across the table to Christine and laid out the facts so she could see what we saw. I pointed out the discrepancies between merchandise received and merchandise in inventory. I told her what the sales people had said about Brian pocketing cash and using fake return authorizations to hide the missing merchandise. "How serious is it?" she asked.

"A couple hundred bucks a month," I said. "As best I can tell."

Christine sighed, her mouth a tight line. She looked around the table. "Any suggestions?"

No one spoke. Finally I said, "I should double check. Make sure I haven't missed something." I hadn't, but it wouldn't hurt to be sure. I mentally cursed Otto. If the man had decent controls, Brian wouldn't have been able to steal so successfully, and I wouldn't have to tell his mother he was a thief.

Christine indicated with a little head bob she agreed, and slid my notes back across the table.

I couldn't let Christine think Brian was in this alone. "There's still Vernon," I said.

I imagined that behind Christine's troubled expression she was thinking, "Oh, God, what now?" At her raised eyebrow, Dan picked up the story, "He's been cooperating with Brian on the cage racket." Christine closed her eyes and lowered her chin, listening as Dan outlined the situation, not commenting or changing her expression. When he finished—I noticed he didn't go into detail about the missing high-end audio gear—she addressed us as a group: "What do you think I should do? If you owned this store, what would you do?"

I preempted everyone: "I understand Vernon is a good technician and Dan says the guy runs a well-oiled service department, but you just can't keep him. He's a cancer that'll eat away at the business." I think I sounded like Dad.

Christine nodded in acceptance, but said, "Still, we need a service manager."

Dan had been giving this some thought. "How about this guy—" He had to look through papers. "Jason Durso? He's been on vacation, so I haven't talked to him. But I looked through his file and he's got about ten years with the store."

"Jason?" Christine looked thoughtful. "I don't really know." She frowned. "When's he due back?"

Dan said he expected Jason in the morning and he could interview him, get a sense of his potential. That opened up a general discussion of the service department I found incredibly boring. The pace picked up when they concluded that Christine and Dan would meet with Vernon when he arrived tomorrow morning, tell him he was fired for cause, collect his keys, and watch over him as he packed up his personal tools and property.

Joanne suggested that if Vernon caused any trouble, Christine should threaten to bring charges. If Jason wasn't interested in the promotion or if Dan questioned his ability, the store would begin running an ad. We didn't make any recommendations about what, if anything, Christine should do about Brian. My first impulse was to suggest she fire him. But of course Brian wasn't my son, and anyway, there might be some other explanation for the missing merchandise. Better to let the family work this out on their own. Poor Christine. Poor Wendy. What a mess. They sure didn't need this heartache piled on top of their grief over Otto. I could feel my indignation flaring up again. What were those cops doing about Otto? About Dad? What could I do?

Before the meeting broke up, I slipped out to look for the dark blue folder in Otto's desk. It was right where I'd hidden it. I took it out, opened it, confirmed it still held the obscene Polaroids and wondered once again, What the hell was this? Otto's harem? His hobby?

I closed the folder, sealed the three open edges with tape, took the package out to the Buick, and slid it under the driver's seat for a trip to the hotel where I could cut them up in the privacy of the room. I thought for a moment about taking them to Wilkins; they were evidence of something. Then I decided: screw it. He hadn't give me a lot of help, why should I help him? Besides, with Otto dead, why bring these women into things?

Back at the hotel, I borrowed scissors from the desk clerk, and spent fifteen minutes in a men's room stall cutting the Polaroids into tiny pieces and flushing them away.

22 / Monday morning

As I dragged myself out of sleep to the buzz of the alarm on Monday and shuffled to the shower, it felt strange—uncomfortable even—to have the room to myself. I'd started the weekend bitching about wanting my own hotel room and now I wished I could hear Dad snoring in the next bed instead of visiting him in the hospital.

I unclipped the drapes to dress in the morning's weak light, carefully returning Dad's clothes pin to his kit. The rain had stopped, but gray clouds still roiled in the sky. The Weather Channel said it was supposed to grow colder as another front moved in slowly right behind this one. Possible flurries at the higher elevations. The street below was littered with sodden leaves that the night's storm had stripped from the trees—an icy mess in the making.

Table talk at breakfast concerned Dad's condition, plans for the day at Jonker's, reports from the businesses back home, and conjectures about the police investigation into Dad's shooting. "Not to mention Otto's accident," I prodded, determined to stir things up and get some reaction to my thinking on the subject.

"Otto's accident?" Nick did a double-take. "What about Otto's accident?"

"That's just it. What happened to Otto wasn't exactly an accident." With everyone's attention now on me, I told them Andy's story. I said I'd actually checked out the accident spot myself and if something big like a Jonker service van had stopped on the road, there was no way even a bicycle could have passed. "Otto would have come around the curve and not been able to stop."

Joanne and Nick spoke together: "Why was a van blocking the road?"

"Did you tell the police?"

"I talked to the detective who was at the hospital Saturday night and he's looking into it."

"But a Jonker van?" Nick asked.

I shrugged. "Could be. The guy who told me about it didn't know a lot. It was dark, he wasn't paying a lot of attention. But you have to admit, it's pretty suspicious. Otto gets killed, then my dad gets shot." I looked at the three sober faces.

"Glen Kieffer had a van." Dan's tone was accusatory.

Joanne rapped on the table and looked around at the group. "Wait, wasn't Steffie's husband driving one of those vans?"

"Hey, everyone in the service department drives a van." Dan sounded as if he had to protect the technicians. "And Tommy, you don't know for a fact that it was a Jonker van." The clincher, as far as the group was concerned.

What could I say? Andy could've been wrong about the time, or mixed up the sequence of events. Come to think of it, he was probably stoned, and in any case he was—as he'd said—more than a little distracted. We left it at that, Dan signaled for the check, and I walked to Dad's car.

At the hospital, Mom was already fussing around Dad's bed. He was clean-shaven, alert, and he'd cleaned off his breakfast tray. "They won't give me coffee. Breakfast with no coffee—what kind of a joint is this?" Grins all around. I felt my stomach begin to unclench and my mood improve.

Kissing Mom, I asked, "How'd you sleep?"

She gave a broad smile and said to Dad, "Christine's spare bedroom is really comfy. You'll be happy. The bed's as big as ours."

That didn't seem to help his mood much. "That's if I ever get out of here."

Mom said, "Let 'em give the bed to someone who's not such a grouch."

"I'm not a grouch. I just want to get back to work."

"I hope you're not such a grouch at Christine's. The way we're imposing. I apologized, but she won't hear it, not after what you've doing for the business."

"I haven't done much."

"Fired a bunch of people," I said.

"Yeah, there is that," he said with a bleak smile.

"Christine clearly needs people around her, with Otto gone," said Mom. "She wants noise, activity, company—her sister, you, me. She wants to keep herself busy at the store. She says we're doing her the favor by staying at the house."

Dad started to grumble something about our own business but Mom cut him off. "You know the business can run without you for a few days. Anyway, I'm less than three hours away if it *does* need me."

Catching up on Christine's situation, Mom told us Wendy had driven away at dawn, returning to Worcester for a seminar she said she couldn't miss. "Christine didn't want to let her go," Mom said. "She wants Wendy to finish her MBA, but she also wants to have her around—especially this week. Wendy said she'll be back but she couldn't let her team down."

I was surprised to realize how sorry I was not to have spent more time with Wendy. Patience, I told myself. You'll still be at Jonker's when she returns. The Gloucester business doesn't need me. Jonker's does.

I offered to sneak a cup of vending machine coffee into Dad's room, but Mom vetoed that idea. Dad squeezed my hand goodbye, I pecked Mom's cheek, and left. Time to return to saving Jonker Appliance & TV.

Bumping over the curb into the store's parking lot, I observed my surroundings with new eyes. The big delivery truck was gone, off on its rounds. A fairly new service van (the one Steffie's husband had been driving?) was parked by the loading dock. The battered van Vernon drove was missing. Brian's little red car and Joanne's convertible occupied slots next to each other. I put the Buick next to the convertible.

In the service department, Dan was interviewing a technician I didn't recognize but assumed was Jason Durso, his first morning back after his vacation. I couldn't imagine what the guy might think about all the changes. Had to be a shock to the system.

Joanne and the former Sears salesperson—Angelina something?—were leading an intense sales meeting in the break room, the first weekly Monday morning pre-opening training/update session. I stopped at the door to catch a bit of Joanne's sermon: "You want to remember you're not trying to sell anything. You're here to help people buy. Someone walks through that front door because she has a want she thinks we can satisfy. It's our job to ask questions, listen carefully, uncover that want and then to help them understand why a certain product satisfies that want. Selling is teaching . . ."

Two or three of the salespeople nodded in agreement. Even Brian, huddled at the back of the room, seemed to be paying attention.

I found Christine and Nick in Otto's office looking at newspaper ad tear sheets. Christine perked up when I rapped gently on the open door. "Tom doing better?"

"A lot better. He wants out, but there's no word on that." I hesitated, looking around the office, now noticeably neater than it had been Friday morning. "Anything special you need me to do?"

Nick looked at Christine, then back at me. "Nothing special. We've still got collection calls. It wouldn't hurt to follow up with some of the people where we left messages."

I hoped my face didn't show my disappointment. "Okay. Sure. I'll get right on it."

Steffie was at her desk at the back of the showroom, cradling the phone on one shoulder while writing a service ticket. When she hung up, I asked, "Where's Vernon this morning?"

Steffie looked surprised, swiveling her head toward the service department. "Isn't he in the back?"

"Nope. And his truck's not in the lot."

"Well then, I guess he just hasn't come in yet."

That was odd, but I kept my expression blank. Steffie didn't know he was supposed to be fired first thing this morning—that should have happened already. "Does he usually come in late after the weekend?"

"Vernon?" Gilberti sounded shocked I'd suggest such a thing. "No, he's always here."

"Maybe we should call his house and find out when he'll be in." Let's get his thieving ass in here so we can fire him and move on.

"I guess." Gilberti didn't sound enthusiastic, but since I was standing over her, she reluctantly pulled out a list of phone numbers. She'd already used a ruler to draw lines through the names of the people Dad fired on Saturday. She ran her finger down the list until it reached Claridge, Vernon, and dialed his number. After what seemed like five minutes, she hung up. "No answer."

I wasn't going to let this go. "Does he have a pager?"

"Oh, yes. They all do." She located that number, called it, pressed a bunch of her phone's buttons, then hung up. "He'll call as soon as he gets to a phone." She sounded confident. I wasn't.

I was about to take over a desk and start on the collection calls, when I had a thought. "Is he married? Vernon?"

"Oh, yes. She used to work here—Peggy Sodoski. She quit when she got pregnant."

"How about a home address?"

"I can dig it out." It wasn't on her list of phone numbers, but she went into her desk drawer, pulled a file, and after a moment gave me a number on a Summit Avenue here in town.

I scribbled it on a pad, thanked her, and started toward the back. Getting Vernon fired was way more important than another collection call, at least on my list of priorities. I popped my head into the office to tell Nick and Christine that Vernon hadn't come to work, wasn't answering his phone, and I was going out to his house.

"You think that's necessary?" Nick gave Christine a meaningful look. "I mean, he doesn't have anything to do with the store any more."

"Yeah, well, I think there's something wrong." I didn't add that I was much happier chasing Vernon than being lied to by creditors or talking to their answering machines.

"Well, when you see him, don't drop any hints about his job. Just tell him we want to see him as soon as he can get in." I was half out the door before Nick finished his sentence.

In the car's glove box, I found my map of Pittsfield and traced the route to Summit, a one-block street no more than five minutes from where I was sitting in the Buick.

I drove slowly to the end of Summit, squinting at house numbers and looking for a beat up Jonker service van. The Claridge house was a small two-story brick bungalow. There was a one-car garage at the back of the property, but I could see from the street that the door was open and the garage was empty. No van. No dog barking, either.

I parked at the curb in front of the house and sat for a

minute. Thinking about the situation, it occurred to me that if Vernon had shot Dad, visiting his house might not be the best idea I ever had. But by this time, I was already out of the car.

The walk to the Claridge front door was lined with still-bright pink begonias. The doorbell button looked new and I could hear the chime deep inside the house when I pressed. And pressed.

Nothing happened.

I pursed my lips and looked up and down Summit Avenue. A young mother had come out of her house and was pushing a stroller toward the playground at the end of the street.

I tried the bell again and brought my nose to the glass of the narrow window beside the door. A sheer curtain allowed me to see a hefty figure moving in the hall, so I continued to linger, shifting from one foot to the other. I was about to knock when the door's deadbolt snapped, and the door cracked open, checked by a chain. "Hold your horses, just hold your horses. Who is it?" Not a warm welcome, but what did I expect?

I could see the outline of a woman in the dim vestibule. "Mrs. Claridge?"

"Who're you?"

"I'm Tommy Lovell. I'm working with Vernon down at Jonker Appliance." Close enough to the truth my conscience didn't bother me. "We're a little worried. He didn't come into work this morning."

"No." This wasn't news to her. "He's gone hunting."

"Hunting?" I wished I could see the woman's face. "When did he leave?"

"Saturday. After work." She sounded suspicious, as if this was all information I should already know, and if I didn't know it, who was I?

"We . . . I don't think he said anything."

"Well," she snorted. "With all the confusion down at the

store, I'm not surprised."

I tried to think. "Did he take the van?"

"Otto never said no. Vern pays his own gas." She paused, then added in an accusing voice, "Are you one of them? Those meddlers from out of town? Come here to stir things up?"

I tried to sound reasonable and friendly. "I'm from out of town, but I didn't come to make trouble."

"Well, you can just go back where you came from. We don't need you. Vern don't need you. The store's doing just fine, he says." She began to shut the door, but I was ready and wedged my shoe into the crack.

"Wait! Wait! Mrs. Claridge. Just one question. Then I'll go away." She pressed the door as hard as she could against my shoe, but hesitated when a small child began to wail deep in the house. "One question!" I repeated. "Was Vernon home Thursday evening? You know, last Thursday?"

"Thursday?" She stopped to think for a few seconds. "He helped a friend install a dishwasher that night after work, didn't get home till late. I was already in bed. Asleep."

I wanted to ask more. What's the friend's name? Where does he live? When did you go to bed? What time did Vernon get home? Where'd he go hunting?

But I suspected I'd asked as much as she'd answer and pulled my foot free. "Thank you for the help." I tried to sound sincere, but the door banged shut and the dead bolt slammed back into place.

As Mrs. Claridge turned back into the house, I caught a glimpse of her shadowy form moving away. Another hefty woman. Like Christine. Like Stephanie Gilberti. Like the women in the Polaroids I'd destroyed.

Did the police suspect Vernon? Time for a little showdown. I drove to the police station and told the desk sergeant that I needed to talk to Detective Wilkins. The sergeant gave a little shrug, picked up his phone, and a minute later Wilkins came out to the reception area.

He seemed less annoyed by my presence than he had Saturday morning. He also seemed bone-tired, the lines on his face deeper, his thinning hair lank. I wondered if Wilkins had slept at all since our late-night session at the hospital. Under other circumstances (and with another person), I'd have commiserated: Jeez, you look like hell.

Wilkins invited me into the inner office, pointed to a chair beside his desk, and sat heavily in his own chair. "Okay, what you got this time?" His tone suggested that he didn't expect much.

I leaned forward. "Vernon Claridge, the service manager at Jonker's. He's been stealing from the company. We think he had a deal with one of the technicians, and he's been selling rebuilt parts as new. It also looks like he had a deal with Brian Jonker to skim cash from the audio department."

Wilkins didn't look impressed by my recitation, but I wasn't done. "It was Claridge's van blocking the loop road when Otto was out on his bike Thursday night. And I think he's the guy who shot my Dad Saturday night."

No response, but he hadn't heard the clincher. "Claridge didn't come to work this morning, so I just went out to his house. He's not there. The Jonker van's not there, either. His wife said he took off to go hunting after work Saturday. And she said he wasn't home Thursday night, the night Otto got killed. She said he was helping a friend install a dishwasher, but you can check that."

"Oh, don't worry, we will."

I could feel my face coloring as the anger welled up. Otto's dead, Dad's in the hospital, and that's all you can say?

"I thought you'd want to know because Claridge didn't tell anyone at the store he was going hunting. He just didn't show up this morning."

"You know where he went?"

Now my face was red hot. "I didn't ask." Not that his wife would have told me. "But isn't that your job?"

Wilkins ignored this as he glanced over at a wall calendar. "It's a little early to go hunting. Nothing opens until later in the month. Even bow hunting doesn't start until the twenty-first."

I'm talking about a dangerous fugitive, a killer, and this guy is talking about hunting season? As if an asshole like Vernon would care about something like a season. Barely controlling my tongue, I asked, "Did you find the time to check with Andy Panetta about the van backing up the loop road Thursday night?"

For a few seconds, I wasn't certain Wilkins was going to answer. Then he admitted, in a tone more civil than mine, "Sure did. Wasn't a lot of help."

"What about Glen Kieffer? He was really pissed about getting fired."

Wilkins sat up straight and put a stop to my interrogation. "I'm afraid I can't talk about an ongoing investigation."

"So what are you going to do about Claridge?"

Wilkins stared me down with a long look I took to mean: Just go away and let us do our job.

"We'll be talking to him," he said with a straight face.

Talk to him? When he's disappeared? I thought I'd seen a flicker of surprise in Wilkins's tired eyes when I said Claridge had gone hunting. But now I was too steamed to think coherently. I got to my feet without a word.

Wilkins waved his hand irritably, deadpanning, "Thanks for stopping by." I didn't feel thanked. I felt like a ten-year-old who'd been distracting a busy grownup from important business. Here I was interviewing witnesses and uncovering vital clues to tragic crimes. I truly thought it was worth a few minutes of Wilkins' precious time.

23 / Monday afternoon

Back at the store, Dan and Jason were sitting together at the service department desk. Dan was explaining his system of compensating and motivating service technicians when I barged in. "Vernon isn't going to be in. His wife told me he went hunting. On Saturday. Did he say anything to you about taking off?"

"Nothing, zippo, nada," said Dan. "I expected to see him in here bright-eyed and bushy-tailed first thing this morning so we could can his ass."

"Hunting?" Jason, a thin-faced guy with a bushy mustache, looked from me to Dan and back. "Deer season doesn't open for another two, three weeks."

"Well, that's what his wife told me. No sign of his van out by the house."

"Sounds like he's taken off," Dan muttered.

I rolled my eyes and turned my attention to Jason. "You work with him, where would he go?"

"Beats the shit out of me." Jason pursed his lips. "Hey, you could try his ski house. He's got a place up in Vermont. One room and a sleeping loft. More shack than cabin."

"You've been there?" I asked.

"Once. Maybe four years ago." Jason shook his head at the memory. "We were going to hunt bear. Black bear. Froze my ass off—season's late November—and we never saw a bear. Never fired a single shot. Not at a bear, anyway." He gave a knowing grin. I visualized a road sign pocked with bullet holes. "Drank a lot of beer, though."

"So where's this shack?"

"Way the hell back in the hills somewhere. You'd need a snowmobile to get there in January."

I wanted to shake the man, but kept my tone level—just barely. "What's it near? How'd you get there?"

"Lemme see. We took my pickup 'cause all he drives is the van. Up Route Seven to Bennington, then west—no, east on Nine and . . ." Jason closed his eyes and frowned. He finally looked at me helplessly. "Just can't remember the details. Sorry. Somewhere up in the mountains around Mount Snow, that's all I can remember. Vern's wife'll know."

Maybe she did, but she sure wouldn't tell me. I said a polite thank you and waved goodbye, and before Dan could open his mouth to question me, I was out the door and back in the Buick. Detective Wilkins might be moving like molasses in January, but not me. Otto dead, Dad shot, and Vernon missing. No time to waste.

I unfolded the Massachusetts/Vermont/New Hampshire road map and traced Route 7 north, Route 9 east, then north to West Dover and Mt. Snow. It was something like an hour-and-a-half drive. Start out now, and I'll be there by mid-day. But where the hell am I going? I balled the map up and squeezed it till my knuckles turned white. No address, not even a town name, no idea what the house looks like. Stupid idea.

But I do know what a Jonker service van looks like. It's white. And something big and white like an appliance service van would be easy to spot from the air.

I could take the Cessna up and hunt for the van. With so many leaves down, a white van would stand out against the brown earth—and up north the trees would be even more bare than around here. By plane, West Dover was maybe half an hour away, and I had lots of daylight left.

As I edged the Buick into traffic, I turned the plan over in my mind. One small problem: from the pilot's seat, I could only search the landscape on the plane's left. If I had a passenger, she could scan the ground on the right. Make the search twice as effective, find the bastard twice as fast.

Brandi would be ideal. Someone who works with tweezers to make jewelry would have to have eagle eyes. Plus she'd be overjoyed to go up. I could imagine her excitement when I invited her.

I had to slam on the brakes as the light changed just ahead. Maybe taking Brandi wasn't such a hot idea. Flying with a passenger when all I had was a student license could cost me my license and ground me forever. But that was nothing compared to how I'd feel if Brandi got hurt because I did something dumb in the air. A truly bad idea.

Still.

Waiting for the light to change I carried on a muttered debate with myself. This was an emergency. The guy was dangerous. He tried to kill my Dad. I could find him. I knew I could. I had to try. Fuck the legality. And I couldn't do this alone.

The car behind honked because the light was green. I jerked back to reality and turned the wheel toward Dunkin' Donuts.

Brandi's eyes lit up when she saw me come in. "Hi, there. Long time no see."

I leaned across the counter and lowered my voice. "You want to go flying? Now?"

"Right now?" She looked around the empty shop. The same older woman from the other day was fussing at one of the machines.

"Yeah, right now. It's important. I'll tell you about it on the way." Brandi bit nervously at what was left of a nail. "I really need your help."

Look at me, Brandi. Look at what I'm offering. Your heart's desire. A chance to go flying. A chance to track down a killer.

For a second, I thought she'd laugh, or ask me what I'm smoking. Then she smiled slowly in a way that showed off her dimple, gave a little why-not? shrug, and turned to her scowling boss. "Megan, I gotta take off."

Megan bristled. "Hey, you can't just walk out. It's your shift."

"Watch me," Brandi said over her shoulder as she headed for the back room, mouthing to me, "See you out back."

On the ride to the airport, I told her about Vernon, the shooting, the van. She drew in her breath sharply when I mentioned Dad's shoulder but let me go on with my summary. "With you searching the right side and me searching the left, we ought to be able to spot it from the air without any trouble." Not exactly true—especially the no trouble part—but if I could convince her, maybe I could convince myself.

I sent Brandi on to the plane rather than have her come into the terminal in her Dunkin' Donuts uniform and PHS jacket, to avoid awkward questions. I told the airport manager I was taking the Cessna up for a practice flight and I'd be back in a couple hours. "Maybe do some touch-and-goes."

She said they'd topped off the fuel, checked the soft tire, and handed me a current FAA information sheet with the field's radio frequency, altitude, and more. I was boiling with anticipation, afraid it would show and she'd begin asking questions. But she treated me like any other pilot. Her only comment: "There's another front coming through, probably late this afternoon." I mumbled something about watching out for the weather.

Walking past the other planes, I felt like shouting or jumping or doing something wildly inappropriate—skipping, or turning a cartwheel on the tarmac. I unlocked the Cessna's doors, helped Brandi into the co-pilot's seat, plugged in two headsets so we could hear each other, and found the plastic-protected checklists. "First, preflight checks."

It was the first time I'd ever done them unsupervised, and I walked around the plane to run down the list meticulously. Rudder gust lock, tail tiedown, control surfaces, right wing tiedown, fuel sample, fuel filler cap, engine oil level, prop, nose wheel strut and tire, left wing tiedown, fuel, pitot tube cover, stall warning opening . . .

Seated in the cockpit, I experienced a massive surge of doubt. What was I doing? I hadn't soloed for ten years, and when I had, I'd been far more confident (or heedless) and anyway in those days I flew pretty regularly. Did flying with Dad twice in the past six weeks give me enough experience to do this? A month ago, the first time I'd taken the controls, Dad reassured me, "Just like riding a bicycle. Once you've done it, you never forget." Finishing the preflight checks, I felt fear turning my guts to mush.

Thankfully, Brandi watched everything without a word or even a question, as if speaking would distract me from a key detail or rouse her from this waking dream. I checked to make sure she was belted in good and snug, then adjusted my own seatbelt.

The engine started without a cough. I let it idle while I set the altimeter and heading indicator. Finally, I radioed the airport manager, who said the taxiway was clear and confirmed that Runway 8 was the active. With a heavy sense that right or wrong I was committing us to an inexorable course, I released the brakes, taxied to the end of the runway, ran the engine up to 1800 rpm, listened to the smooth rumble, throttled back. The airport manager said I was clear.

"Here we go," I said aloud to Brandi and myself, released the brakes, and pulled the throttle to full. The Cessna began to accelerate. I had to make tiny adjustments for a light cross wind. At 55 knots, I eased the yoke back, the nose lifted, and we were flying. I looked over to Brandi for an instant, but couldn't see her face. She was staring at the ground falling away beneath our wings.

I did a gentle climbing turn until we were headed north, continuing to climb until I reached 5,500 feet. We passed over a lake. The road map I'd asked Brandi to follow showed it had to be Pontoosuc, north of Pittsfield. Which meant the highway beside it was Route 7. All I had to do was follow the road through the Berkshire hills to Bennington, pick up Route 9, and look for the Mt. Snow ski area.

Flying straight and level, alone in the sky, I felt more confident. Mount Graylock, at almost 3,500 feet, reared up on our left. Cars crawled along the road far below. A rough calculation told me we could fly safely for about four hours. I touched Brandi's arm, and she started against her seatbelt. "What do you think?" I asked, wondering whether she felt uneasy or maybe just plain sorry she'd come along.

But her face was like a child at Christmastime. "It's wonderful!"

"Yeah, there's nothing like it." And it was getting better because I could see more rips of blue in the clouds ahead. It would be great if we could search in sunlight rather than in the dull light under a slate-gray overcast.

"Tommy, do I get to say 'ten-four, good buddy' or just 'over-and-out'?"

"Only if we have to call Houston from the moon," I told her.

Over Bennington, I circled until Brandi pointed down at what had to be Route 9 heading east. According to the map, there were no towns between Bennington and Wilmington, and Wilmington looked like a village. There was a big reservoir west of Wilmington, and only minutes after I told her it was our next landmark, Brandi pointed ahead at the water-filled valley. As we passed it, I banked and set a course north.

In another few minutes we could see ski trails cut through the trees, Mt. Snow. The mountains seemed higher than I'd expected. Mt. Snow was almost 3,600 feet. We needed a good topological map. We needed to fly along the valleys, stay high enough to avoid the mountains, low enough to see something. As I'd hoped, the trees were nearly bare and we could see houses, cars, and trucks on the ground. A hundred miles further north than Pittsfield and a thousand feet of altitude made the difference. I watched what looked like a toy pickup truck chug up a long switchback driveway to stop at a house.

An instrument check showed I'd lost altitude, as if unconsciously trying to get closer to the ground. I felt a momentary stab of nerves as I climbed back to 4,000 feet and tried to follow the valley's course. "You watch your side," I said. "It's a white service truck with black letters on the side. A big *Jonker's*." Brandi nodded and turned back to survey the land.

But a few minutes following the valley meant I had to focus on flying the plane and couldn't scan the ground. The wind out of the northwest hit the mountains and eddied, buffeting the plane. We rocked and I heard Brandi gasp. I reassured her with a light touch on her leg. "It's only a little turbulence. You okay?"

I could see her swallow. "Yeah, I'm okay."

After another minute when I had to focus on flying, I decided it was more important to set a heading and just hold it than try to follow a valley.

Ten miles beyond Mt. Snow, I did a slow 180 to head back south. When I reached Route 9 and the reservoir, I did another 180 to head north again and search the next strip of landscape.

Brandi consulted the map and told me we were over Green Mountain National Forest, which seemed to be mostly wilderness. Dirt roads. Old logging roads. The widely scattered house roofs, usually in a clearing, stood out among the bare trees. We could see parked cars, abandoned farm equipment, a child's backyard trampoline, hot tubs on ski house decks, an isolated graveyard. Nothing resembled a service van.

Our flight pattern was a loom's shuttle, back and forth across the sky, weaving a search square.

No van.

When I realized we were back over Bennington, I retraced our route to Wilmington, flew north, and began a search north and west of the area we'd just covered. Ski trails of another area scarred the side of a mountain. Condos and large buildings crowded around the area's base.

But no van.

I imposed another imaginary search square on the roadmap and started shuttling north and south, generally following the ridges and scanning the valleys. The sun disappeared entirely and I could see the new cold front building to the north. After another exceedingly boring hour, the only chore to maintain altitude and heading, I muttered into my mike, "We're wasting our time. Jason didn't know what he was talking about."

"What?" Brandi's voice in my headset sounded tense. "About the ski house?"

I was disgusted with myself for taking off on this wild goose chase. "Or we're looking in the wrong place. Or Vernon didn't drive to Vermont. Or the van's under cover. Or we missed it. Or . . . or . . . or . . ." I couldn't think of another reason. "Time to go home. Sorry it's not more interesting."

Brandi gave me a what-are-you-talking-about look. "Are you kidding? I'm up in a plane with you, getting an incredible view of . . . everything, miles and miles of mountains and sky and all. And I'm helping you look for a fugitive. Does it get any better?" Her grin made me grin.

I was about to make some smart remark when I sensed the

engine's hiccup through the yoke and rudder pedals before I heard it. I glanced at the RPM gauge. Shit, oh shit, we're losing power. Now I could hear the engine beginning to run rough. I goosed the power, but the engine seemed to be gasping for air. Panic started to form, a black mist rising to erase every coherent thought racing through my mind.

We're going to crash.

I scanned the ground. Nothing open. No possible place to land.

We're fucked. I'm going to kill Brandi and myself.

"Panic and you're dead."

"What? What's the matter?" Brandi sounded alarmed.

It must have slipped out before I realized I was speaking into the mike. Panic and you're dead, I repeated silently, beating back the black mist. I flashed Brandi a tight smile. "It's okay. Just kidding. Something my Dad always says when we're flying together." She nodded and turned back to the valley scenery.

What the fuck was happening to the engine? With the loss of RPMs, we were losing altitude, and adding throttle had no more effect.

Water in the fuel? But I'd checked that on the ground.

What else? What else?

The engine was running more and more rough. Any moment it would stop and we'd become a glider. A glider plowing into trees and rocks.

Ice!

The thought popped into my mind as I was already reaching to switch on the carburetor heat.

"Turn on the carburetor heat before making a significant power reduction," my instructor had drilled me years ago. "At the first sign of carburetor ice, apply full carburetor heat *and leave it on*." Did I switch it on in time?

Though I held the plane straight and level, we were dropping lower and lower, down to almost 3,000 feet, heading down a valley, still under control, but the hills growing higher beyond both wingtips. Good thing Brandi was still intent on finding that van, not frightened by our downward drift, slow but definite. Not good.

After what seemed like forever but was probably only a few minutes, I noticed a tiny change in the engine sound. Smoother, not so rough. I throttled back slightly as the RPMs continued to rise and felt my jaw unclench. We weren't going to die. I would've whooped but caught myself and changed it to a throat-clearing noise. Brandi never even looked my way. She just kept moving her head back and forth in a slow arc, checking the ground below.

Except now we were much closer to the ground than I'd dare fly before, only about 500 feet above the trees. It was easy to see the river below, with railroad tracks and a country road alongside. All this had to be on the road map, but I didn't want to distract Brandi, and besides, nursing the engine required all my concentration. The way the mountains crowded in, I had to turn with the valley, one hand ready to give full throttle and hoping the engine would respond if I needed to climb suddenly.

"There!" Brandi's shout boomed in my headset. She was pointing up the valley at one o'clock low. "You see it? A white van?"

And there was a white service van with black letters on the side panel, parked outside a small brown A-frame. "Ten-four!" I told her. We locked eyes for a second, then I put the plane into a climb until we were well out of the valley and could turn safely. "Are you sure that was it?" I asked. I was sure I'd seen the van, but was she sure it was the right one?

"Yes!" She was laughing with excitement. "That was it! I could almost read the other stuff under 'Jonker.'"

"Okay, now where the hell are we?"

She began inspecting the road map. I thought of taking another low-level pass through the valley to get one more look but I was afraid I'd spook Claridge if he heard the Cessna come by low and slow again. Not to mention how I was spooked by the ice. No, I sure didn't want to go back into the valley.

So I turned 90 degrees and crossed the valley at 4,000 feet. Seeing the parked van and the cabin again confirmed my impression. They had to be Vernon's. At this height we couldn't read the letters, but the pattern sure resembled the writing on the Jonker trucks.

"Is this it?" Brandi had folded the map to just our search area and was pointing to a spot.

I looked at the map, then at the landscape below, feeling an electric rush of elation. "Yup. Here. We're flying along a line that would go like this." I showed her our course on the map.

"Yippee! We did it! We actually found the creep. Now what?"

Good question. Now what? Too bad the Cessna isn't a fighter plane with a machine gun—I'd love to strafe the asshole's house once or twice. Yeah, right. "We've got to call the Pittsfield cops."

I climbed to 5,500 feet and began a gentle 180 to be sure I knew exactly where we were. I tuned the radio to 122.8 to call the Mt. Snow Airport. When the ground answered, I identified myself, and asked to land. The manager told me Runway 1 was active.

We flew south for less than ten minutes. I saw the field, one north/south runway. I flew parallel to the runway bleeding altitude until I was a half-mile beyond the numbers, did a careful 180, and lined up on the runway's center, added flaps, throttled back, and pushed the nose gently down. Just beyond the numbers, I pulled back on the yoke, throttled almost to idle, and we bounced onto the asphalt.

Only when I began to taxi toward the little terminal building did I realize Brandi had a tight grip on my arm. Really tight. "Not a bad landing," I said, my tone much more devil-may-care than I felt. "I think we can use the plane again."

At the terminal, I shut down. "Stay here. I'm going to call the Pittsfield cops." I didn't want any questions about a passenger.

"I've got to pee." She climbed down awkwardly and stood on the pavement as if it were rocking. She should only know how close we came to dying.

We sprinted into the terminal, where she headed for the bathroom and I fished for coins as I asked for the pay phone.

When I reached the police switchboard, I said, "I've located a fugitive," and asked for Detective Wilkins. I was switched to his desk right away. "Hi, this is Tommy Lovell. I found Vernon Claridge. He's in his cabin in Vermont."

"Where the hell are you?" Wilkins grunted.

"In Vermont, at the Mount Snow Airport in West Dover. In Vermont. I flew up here in my dad's Cessna. I found Claridge's van. It's sitting outside a cabin north of here."

"Any sign of Claridge?"

Damn. I hadn't seen any movement around the cabin. No smoke from the chimney. "Uh, no, but I got a good look at the van. It's Jonker's van all right."

"Vermont's not all that big a state, but could you give a more precise location?" Now Wilkins sounded almost good-humored. "Better than 'north of here.'"

"Here's the thing. I can't give you the exact spot. The valley runs generally north/northwest-south/southeast. There's a river in it and there's a road on one side and rail tracks on the other. Northeast of the Mt. Snow Airport. Maybe ten miles. When I get back, I can show you on a map." But surely local people—not to mention the local cops—would know what I was talking about.

"Okay," Wilkins sounded resigned. "I'll talk to the Vermont State Police. Have them go check it out while it's still light. Can you hang around the airport till the Vermont guys get there?"

There he went again, making a question sound like an order. But this time, I was more than happy to stay right where I was.

24 / Thursday afternoon

The excitement of tracking a killer on Monday had faded by the time Otto was buried on Thursday morning. A Chamber of Commerce dignitary gave the eulogy, speaking directly to Christine, Wendy, and Brian in the front row. The stone church's pews were well populated with friends, neighbors, and business associates. Mom and Dad (with his arm in a cast), Joanne, Nick and Dan were right behind the family, staying close for support. I sat directly behind Wendy, watching her alternately stare into space and look down, eyes anywhere but on the polished coffin. Jonker Appliance & TV was closed for the day, and it looked to me as if all the employees attended—including two people who Dad had fired. I thought that showed class.

Standing around before the service, Christine almost broke down. By the end, she needed the support of Wendy on one elbow and Brian on the other as she stood to accept condolences from the dozens of people who'd come to pay their respects. A week ago, I'd only known the Jonkers as friends of my parents. Barely remembered meeting Wendy as a shy little girl, let alone saving her. Now it felt like Dad and I had traveled through a long, dark tunnel with them. Dark and sad.

I hugged Christine and Wendy, shook Brian's clammy hand.

It was a relief not to have to ride out to the cemetery, having been summoned to the police station to go over my formal statement one more time. That took a couple of hours, and then I drove back to the Jonker home. As I came through the front hall archway into the living room, Nick hailed me, "Tommy! How'd it go?"

That set off a flurry of questions from the Jonkers and Dad's friends: "What happened? . . . What'd you find out? . . . What'd they say?" Until that morning, we only knew what we'd read in the paper or seen on TV: that Vermont state police had arrested Vernon and transported him back to Massachusetts for arraignment. The news stories had paid special notice to Wilkins' outstanding police work.

All faces turned to me. I took a deep breath, not sure where to begin. "I had to give a full statement, then Detective Wilkins talked to me off the record—now that we're best buddies."

"Well, are you going to tell us, or just stand there?" said Nick.

I sat beside Dad on the living room's enormous sofa. "It was Vernon's service van on the loop road last Thursday night. Wilkins says everything's in Vernon's statement. Full confession. He did help his buddy install a dishwasher—that checked out—but they got to talking about the store and about Otto and how the business was going. When Otto told the staff that we were coming to look over the business, Vernon—and his wife—began to get worried."

"Why would Vernon's wife care?" asked Joanne.

"She told him she'd let Otto take some pictures of her one time, pictures she wouldn't want anyone to see. She swore nothing had happened, and it was all before they got married anyway, but that didn't help Vernon's attitude. Everything was falling apart. We were going to find pictures of his wife, and once we fired his buddy Keiffer, he thought he might be next."

"Might be?" said Nick. "Might be? He was already toast by

Saturday night."

"I'm just telling you what's in his statement."

"But why?" asked Joanne. "All that stuff—the knock-off parts, Keiffer's time scam—it was all penny ante. Even the return authorization scam—" She broke off. I saw Brian was listening as carefully as the rest of us.

I glanced around, trying to organize the story. "I guess Vernon was afraid of what would happen once we started really poking into Otto's operation. So when he left his friend's house, he decided to drive over here to talk things over with Otto." As I was speaking, I had a thought. "Maybe he thought he could use Otto's pictures of Patty, his wife, as some kind of leverage."

Out of the corner of my eye, I could see Christine's hand fly to her mouth. Brian was leaning against the wall, arms crossed, casual as can be. I continued with my story.

"But when Vernon reached the house, Otto was just heading off on his bike. Vernon had to turn the van around and chase after him. He was afraid of missing Otto, so when they got to the state forest and Otto headed up the loop road, Vernon knew he could cut him off at the bottom. He backed the van up a little way to block Otto. Make him stop. Vernon claims he didn't mean any harm. He says all he wanted to do was talk things out, explain, and everything would be fine."

"What?" barked Nick. "He thought Otto would just forget about the stealing?"

"I don't think he was thinking," said Dan. "I spent time with Vernon during the weekend. Seems to me he's a whiz at following a wiring diagram or repair manual, but unless everything's laid out for him, he gets flustered."

"Anyway," I went on, "he sure didn't expect Otto to come tearing around the curve, try to stop, hit the guardrail, and . . . um—" I was going to say, 'and go flying into the woods,' but I stopped to glance at Wendy and Christine and adjusted my tone.

"Vernon told the cops it scared the heck out of him. So he just came home and went to bed like nothing happened. Wilkins says that if Claridge has said it once, he's said it a thousand times, 'I didn't mean him to get hurt. I didn't mean it.' Of course, he's being charged with leaving the scene, plus manslaughter."

"So what about shooting your dad?" Nick asked.

"Vernon claims he had nothing to do with that—and it looks like he's telling the truth." That caused a stir.

Dad looked skeptical. "How do you know that?"

"The Vermont cops searched Claridge's cabin and found his rifle. But it hadn't been fired in months." I looked around the room to see the effect I was having. Seven rapt expressions, one agitated face.

"Then who?" asked Joanne.

"The police found a rifle under the mattress in Brian's apartment." I was watching Brian, whose face had gone white, his eyes wide, his mouth open. "They haven't done the ballistics tests yet, but Wilkins says it's the right caliber. And it had been shot recently."

Everyone looked at Brian who appeared about to cry.

"It was just a scare! I was just going to shoot, and—"

"Bullshit!" Dad broke in. "I was silhouetted in the doorway. If I hadn't seen the muzzle flash and dropped, I'd have caught it in the chest."

"Why, Brian! Why?" Christine's cry was an animal in pain.

Brian could barely speak. "I just wanted to make you go away."

I couldn't keep the disgust out of my voice. "You don't know my Dad if you think shooting him would make us go away."

Mom took Dad's free hand and patted it.

"Because you were stealing from your father's business."

"It was Vernon's idea." Brian was staring at the floor. "He'd caught me, and he said he was going to talk to Pop if I didn't split with him. I told him I wasn't going to do it any more. I only did it once or twice because I needed some quick cash. But he said I had to keep on doing it. It'd be just between the two of us, and there was no way anyone'd find out."

I thought that was a pretty story and didn't believe a word. But it didn't make any difference. "Detective!" I called.

Wilkins, who'd been listening in the hall, came through the archway, followed by two uniformed officers. He went directly to Brian, whose shoulders were shaking. "Son, you'll have to come with me."

Two hours later, after Nick, Joanne, and Dan had cleared out and Christine was back from the police station, I brought Mom's suitcase and Dad's bag down from the guest room.

"My work here is done," Dad told Christine, trying to keep his tone light.

She looked as if she wanted to hug him but was afraid she'd hurt him. "Thank you for everything." Wendy kissed him on the cheek.

I carried the bags out to Mom's car where Dad turned to give me his most serious stare, "You going to be all right?"

I shrugged. "Who knows? The store's got a new service manager, essentially a new sales staff, an office manager who's in secret mourning, and a new general manager—at least until I decide if I want to stay on or open another restaurant or what."

I took a deep breath. "I'll be fine."

Acknowledgements

My deepest gratitude goes to the faithful members of my writer's group; Kay Abella, Don Blinbry, Tiffany Douse, Terri Garneau, Vinton Rafe McCabe, and Linda Strange all offered valuable comments, suggestions, and ideas as this manuscript evolved.

My ski-buddy and pilot friend Peter St. Pierre not only suggested that it would be possible to search for a white van from the air, but took me up in a Cessna to show me what it would be like.

Susan Brier, The Write Design Company, not only designed the jacket but also made invaluable editorial suggestions.

Liz Arneth, Mary Maki, and Cyndy Kryder, my faithful and true first readers, gave me invaluable feedback and saved me from the hell of typographic errors. Any remaining typos are my own fault.

My wife Marian read every draft and helped me see the characters and the story I wanted to tell more clearly. Every author should have such a careful, thoughtful, and helpful reader. I am blessed.

Appliance-TV retailers Dick Cox, Richard Donaldson, Bill Fisher, Leonard Geiser, Jack Hackett, Stewart Hall, and Dean Ridgeley gave me the background to write about Otto's business from the inside. They will never know how deeply they influenced my life.

Look for the next Tommy Lovell mystery

Six months after the death in a family business, Tommy Lovell has his hands full running Jonker's Appliance & TV and juggling the two women in his life. Then he gets a frantic call from one of his service technicians. The technician was supposed to repair a customer's broken TV, but he's just found the woman's body in her living room. Tommy warns the panicky technician to touch nothing and call the police. But when Tommy arrives at the house minutes later, the front door is wide open, the service van is gone, and there's no sign of the technician. At that moment, a neighbor walks in—and Tommy becomes the top suspect in a baffling murder that pushes him to the limits of loyalty and endurance.

About the Author

Wally Wood has published two novels and worked with a number of authors as a ghostwriter and collaborator on 21 business books. As a volunteer teacher, he worked in two men's state prisons for almost 20 years teaching business and writing subjects. He regularly leads a creative writing workshop for middle-school students and serves as a SCORE volunteer advisor.

He maintains a blog about writing and mysteries at—where else?—www.mysteriesofwriting.blogspot.com. The website has a discussion guide for *Death in a Family Business*.

Other books by Wally Wood

The Girl in the Photo: As Abbie and David go through their father's effects after his death, they discover a memoir he was writing about a love affair he had with a Japanese when he was a young surgeon in Japan during the Korean War. They find a picture of the woman and a letter from the time that suggests they may have a sibling they never knew existed. Even as they mourn their father, David and Abbie question what they thought they knew about his life--and theirs--  as they struggle with conflicting memories, unexpected emotions, and new possibilities.

Getting Oriented: A Novel About Japan: Phil Fletcher's debut as a tour guide takes his life in unexpected directions after an old college buddy persuades him to guide a group of Americans traveling through Japan. The group includes a high-powered career woman who finds far more than historic sights in the Land of the Rising Sun; a man who discovers a hidden interest in Japanese erotica; a neglected wife and a Southern belle vying for attention on Phil's 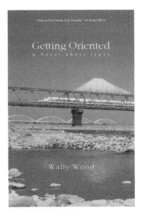 futon; and a retired couple facing their deepest fears on the much-anticipated trip of a lifetime. Private dramas provoke crises and life-changing decisions during this twelve-day tour of Japan.